THE SECRET HISTORY OF VICTOR PRINCE

JENNIFER R. POVEY

AITUNE

PROLOGUE

CHRISSY KNEW she shouldn't go jogging late at night.

She knew she shouldn't take a short cut through Tompkins Square Park. That was how you got raped, especially when you were new from flyover country and hadn't developed your big city senses yet.

The fact that she did it anyway said something about her sense of self preservation. She circled around the Hare Krishna tree, her heart pounding and her limbs starting to burn.

A moment later, her screams echoed through the trees. Nobody came rushing to her aid immediately, which says more about big cities than human nature.

She finally stopped, and looked down once more at the thing which had made her scream. Bile rose to her throat.

She was looking at a body. There was no question as to the deceased nature of said body. It was that of a woman, a young one. Blood had already started to congeal around the form, blood that came from multiple stab wounds. Chrissy could not tell whether she had fought back or not.

She could only tell that she had been quite brutally and methodically killed.

Chrissy had been an avid reader of mystery novels. She would never pick one up again.

Finally somebody came running, a young black man wearing a red hoodie, the hood down over his shoulders, his chest emblazoned with the logo of a comic book character.

He hesitated. Looked at her. "Could you call the cops?"

Given his skin color, it was unsurprising that he would hesitate about calling them himself.

She swallowed, the vile taste of almost-but-not-quite vomit circling through her mouth. Then she pulled out her cell phone. "Police. Tompkins Park. There's...there's..."

"What is there?"

"I..."

"What is there?"

The repeated words finally got through to her. "A body. Please."

"Are they dead?"

"Yes. They're...all..."

"I'm sending police and an ambulance. I need you to...is anyone else there?"

"There..." She glanced around, but the black man had left. "Not right now."

"Where exactly in the park are you?"

"Right under the Hare Krishna tree." The dispatcher was so calm. There was a dead body at her feet and she wanted to scream again, to cry, to throw up. To know who she was. To find who killed her and give them the same treatment. To run and hide.

"Okay. Stay put."

She stayed put. She stayed put until they showed up. She let them take her statement.

She let them walk her home.

She never went jogging at night again.

1

Detective Judy Eidelman let the uniforms take care of the near hysterical witness.

The poor woman had clearly never run into anything like that before. From her Dakotas accent, she wasn't even used to being in the City, let alone encountering the worst men could do to each other.

She was pretty sure this was the worst. The victim had been young and pretty. Forensics would determine whether she had been raped before being killed, but Judy already knew where to place her bets.

Young, pretty, and white. This one was going to make headlines, there was going to be a tremendous amount of pressure on them to solve it. Cynically, she thought of the number of times it happened to a black or indigenous girl, and the pressure was to forget about it, to put it in a drawer. That pressure got to her sometimes. It wasn't right, but she couldn't fix it if she...

She glanced at her new partner. Darrell's dark face showed his tension. He'd seen a dead body before, but this was a bad one.

He had to learn. She steeled herself and looked at the body again. Multiple stab wounds to the torso. The medical examiner would have a lot to say, but Judy knelt and looked at the hands.

Yes, there was debris under the fingernails. She'd fought back. It hadn't been enough, but she'd fought back.

She stepped back, letting them take the body. Forensics would match the DNA, would get her identified.

"Psycho bastard," Darrell said, finally.

"I honestly hope not." If it was an actual psycho there would be more. More likely the murderer had known the victim. They almost always did.

But this was a perfect setup for the New York Panic. A young, pretty jogger murdered in a park. Admittedly, it wasn't Central Park this time.

It was going to bring up all those old stories. "But it does look like a walking urban legend, doesn't it?" Darrell shook his head.

She took a deep breath. "Can you go with the body? Lean on the medical examiner until we get results."

"What are you going to do?"

"I'm going to see if nobody saw nothing," she quipped, eyeing the bank of walk ups on one side of the park. It wasn't that late; some people would have been awake. The trees might have kept them legitimately oblivious, though.

Darrell laughed weakly. "It's New York."

She saluted him. "You're learning." A uniform fell in next to her as she walked towards the apartments.

For once, she did not argue with the extra protection.

───────────

THE BUILDING WAS a classic New York tenement with the fire escapes on the front. And no, nobody saw nothing. Knocking on a few relevant doors gave her precisely that. People were absent, asleep, or had been disturbed only by a scream that had occurred right before the dispatcher was called, and distinctly after her guess at time of death.

That scream had been the poor innocent who found the body, not the victim. So, the victim had fought back, but done so relatively quietly.

You were supposed to scream. Why hadn't she? Screaming was part of self defense, it drew attention.

It led back to the obvious conclusion. She had known her killer. Leaving forensics to search the scene, she walked back over to the tree. Leaned against it.

She wished she could ask the tree; it had, no doubt, witnessed the murder but, being a tree, had little to say on the matter. She'd had a college roommate who believed in such things. Animism.

Judy's personal jury was out, but it didn't matter whether the tree saw anything. The tree could not talk.

The uniforms were canvasing the area, but nobody saw nothing. Nobody ever did, not even when the victim was young, pretty, and white.

Blonde even.

Judy tugged at her own dark and vaguely curly locks and shook her head.

"Okay, here's one thing we do have. Somebody saw a young black man leave the area right after whoever screamed stopped screaming."

"I'm pretty sure that was that poor jogger. And I'm not going to be too suspicious of a young black man who leaves an area that's about to be crawling with cops. Identify him anyway."

He was probably just a witness, but if he'd stuck around, things would have gone bad. He would have been far too convenient. She was not going to let "convenient" win. "We can track him down and get a statement, but my guess is the body had already been there some fifteen minutes."

"You'd think it wouldn't have stayed there that long without being found."

"Late on a Thursday night. If it was Friday I'd agree with you." Thursday was a dead night for night life.

"I think I've done everything I can here," she added. "We have an ID on the jogger?"

"Chrissy Voltaire, born in freaking North Dakota, moved here to find work. I'm pretty sure she's just an unfortunate bystander." Clark was a senior uniform. She listened to his words.

She nodded. "So, until we get the body identified. I don't think this is a mad rapist. More likely her boyfriend."

Clark nodded himself. "More likely. You go do what you need to do. I'll handle things here."

She finally left. To get some rest and deal with the nightmares that so often stalked her.

They didn't get as many murders a year as people thought.

It only took one.

"Dani Martin," Darrell pronounced. "Freshman at New York University, born in Philadelphia. Only child."

Judy winced for the parents. "Has somebody contacted the parents yet?"

"Yes. They've been notified and are thinking about anything she might have said."

She was still working on the boyfriend hypothesis. It seemed the most likely. Boyfriend or somebody she'd rejected.

"Interesting thing. She wasn't raped."

Judy raised an eyebrow. "She *wasn't*."

"No." A pause. "I have the medical examiner's full report. She wasn't raped, she definitely fought back, and she probably fought back well. Black belt in Tae Kwon Do."

That might explain the lack of screaming. She probably thought she could win. "What dan, or don't we know yet?"

"I don't know that much." He almost looked sheepish.

So, the woman had been in the park, had been jumped, had fought back, and the guy had killed her instead of raping her.

Plausible scenario. But she was still hung up on this being somebody the young woman...seventeen...had known.

At her age, she could have been second or even third dan, depending on when she had started. Or not. Judy didn't know a lot about martial arts, but she knew there were minimums. And she knew who she could find out more from.

"Okay, I want to talk to her roommate, her...I forget the term in Tae

Kwon Do." Her instructor. It might be part of the picture. "And any romantic partners, current or recent."

He nodded.

"Forget her professors, she was a freshman, none of them would have known her. But find out if she had an advisor or a counselor." She smiled at Darrell. "Thank you."

The question was, of course, who to talk to first. Common wisdom said the roommate. Her gut, which seldom let her down, said the instructor.

She needed to build up a picture of who Dani Martin had been if she was going to work out who killed her.

"But before that, I'm getting myself a bagel." She'd pulled an all nighter. "Coming?" she asked of her partner.

He nodded. "Noah's?"

"Where else?"

He grinned. "Hey, I trust your judgment on bagels and lox."

"Stereotypes," she mock grumbled.

"This one's true," he pointed out.

He was right. She really was a better judge of good lox than he was. She was also right about it being a stereotype. It didn't matter.

They stepped out into New York's late summer dawn. For a moment, she could forget she had a case.

But no, she would not forget Dani Martin's accusing face.

2

In a dreary rental space in East New York, a somewhat overweight man with wispy blonde hair was fiddling with something on a work bench.

A slender, dark haired man entered the space unannounced. "Not about to blow anything up, are you, Richard?"

"Only you if you keep walking in on me like that!"

The man laughed a dry, empty laugh. "You know you wouldn't do that." He walked over to the bench. "Ah, not a bomb. What little *treasure* are you working on?"

"Spider tracer," the man quipped.

This elicited another dry laugh. "Looks a bit big to put on a person. Vehicle use, then?"

"So, what have you been up to?" Richard asked, rather than answering the question.

"Narrowly avoiding being framed for murder," the black-haired man said. "Might not be off the hook yet."

"Crap." Richard stopped working, turned his chair. "Victor, what *happened*?"

"I tracked down the young Guardian who recently showed up in south Manhattan. Just in time for somebody to take her down."

This time Richard's swear word was stronger. "Look, some of us *do* have to worry about Guardians killing us. *Minor inconvenience* right..." He glared at the man.

"Oh, I planned on convincing her to let us stay below her radar. But..."

"But of course everyone's going to think you did it."

"Relax. It's true nobody saw the actual culprit, but I doubt they looked like me in any more than circumstantial way. If they'd had a glamor up, Martin would have sensed it and known to be on her guard. I suspect she was killed by a mundane."

Richard nodded slowly. "But if you're wrong...I can't alibi you, well..."

"We could be in bed together," Victor quipped. It was both a suggestion for a lie and an obvious if casual invitation.

"After I finish this," Richard promised. "You worry about getting that cleared up."

Victor nodded slowly. For once he wasn't sure how. But fardle it, if he was going to get arrested and sent down, it should at least be for something he actually did.

Which left him with only one option.

He had to find the murderer himself. With proof the police would believe.

"I hate cops," he added, perhaps inexplicably, and stepped back out of the space. 'Flexspace' they called it, cheap for small scale storage or manufacturing.

Not in prime territory by the docks. But in a nothing industrial park between a wheelchair repair company and what he suspected was a grow op, where nobody would look for them. Or where everybody would, but not until it was too late, until they were done with why they were here and moving on again.

This time they might have to move on from New York, and Victor felt a pang of grief. He was from here, from here and not at the same time, but the memories of this life were clearer than all save...

He walked past the high school, carefully keeping to the opposite side of the road. He thought best while moving. The air was clear, the sun fading but bright, offering not that much heat but plenty of psychological warmth.

She'd fought back in near silence, but she hadn't been able to defeat her foe.

With that powerful a cloaking field this was no mortal witch. Only four possibilities remained: Demon, fairy, rogue Guardian, or a *highly* skilled mundane.

Victor's fear was that it was the first. That would put him against something dangerously close to his own kind.

If it wasn't his own kind.

His reassurances to Richard aside, he knew this was going to end with somebody in Hell.

He knew it was likely to be him.

IT WASN'T DIRECT or easy to get to Manhattan or, to be more precise, to New York University. He had to take a bus, then the subway. This was not the best part of Brooklyn. But his route took him that way none-theless, from dreary streets to, well.

More dreary streets. New York was his home and heart, but he had to admit that the city, the sprawling great metropolis was womb and lover and trap for him, as for so many of her children. Some people never sought to leave New York.

Some people simply couldn't.

He might be forced to. Or worse. He did not want to think of the reaming out that would come if he took on a ranking demon and lost. He was only lilin, once mere mortal and the lowest of the minions of Hell.

Yet the easiest to send out into the world. He had found Richard, and would never regret *that*. Richard did not need any help from him to wickedness, he had already found his own way into the shadows. All Victor had to do *there* was make sure he never escaped.

Other challenges were greater. He emerged into the light from 8 Street Station. Into the mess of buildings and people that was Manhat-tan, although at least not Midtown.

No sane New Yorker went anywhere near Times Square. That was left for the tourists. Southern Manhattan was better.

There had been no question as to why a Guardian had suddenly arrived in south Manhattan. You always looked at the universities first.

Richard was right; one should stay out of the way of Guardians. Richard, though, was barely more than a mundane. Aware, yes, powerful, no. Victor kept him around for his skills...in both technical matters and bed...not for any supernatural talent.

The sky was clouding up, threatening rain. Victor scowled at it and kept walking. He was alert to trouble, but any outward observer would have seen complete relaxation. He turned down a side street, past student housing and up against the edge of campus in the form of a large red library that towered over him with the promise of learning but also of tomes so boring that even a good student might fall into a doze. A couple of students walked past. One of them eyed him.

He smiled at the young woman, a predatory and inviting smile. He shouldn't, given he was more-or-less exclusive with Richard, but it was hard to resist. It might affect her equilibrium. She blushed and looked away.

He could never forget what he was.

VICTOR COULD NOT USE magic to find his target; he had never been good at the fine control needed for scrying. The power tended to rush out of him, destructive and exhilarating. It felt good.

It killed.

Which left him his mundane skills, the training he had given himself. He would find them, but he had to do it the slow way, the patient way.

No matter how much he wanted to start taking this place apart, it would not serve him well to do so. It would attract all kinds of attention.

On top of whatever had already been attracted by the premature death of a Guardian. At least her new incarnation would have to grow to something close to adulthood before they became something he had to worry about.

Except that was a bad thing. If she was here she could tell people he didn't do it.

Nobody would believe a lilin who said he hadn't committed a murder. They would, in any case, be looking for any and every excuse to send him back to Hell. Amongst those who didn't know the truth, he had a record and a reputation. He was known to be a professional, and the cops would put him high on the list.

There was, for him, no guarantee of another escape. A shudder went through him. But he deserved no escape, not after what he did.

And each step he took sealed his fate further. Agreeing, not fighting. Being what he was was, in and of itself, a sign that Hell trusted him. Which was a sign that he was willing to stay damned.

Even to damn others, although in truth lilin were instruments of destruction not temptation.

He stopped and looked upwards, fighting against the distraction circling in his mind. Then he looked around, blinking.

One thing he could see were the faint flickering auras of souls. Sometimes they had their own disguises; more than once he'd been fooled by an expert shield or even by the deep repression of something a person had once been.

But around here? Young people, innocents for the most part. Uninvolved in the ancient battles of Hell and Heaven and Faerie. Some of them had faith, glowing a little. A couple already had deep taint; or perhaps taint from a previous life they were being given a chance to get rid of. One or two had definitely dabbled in witchcraft.

If there were any experts here they were well shielded or even cloaked. But what he was looking for was...not, this time, the vulnerable.

Not those with faith, as there was no guarantee they would not subconsciously sense what he was, react to it.

There.

That one had the kind of cynical shell already built that he was looking for. He quirked his lips into something between a smile and a smirk and crossed the street towards the young man, hands in his pockets.

Yes, this one would do well enough.

3

THE BAREST HINT of fall was in the air as Judy and Darrell got out of the car. Driving in Manhattan was a game of Russian roulette, but there were certain things you didn't do.

Like take the subway when you had people to question. It was rare for the system to have problems, but every time Judy had tried that... She shook her head. New York University's campus was their first destination.

She was still trying to locate the martial arts instructor. The roommate had proved easier.

Jill felt an odd prick on the back of her neck, something vaguely familiar. She glanced around and saw him. Dark hair, just enough facial hair to highlight his angular chin, relatively slender build.

A man she'd seen once before, and never been able to pin to anything. There had been a murder that time too.

He might have done it.

He might have done this one.

He might be a ringer for the man she remembered, but there was something, an odd tingling fog in her brain. He was talking to a young student.

"Judy?" Darrell asked.

She shook her head. "See the dark-haired guy over there. I'm pretty sure he's not on the side of the angels. But he's probably nothing to do with the case."

Darrell nodded, turning to look at the man for a moment. "Hot, though."

"Ahem," Judy said.

"Well, he is." Darrell sounded a little bit defensive.

"I wouldn't."

All of her instincts told her getting involved with that guy would be a bad idea. Hot, but a bad idea. Shaking her head, still trying to place him, she headed towards the dorm office. Hopefully they'd gotten Lacy, the roommate, to stick around.

Hopefully she wasn't terrified of cops. Judy knew many people had reason. She tried to be one of the good ones, but she knew her fair share of cops who were more interested in arresting people than solving crimes, who were racist or sexist or anti-semitic or anti-*something* or who were just plain incompetent.

She knew what happened to good cops who pushed too hard against it. She couldn't help anyone if she got fired or worse.

She reached the office, putting the dark-haired man out of her mind. The door opened on a slightly fusty smell and a receptionist who was clearly a second- or third-year student paying off some of her tuition. She had her ears not just pierced, but elongated. "Can I help you?"

Judy tugged out her badge. "We're here to talk to Lacy Wilcox. We called ahead."

The receptionist shuddered. "I heard what happened to Dani."

Judy nodded a little bit, putting on a sympathetic face. This person might not have known Dani well, but they had definitely known her.

"I mean, she...okay, she was a little bit reckless, but nobody deserves that."

She made a mental note of that too. Reckless could have been what put her there to be a victim, but you didn't blame them. You didn't ever blame them.

No.

You did.

You just didn't do it where the public could hear you. You saved those whisperings for the back of the canteen.

Sometimes they really did have it coming.

Dani Martin had, worst case, messed up.

LACY WAS a slender young woman dressed in full loligoth fashion except for the pale skin, which she did not come with naturally. She pushed back her locs as she regarded Judy.

Judy could see that she was pale under her significant melanin. And suspected the dressing up was a defense mechanism against her grief, against the cops, against the risk of being somehow blamed for this.

They were roommates. That did not mean they were friends. They could be enemies. Judy watched every minute reaction and motion. "Darrell, please stay," she said quietly.

Lacy relaxed a little bit. She likely saw the African-American cop as at least...at least a bit less likely to judge her.

"Relax. You're not a suspect."

Lacy's second defense mechanism was snark, "What, because I'd have killed her here? I'd never have got the blood out the carpet."

Judy managed not to laugh. "It's hard to clean up." Sadly, she knew from occasional experience. "Truth is, you had opportunities to kill her in a much less messy way."

"I could have poisoned her," Lacy mused. "Look..."

"Be honest. You didn't choose to be her roommate. I *hated* mine," Judy confided. "She liked to play cards until 3am. On weeknights."

Lacy laughed. "Oh man, that's worse. I didn't hate Dani. We just had absolutely nothing in common and I didn't like her much. I was considering putting in for a change. I'd like to share space with somebody I actually get along with." She closed her eyes. "But I didn't want *that* to happen."

"Why didn't you like her?" It was a possible clue.

"Oh, well. She was odd." Lacy glanced down at herself. "The wrong *kind* of odd," she amended.

Judy could see where her eyeliner had been damaged by tears. "A different kind of odd from you."

"Right. I'm into depressing music and World of Darkness role playing games. She was into meditation and crystals and New Age stuff. And martial arts." Lacy closed her eyes. "She thought she could win the fight, didn't she."

Judy didn't answer that almost-a-question. "So, she was into New Age stuff?"

"Well, she was into occultism. She claimed she wasn't a fluffy bunny, whatever that means, but she did wear crystals."

Judy nodded. "I know the type."

She even thought she might have heard the phrase fluffy bunny, but she wasn't sure what it meant.

"I need to ask you...I *do* need to ask you where you were when she was killed." A pause. "And if you knew anyone who hated her enough to kill her."

Lacy shook her head. "I was in the library studying. Just check with the librarian. As for the other? No. Nobody hated Dani."

Sadly, they often said that even when it was true. Or even believed it. No help here, then.

Unless the New Age thing was a clue. "Can you tell me where she went to study Tae Kwon Do?"

Lacy told her.

<hr />

"No REAL LUCK?" Darrell asked as they left...armed with the name of Dani's sodam and dojang.

"We have a place to go next."

He nodded. "Where?"

"Her Tae Kwon Do studio.Maybe her instructor knew something, or one of the other students."

Maybe.

She was starting to think this wasn't going to be one of those simple "the boyfriend did it" cases. She wished it was, but...

Into the occult. "Also, she was apparently into New Age and occult stuff. Probably not connected, but..."

Judy felt the hair on the back of her neck prick up.

Darrell frowned. "Are we sure it's not?"

Judy pursed her lips. "I don't think so."

He shrugged. "Some of those wiccan types can get into some quite nasty fights, although they don't generally resort to violence."

Maybe one of them did came a small voice in her head. She silenced it. She would follow the lead if it showed up, but it wasn't a priority.

They walked back to the car. "Next step the martial arts studio." What were they called in Tae Kwon Do? Dojo was Japanese.

She couldn't remember.

There was a skinny black guy watching the car. She didn't know him, but her hairs pricked up again. He was watching the car intently, hands in his pockets, leaning against a wall opposite. Slightly too old to be a traditional student. Late twenties, maybe thirty. A bit of nervousness in his motion.

She glanced at Darrell. At the car. It wasn't marked as a police car, but some people were experts at spotting unmarked cars.

And some people didn't trust cops. With a very good reason, especially given the amount of melanin he had. Darrell's skin color would not help him feel any better. She quietly checked under the car before she got in, just in case. Likely all he'd done was watch.

But there was something about him. She'd remember his face.

Even if she wasn't entirely sure why.

4

VICTOR WASN'T AS worried about the two obvious cops who came out of one of the dorms as he was about the guy watching the cop car.

Oh, that one. That one was a real danger to him. Which was kind of a shame because he was also seriously hot. On the thin side, but enough to make Victor want to lick his lips a little.

No.

That was a fire that would burn him, would burn both of them. He changed direction to go an entire block off to avoid the man. At the same time he knew he wouldn't have seen the last of him.

He saw the man's head lift as he turned away. Saw him sniff the air.

Not a werewolf; they were extinct and this guy almost certainly lacked the specific qualifications needed to shift. But there were some spirit workers who could do more or less what they had done.

It could have been worse. The guy could have had a rider, and then Victor would have been really screwed. The loa and orisha did *not* care for things like him.

Deep breath.

He'd been made, of that he was sure. Which meant he was probably going to have to deal with the guy by some means, whether by corrupting him, killing him, or convincing him Victor wasn't worth his time and effort.

He generally preferred the last. Although he'd enjoy the process of corruption with that one.

Stop it, he told himself. *You have a boyfriend.*

Of course, he didn't anticipate spending the next fifty years with Richard. But he wasn't ready to cut him loose just yet.

And not just because he was useful.

So. The cops had gone into that particular dorm, which told him that was her dorm. If he could find out who the cops were going to see...

He wished for a moment he had a fae or faeblood's knack for glamor. He didn't. So he would just have to brazen it out. He walked around the block.

Curse it, the guy was still there.

Brazen it out. Victor firmly ignored him as he walked into the dorm. There was a common area in the lobby. A receptionist of sorts, clearly a student making her rent. He moved to look at some of the posters instead, trying to look casual. He appeared too old to be a student, but he could probably pass as somebody's older boyfriend.

His break came a few minutes later. "So, I saw the cops." The girl leaned over the desk, her pink braids dangling.

"There was a *murder*," the receptionist said. "A girl in this building. Don't go jogging late at night."

"I never do," said pink hair.

"You're smart. Unlike the girl who got killed."

She hadn't been jogging late at night, Victor reckoned. She'd been hunting and the prey had turned on her.

Or he was right and a mundane had killed her. But he still suspected she had been hunting.

He wished he thought it was just that she had been taken out by some unseelie fae, some minor creature.

He didn't think so.

But he wished so.

LISTENING for a few more minutes got him a name. Dani.

Her name of the time was Dani. Not her true name, of course, Guardians kept them as close as did demons and, for that matter, lilin.

But the name her parents had given her, thinking her nothing more than their child.

Dani.

Part of him wanted to know everything about her, wanted to feel her life. He wished this had been a hunting accident. There were even a few vampires left in New York. The modern world was not kind to beings which messed up cameras by their very nature. The MO, however, did not match a vampire.

It matched somebody who knew that the best way to take out a Guardian was *not* with magic.

It was pretty close to what he might have tried, although he was sure he would have lost. She would have felt him coming, would have known what he was. Would have acted in self defense.

Likely froze him.

But the police did not know that and sniffing around was dangerous. Still, a hunting accident.

Or.

Or she really had been killed by a mundane. She would not have sensed one, would not have known she was going to be attacked until she was. Guardians sometimes had training in mundane combat.

She had not. She had been studying to fill the gap and it had not worked. He almost felt sad for a moment.

Even though he would have probably ended up either killing her or being killed by her. But all part of the cycle.

For those who remembered, it was exactly that. A cycle of life and lives, and enemies always came back to haunt you.

For those who did not? They saw only the edges.

Guardians. Lilin. Some of the more powerful witches and spirit workers. And occasionally somebody almost mundane would suddenly *remember*.

That could also be what happened.

But he had investigated all he was willing to for now.

When he came out, the spirit worker was still there. He brazened it out, heading straight for the nearest subway station, or as straight as streets and crowds allowed him.

The man did not follow.

He regretted that.

"COULD HAVE BEEN A HUNTING ACCIDENT," Victor said brightly as he entered the workshop. "You done with the tracker."

"If so, what was she hunting?"

"Not vampire." Victor took a deep breath. "Not the right MO. And I'm still a little concerned. If she *was* taken out it was by somebody who knew that mundanes are the best weapons against Guardians." Or it had been just... "Or she ran into another of my kind. Which would not be fun."

Lilin did not work together well. They weren't supposed to intentionally kill each other, but there were ways to deal with a rival that weren't killing.

Like, say, framing for murder. Not that killing each other didn't happen. A fight between lilin often ended up with serious damage.

But nobody seemed to be *setting out* to frame Victor. "Point is, nobody's trying to frame me and I think we can relax. Well, except for one thing." Unless, of course, somebody saw this as an opportunity. Bridge, cross, come to.

"What?"

"Skinny black guy, smells of wet dog. He shows up, I'd just go out the back door and pretend there was nobody here."

"Werewolf?"

"I've already told you, there *are* no more werewolves. Spirit worker of some kind. He made me outside the university and I don't think he's on our side." He didn't mention to Richard the other reason they guy couldn't be a werewolf. It didn't matter, not since they had been hunted to extinction.

Richard sighed. "Let's finish this job and blow this joint."

"I couldn't agree more. But you done?"

Richard set down his tools. "I am now." He melted out of the chair and into Victor's arms, their lips touching, mouths open.

He wasn't the most attractive lover Victor had ever had.

He made up for it in other ways. Like the kissing. Richard was a *very* good kisser. He smelled of male musk and, faintly, welding torch.

He slipped an arm around his lover's waist and started to guide him towards the cot they had upstairs. It would do for now. He couldn't wait any longer. He could feel a bulge that indicated Richard probably couldn't either.

They went upstairs, leaving a trail of discarded clothing behind them, excitement growing before Richard, for once the more dominant one, pulled Victor down onto the cot.

He allowed it, reaching for the lube on the table next to it.

But his thoughts weren't entirely on the lover he had. They were in part on might-have-beens.

And when his climax came it was tinged with more fear than he had thought he was feeling.

5

"NEIGHBORHOOD WATCH," Darrell quipped, indicating the thin guy as they left him behind.

"I'm not going to shoot any black guys, but they don't know that." Judy's lips hit a thin line. She'd always tried to be a good cop, but had she stood aside too much for the sake of her own precious career?

Was she a good cop?

But that didn't explain why the hairs on the back of her neck, which had finally returned to normal, had pricked when she saw him.

She was oddly more worried about the white guy.

"I *hope* he was that," she adds. "Not somebody connected to the case. Last thing I want is to find out this was some kind of conspiracy."

Dani's dojang was tucked down a side street, a surprisingly narrow store front in one of those buildings that went further back than it looked.

The door was open. Classes were in progress, despite it being the middle of the day. A class anyway, which seemed to be mostly middle-aged women.

Must be the housewife class, she thought wryly. Women coming in to learn self defense while the kids were in school and the husband at work. Privileged women by virtue of that fact. Probably paid for this place.

She waited, watching. They didn't seem to be very good, any of them. The teacher was directing two of them in a spar.

One of them didn't want to hit the other. The instructor was encouraging them gently. He seemed to be of mixed Korean and European origin, his hair a lighter brown than she had expected.

Maybe this was a very novice class. She didn't know enough about Tae Kwon Do to judge.

Finally, he stepped back. "Five-minute break." Then his eyes swept towards her. Intent.

She felt a hint of the same prickling. "What do you need?"

"I'm afraid we need to talk to you about one of your students."

He nodded. "Is this urgent or can it wait fifteen minutes?"

Until class was over. She glanced at Darrell. "It can wait."

"Why don't you take a seat in the lounge, then. I'll finish up with this group and then we can talk at leisure."

He seemed unruffled. Or perhaps he was not showing his ruffles in front of the class. Judy headed into the indicated lounge. There was mismatched furniture inside, and she flopped onto an armchair. Darrell stayed standing, looking at the various certificates and trophies in the room. Was that.. "Oh, wow, I've never seen one of those in the flesh before."

She looked up and blinked. "Neither have I." She couldn't resist standing up to look.

In a securely locked case with several other trophies was an Olympic medal. Gold.

———

"SHE WAS ONE OF MY STUDENTS." The instructor came in while Darrell was still admiring the award. "As a child. She let me put it on display here to motivate the students."

"Tells everyone you're a good instructor, too." Judy had sat back down.

"So, which of my students is this about?"

"Dani Martin."

His eyes clouded over. "She didn't show up for class..." He looked between the two of them. Sat down, heavily. "Is she..."

"I'm afraid she's dead. She was murdered two nights ago in Tompkins Square Park." Judy didn't want to go into the details, but did add. "She tried to fight."

"She would." He closed his eyes for a moment. "But we all come up against a superior opponent at some point. Or one who is armed when we aren't."

Judy nodded. "We don't think it was random, although it could have been."

"What time did it happen?"

"Sometime between 6pm and 9pm last night."

"I was teaching that entire time, just to get it out of the way. Stopped for dinner at 7pm, ate with a couple of my students. Dani was supposed to be here for morning class."

Judy wondered when this guy slept. Probably in the afternoons. "So you do class..."

"Early morning and late night, plus the late morning class a couple of days a week. All day Saturday and Sunday when there aren't tournaments."

"So, what kind of student was Dani?"

"Driven," he said. "She felt unsafe, I think. And apparently she was right. Her old instructor said the same thing about her. She wasn't the best student I had, but she was one of the most dedicated. I...called her when she didn't show up. I suppose her phone's in evidence."

"It is. Did any of the other students...did she have any nasty rivalries?"

"Dani? Nah. She didn't exactly have friends either."

"Dating anyone?"

"Oh..." He shook his head. "Probably. At least one, anyway."

That was also a clue. Some people would have a low opinion of somebody who had more than one partner at the same time, if that were true. She made a mental note of it. "Her roommate told me she always wore a crystal necklace."

"Quartz crystal on a thong, nothing special. She thought it was lucky or something."

"So, nothing of value."

"Only to her." He frowned a bit, looking like he was about to say something else. Studying her with an odd intensity to his gaze. Finally, "Detective, be careful."

"You think..."

"I think that anyone who would kill somebody like Dani might not stop at cop killing." He shook his head. "Of course, if it was random that's another matter."

Robbery for the necklace no longer seemed to be a good motivation.

Then he raised his head. "Detectives. Leave the building now. Through the back. *Trust me.*"

She looked at Darrell. "You go. I need to see what's going on."

"No," he said. "You don't."

"EVERYONE OUT THE BACK."

Judy glanced at Darrell. "Get them all clear."

She had no idea what was going on. She didn't want to know what was going on.

"Go," he insisted, turning dark eyes towards her.

"No." She took a deep breath. "This may be connected to my case. And I'm not afraid of..."

"You don't even know what to be afraid of." His eyes bored into her as the students who had been practicing vanished through the back door into some alleyway or other.

The knock on the front door came a moment later. Without waiting for an answer four men came into the room.

She made sure her badge was tucked away out of sight. Protection racket was her guess, but how had he known they were there?

"I assume you aren't changing your mind."

"You killed Dani," he accused, very quietly. "You *killed one of my students.*"

"That wasn't us. My word on it."

Judy slipped back towards a corner. She didn't look like a student, wasn't dressed as one. Likely wasn't fit enough to be one, not with all the time she spent behind a desk.

Maybe she should fix that.

"Prove it."

"We can tell you who did it. But you won't like it."

"Who?" He looked from man to man. "No. You'll lie."

"You can judge that for yourself. Or have the cop do it."

"I know if you tell me the truth it's the prelude to killing me." His lips quirked. He seemed oddly unafraid.

"It's the prelude to killing *her*." One of the men strode towards Judy.

"Oh, I really wouldn't," he said.

"She's a mundane."

He just smiled. He didn't say anything.

One of the men grabbed her, pushed her up against the wall. She drove her knee instinctively into his groin.

"I said not to."

The light in the room was changing. The air was growing thick. "Who killed Dani?"

"A lilin named Victor Prince."

That name could be a lie. It could be the truth. It was an angle for investigation and Judy seized on it. But also on the word lilin, which she could *not* have heard right. She didn't have time to think about it. She saw an imperceptible nod from the man.

And he became a whirl of motion. The air chilled, chilled violently, became so cold the breath caught in her throat.

She knew he was right.

She did not want to be here.

She did not want to be any part of this.

She ran.

Behind her, almost the second she was clear, the dojang exploded outwards, glass flying into the street, the building sagging and crumbling.

Nobody came out of the ruins.

6

VICTOR EXAMINED THE BOMB CAREFULLY. He wasn't the expert Richard was, but he was an extra set of eyes to look it over.

He ignored the man himself for right now. Sometimes even he found the intensity in those eyes a little much. Richard enjoyed his job.

So did Victor, but it was different. Victor was what he was; there was no changing it. Richard chose this. No, it wasn't a mental illness.

It was a choice. He felt that in the man, and it had drawn him to him in the first place, but there was some small part of him deep within that was repelled.

Just that small thing which kept him from a true commitment. He already knew if Richard asked for what legal recognition they could get...and if things went the way they were doing then yes, marriage might be on the cards...he would say no.

Besides.

Nothing was forever, and people thought of marriage as that. A binding of souls. Sometimes it was. More often it was not, only until death do us part.

He was very aware that could be any time. "Looks good."

"Wish we could use it right now," Richard said, wistfully.

"You know we have to wait on the client's word." Victor hated that too, but they needed money.

No matter what he was, he still had to eat and buy clothing and pay the rent.

Yet another reason to get out of New York: the ever-climbing cost of living. He was pretty sure that before too long everyone not hyper rich would be in New Jersey or the furthest reaches of Queens.

He didn't want to leave. But he knew it was time. "I don't like it either."

Petulantly, Richard kicked the table.

Victor reached into a drawer, pulled out a pair of joints. Handed him one. "I think you need this."

Richard sucked in a breath, but did not argue, fumbling for his lighter. There was nobody else in the small building to smell the smoke and call the cops or complain.

Marijuana didn't really affect Victor. He smoked out of solidarity. Richard turned to the computer, joint dangling from between his lips.

"Oh. Oh *beautiful*."

"What?" Victor turned, the smoke blowing away from him.

"Somebody blew up a martial arts studio in the Village."

"Sure it's not a gas explosion?" Victor asked.

"Oh, I'm sure it's a gas explosion." Richard air quoted the words. "But check out this video."

Victor watched, but he didn't have Richard's expertise. He did see the woman scrambling away.

He'd seen her somewhere before. "You know I don't see it like you do."

"The explosion epicenter was in the studio itself. My guess would be grenade or spell backlash."

Victor nodded. He looked at the woman again. Who was she? Somebody very lucky. She wasn't dressed as a student.

"Maybe they were teaching something more than martial arts," Victor mused.

"I'd lay bets on it." A pause. "The instructor was in there. But nobody else."

Victor narrowed his eyes. "Play it again."

Richard did.

"I'm seeing at least three bodies in there."

"Ooh. I love a good cover-up." Richard leaned back in his chair, one hand on the joint, the other thrown behind his head.

"Unless it's a cover-up we end up mixed up in."

He got the last word.

AFTER INITIAL EXCITEMENT, Richard was pouty that somebody not him had got to blow something up.

Victor idly decided to research the martial arts studio. Spell backlash. Or a fight. Three dead people that hadn't been mentioned as even existing.

And a familiar-looking woman. Yes, he knew her. And he knew what she was.

Cop.

He was sure of that much even if any other details of the context had escaped him.

So, cop walks into martial arts studio. Cop runs out of martial arts studio a moment before it blows up.

And the press call it a gas explosion.

This told him something plain and simple: The cops had put out the kind of quiet gag order that sometimes worked, sometimes didn't.

To keep certain things quiet until they'd finished investigating. It made far too much sense, in his mind. Organized crime, probably. Tidy, neat, forgettable.

Heck, there would probably be a buy off, a bit more corruption, a bit more darkness over the city. He smiled a bit at the prospect.

Every bit of corruption and darkness made his life and his job easier. But he was half expecting to receive orders. Half expecting to be sent after somebody.

He had all but forgotten about the Guardian. The school had been a good one, the head instructor quite excellent. An alumni had won an

Olympic medal which, one story noted, had been kept on display in the dojang.

Some people would probably be upset about that. Most of all the person who had won it.

Victor didn't care. He cared about signs that something more than mundane martial arts was going on there, some other instruction.

Because he suspected that Richard was right. There was a supernatural explanation here. Ki manipulation could create that kind of effect if it hit the wrong kind of shielding.

And he went hunting, deeper into the dark web.

Surveillance footage of the outside of the store opposite. First two cops, the woman and a black man, plainclothes. They walked into the dojo. A few minutes after that, three men in suits walked in. A few minutes after *that* the woman cop ran out, without her partner, and the building exploded behind her.

So, the black cop and the students? Their bodies hadn't been found.

He frowned. Was there a back door? If so, they must have used it...which meant they had some warning.

Fortunately it was New York. Pulling up street view confirmed the back door and the alleyway.

Yes. A back door, which meant...the men had entered, somebody had evacuated the remaining students through the back. Somebody meaning the black cop, he suspected.

The woman had elected to stay to find out what was going on, and barely got out. Or been pushed out.

He had a picture now, the start of one. Which meant that if he could get a list of students...

Some of them were likely to be dangerous.

Some of them were going to be looking for revenge.

It was none of his business. But he found the list anyway.

And one name on it stuck out.

"WE NEED TO MOVE," Victor said as he came out of his office.

"The bomb."

"It's stable. Get it to the van."

"What's the panic?"

"You know that studio that got blown up? You won't believe who was a student there. Short of a direct order from Hell, we're going to lie *very* low for a while."

Richard frowned. "And if you do..."

"Then *you* are still going to lie low until the client calls, then do the job and get out of town. I'll find you."

The 'if I can' was left unspoken, and wisely so. The fight bubbled under the surface, but did not quite boil. Richard sighed and nodded. "I'll start loading the van."

"Make sure the thing starts first," Victor said, moving into the office and beginning to shut everything down. Had marijuana affected him, he might have gone for another joint just to take the edge off.

Short of a direct order from Hell. Truth was he wanted to clear the area before any such order could be given. He would be unsurprised if something didn't come down. Lilin were expendable, or rather fixable. If he died, they would just send him out again, possibly after a chewing out.

He wasn't supposed to care about staying alive. He wasn't supposed to care about anything but the mission. This was better than a cell in Hell.

It was better than watching his crime replayed in front of his eyes over and over, that being one of the torments that had been visited on him. His wife screaming.

What had he done?

He shook his head. Unplugged and disconnected the computer. They'd be gone before they canceled the lease. Gone to some other property under another name.

Gone altogether, if their client actually bothered to talk to them. Out of New York, somewhere west, somewhere south. Before all of this came to a head.

Unless he got that order.

In which case he was sending Richard away. He had actually come to care for him, no, he would not marry him even if it became legal.

But he didn't want him in Hell just yet.

Even if that was the inevitable trajectory of his life. Even if there was no way they could escape, and he knew Richard well enough. He would not change. He would always be what he was now, always enjoy blowing things up. But Victor could keep him alive for now. Even if he wasn't supposed to care.

There was a knock on the door.

7

THERE WERE a lot of Victor Princes in New York. A lot. It was a dramatic name, fairly unusual, but far from unique and New York was a big city. A very big city.

But there were not many Victor Princes who had the kind of file this one did. And looking at the file, she knew where she had seen the name before.

He had briefly been a suspect in a previous murder, a case of a woman washing up in the river. And she had seen him then.

And again at the college, lurking.

He was involved. But it seemed too pat, and she didn't trust those men. Who were dead.

They were covering that up. Three dead mobsters were not something you wanted too many rumors about until you had some grasp of what was going on. The dead instructor...

One of the mobsters must have had a grenade. It seemed so unlikely, but there was no other explanation.

She hadn't seen what she had seen. But this particular Victor Prince. Suspect in a number of crimes, but they'd never been able to pin anything on him.

She knew what he really was, of course.

A mercenary.

And thus a perfect scapegoat. He was a hit man, the kind of person you got to do your dirty work, paid off and forgot about. If they got caught it was deniable. They had their own code of honor. They would never sell out their employer, whoever they were. Well, almost never anyway. The good ones didn't.

This one had been doing it for years and not gotten caught. Or rather, not gotten caught in a way they could prove. He was one of the good ones.

She left Darrell in the library. She was about to do the dumbest thing of her career. She was probably about to get herself killed. She left a message for the Captain with Victor Prince's name and the location, knowing she would be long gone before he bothered to check.

But some instinct told her that if she took anyone along with her, it would trigger...something. Something that would make things worse. Cops escalated fights. She knew that. She tried not to be one of those cops.

But often she felt as if she was surrounded by them, on all sides. As if they were taking over.

As if they already had. And now she had a suspect, the pressure would be on to simply end this. Even more so if he was black.

So, no, she wasn't going to take any uniforms with her this time, although she would not be able to avoid it for long. She did check her piece, for what it was worth. Against somebody like this?

No, she was going to rely on something other than fighting.

She got out of the car opposite the industrial unit, in East New York. This was where she'd tracked him down to. A dangerous man.

She walked up to the door and knocked on it.

THE MAN who opened the door had one hand out of view and was definitely not Victor Prince. He was a slightly overweight guy with wispy blonde hair.

And she knew what was in the hidden hand. Behind him, the man she was looking for stepped out of an office, emerging onto a small catwalk above the floor.

They were packing to move out. Suspicious behavior, but perhaps understandable. "I'm not here for a fight," she said. "I just want to talk to Mr. Prince."

"You're a cop," the man who was not Victor Prince accused. She could see the glint of the gun now. It was all she could do not to reach for her own, but that would escalate things. That was how you got shots fired and stuff in the local paper. That was how bad cops started.

"I have a few questions. Nobody's going to be arrested, at least not if I like the answers." Confidence was key with people like this.

A harsh laugh from the man on the catwalk. He came down the stairs, moving like a predator. She wondered for a moment what he would be like in bed.

Told her ovaries firmly to shut up. True, she'd been single since Beth had moved to Wisconsin. And she hadn't managed to get a romp between the sheets in a while.

But getting a lady boner over a criminal was just plain stupid. "And I'm alone."

"Dumb and incompetent." The man came down the stairs. "Richard, the van."

Firm, dominant. This was a man who was going to be in charge until he met his match. An alpha, as it were.

Richard went, but kept the gun in his hand. They faced each other.

"No, I just don't trust the uniforms not to shoot somebody."

Again, the harsh laugh. "Ah, so you see yourself as one of the good ones."

"I try." Their eyes met. That feeling of the hair pricking on the back of her neck grew, but this time it was more than that. The feeling of being in the presence of something ancient and dark. There was a smell of cloying musk and brimstone in her nostrils.

"We've met before," Victor said.

"Body in the river." She remembered that case now. Maybe he had done it, maybe not. It would be so easy to bring him in. Or better yet to save the paperwork, as it were.

He nodded. "And now you've come to..."

"Dani Martin."

"I did *not* kill her."

His emphasis was careful. There was no panic in his tone. But also no tell. She couldn't determine right away if he was lying. "Little bird told me you did."

A slow nod. "My alibi went to the van. We were in bed."

He apparently said it, from his tone, hoping for a reaction. He didn't get one. "Convenient. Can't prove it, can't disprove it." She didn't, couldn't take her eyes off of him.

She felt as if she was in the room with a panther. He was either going to kill her or mate with her.

"Very. Unfortunately, I wasn't given advanced warning to come up with something better."

That startled a laugh out of her. "You knew her."

A pause. "Detective. I didn't do it, and if I find out who did I'll point you in the right direction. But beyond that, you don't want to know."

"Yes," she found herself saying. "I do."

***

"So, Dani Martin was a victim of...a sting operation aimed at you." She didn't believe him. There were tells...this man was an expert liar, but she was practiced at seeing through deception.

But she couldn't weave through this to the truth. "Then why kill the instructor."

Victor shook his head. "I have no idea. The entire point of that operation was to give you my name in the hope that..." A pause.

"That I'd blindly come and arrest you."

She still might have to, but she added, "On the word of a mob guy who's now dead."

"You *are* one of the good ones. Thorough, at least. So I'd add that it's possible that they didn't kill her, just used the murder as a convenient thing to hang on me. But why warn me?"

"I was hoping you knew who actually did it. You can't give me a name."

It would be tidy if the murderer had died in the dojang explosion.

Neat. They could wrap it up, finalize the paperwork, and tell the media what had happened.

"Not a personal name, no."

"An organization name." She let out a breath.

"Diabla," he said. A pause. "I can't be sure. I could be wrong. But it's worth checking out."

Devil. In the feminine form. "A gang, then." One of those that had, perhaps, as its membership aged started to challenge the older families. "And one with a grudge against you."

"They tried to hire me. They couldn't afford me."

That bit of honesty might have won her over if she had thought it honesty in truth. He wasn't hiding what he was from her. He was also lying. He didn't know who did it. He was just trying to deflect her from him. Perhaps he intended to find the murderer himself as a way of proving his innocence. A professional like that might be capable. He was lying. He was very definitely lying. She just could not work out what direction the lie flowed in.

Of course, he knew that she couldn't prove anything. "You know I don't believe you."

"I know."

It was a moment of near intimacy. The industrial unit, half empty. The faint sound of the fan that kept the temperature in here comfortable, although it probably couldn't keep up in the summer. There would be no air conditioning here.

She didn't know this man and never would. She didn't know what to make of him. But he had told her a story she could use.

A story she could believe. It wasn't the truth, she was sure of it. A pretty lie, an obscure gang named after the Devil in high heels. Lilin. The actual Devil? She shook her head, not willing to believe *that* just yet.

"But you should."

He was trying to give her an out. A way to wrap up the case. It was the behavior of a guilty man.

It was the behavior of a man trying to protect her.

It was both. She could not tell which. "I strongly suggest you change your mind about moving. I need to know where to find you."

She knew he would be gone next time she looked, to a place rented under a different name. She had to say it anyway.

"Detective." A pause. Something in his eyes. "Drop the case. Tie it off. Find a reason to walk away. Because if you don't then *if* you survive you will never be able to walk away. This is your last chance."

Her last chance for what?

But she already knew she wasn't going to walk away.

8

"SHE'S GOING to end up dead," Victor pronounced as the cop left.

"Going to kill her?" Richard asked.

"I may have to," he said, plainly. He didn't want to, not particularly. He would enjoy the act because it was what he did. What he was created for. But he didn't want to. She was on the edge of something too, he could feel it.

"But I'd rather avoid it. You know how much attention cop killing gets."

"Do it on our way out of town, then," Richard suggested. From his tone, he was quite serious.

Victor considered the matter for a long moment. "It probably won't be necessary at that point. Let's just try to avoid it."

Was he getting soft? No, he was being practical. Sensible. Trying to keep the heat down. Richard was not always good at that.

Richard offered him a bottle. He took a generous swallow without even looking. With his physiology it was near impossible to get him drunk or high. It was Tennessee unaged corn whisky, mind, and he gave his lover a look.

"What? You like that stuff."

"Not without warning!" Moonshine was good, but he preferred to *know* it was moonshine.

"You could have looked," Richard mock pouted, pretending to stalk away.

"I thought I could trust you." He grinned, set the bottle down, and then chased after Richard.

With predictable results.

Later, "Are we still going to move?"

"No," Victor pronounced, "At this point it would make cop lady more suspicious."

He still thought she was going to end up dead, mind. She was the type who didn't make it to retirement. She didn't know when *not* to poke.

But that was probably what made her a good cop. Along with...but perhaps it was nothing.

A good cop was going to have an aura. A bad one, too. The bad ones were so much fun to play with.

He decided that he was really more disappointed that he wouldn't get to play than anything else. This one felt too solid to easily be budged from her course. She'd made it to detective and still thought she could be a good cop.

Which was why he might have to kill her.

"Just make sure that when she comes poking around..."

"Should we arrange to stay longer."

Victor considered that. If they could get out of New York they would be out of her jurisdiction, but... "I think so. She's probably too proud to call the FBI unless she has to, but I'm not counting on it."

Richard nodded. "I'll set that up." He detached himself from Victor, pulling on his jeans without bothering with underpants.

Victor watched him go for a moment, then turned his thoughts back to the cop.

Yeah.

She was going to wind up dead.

VICTOR DECIDED to set aside the thing with the cop. He also decided he needed to get out and do something.

Something not with Richard. Making his way out of the building, he headed towards the subway station.

He wanted, abruptly, to get out of New York *or* to go wander into Midtown. He wasn't sure which he wanted, and he never liked these kinds of feelings. He never liked feeling as if he didn't know what to do.

It was a bad sign, and it usually meant somebody downstairs wanted his attention. He glanced up at the sky, which was clear, and then headed into the station.

The train rattled its way to Manhattan. Of the contrary urges, this was the easiest one to satisfy and perhaps Central Park would prove a good compromise. Green in the heart of the city, rolling, with many places where you could forget you were in the very center of what Victor genuinely believed was the greatest city on earth. Trees. Rocks. The lungs of the city, the place people went to restore their sanity.

But he could feel darkness roiling through him. Maybe not, then. Something was stirring in the depths, something which might have nothing to do with him. Shuddering, he got off at Rockefeller Center, bent on losing himself in the mass of people.

They shimmered around him, some deep in the flames, some bright. Most, of course, somewhere in the middle.

Was there anyone who would be fun to play with? In this crowd it was hard to tell, and he had other urges too.

Not sex, thanks to Richard, but with the dark feelings that came over him, he found himself looking at each of the faces. Looking for somebody who might be at that point where he could tip them over the edge, send them on the path that led to damnation.

Pulling himself back. He had to keep control. Not easy for a lilin, control.

Rockefeller Plaza was a zoo of people, though. Lots of them. Lots of targets, lots of temptation.

He frowned and closed his eyes for a moment.

When he talked about orders from below, he knew Richard envisioned a loud voice in his head telling him exactly what to do.

Sometimes, yes, sometimes it was that. More often it was much more like the sensation he was getting right now.

There was somebody the bosses wanted dealt with, and he'd know how when he saw them. With that realization all of the conflicted feelings inside him resolved.

One way or another. It was up to him how.

He turned down 49th street, where there were fewer people. Those who did see him got out of his way, perhaps sensing the very edges of his dark mission.

NBC headquarters. No. Not there.

He kept moving, stopped to get a hot dog from a vendor, ignoring the fancier food trucks.

There. They were in that office building.

It was close enough to 5pm.

He set up a position opposite and waited.

EVENING STARTED to come early in the canyons of Manhattan, the sun dipping beneath the buildings sooner even in early Fall.

The man who emerged from the building in a pin stripe suit was the target. Victor narrowed his eyes, seeing the faint hint of smoke around him.

Ah, yes. This one was trying to escape his bargain. The easiest way to deal with it would be to kill him. Obviously not here, though. He had to establish identity and routines.

Then deal with it.

He moved calmly along the street, crossed to that side once there was a gap in the Manhattan traffic. He moved with the expertise of the native New Yorker. Easily dodging cars, without any sign of fear. Fell into the crowd behind the man and then past him. A light brush was enough to cause him to turn.

And yes, he was still wearing his building name badge. Christian Hodges. What an ironic first name; there was nothing anointed about this guy.

Lawyer, if Victor had the read right. Although contrary to popular belief, lawyer souls were remarkably hard to secure. They tended to be strong willed people who enjoyed fighting battles. They didn't budge easily.

But this one had. The smoke coming off him smelled quite sweet to the lilin, but he couldn't make his move right now.

He had to start doing his research, as soon as he got back. But he had to see the target first. Like a bloodhound, he had the man's scent now.

There was no escape for him. If needed, he would send Richard out of town ahead. He had to stay and see it through.

He watched the man descend into the nearest subway station and nodded with private satisfaction.

The name was possibly common. The name combined with the work address, he could find. He was a Manhattan lawyer, he would have a website, a LinkedIn profile.

He would have an address, and maybe home would be the best place to get him. A wife or a lover he could use. Children he could use.

He felt no aversion to harming children. Not if it would get him what he wanted. Okay, perhaps, part of him did, but what difference did it make?

Rather than go back straight away, he hung a left and headed for Central Park. His hot dog had long since been consumed. A carriage horse shied slightly as it caught his scent. He gave it a wider berth, not wanting the commotion that would be caused if it spooked and ran.

The faintest hint of blight dulled the leaves around him as he walked into the park.

9

VICTOR PRINCE's enigmatic warning followed her home.

She was sure it wasn't his real name. She wasn't sure it mattered. It was an alias he had used for years, based off of the file. One which might well have become considerably more comfortable than the name he was born with. It worked that way a lot, in her experience.

Heck, she knew old cops whose name might as well be "Officer" or "Detective." Who kept being called that long after they retired. She suspected she might end up one of them. She had no intention of retiring until she had to, until some accident or incident left her unable to do the job. Which was rarer than those who liked to claim cops were always in danger admitted. Or until she was forced out. Some days she thought that she could not last any longer. She had to. She had to fix things. She couldn't fix things.

For now, though? Sometimes you need to take a break from a case to focus on it properly. She took a walk, although she was abruptly nervous about doing so on her own.

That warning could well have included an intent to kill her, although she wasn't sure why.

The sky was clear. The fall sun was starting to descend behind the buildings. It was warm, but not too warm. At some point in the last couple of days the air had ticked over from late summer to early fall, just in the way it felt. That crispness. That faint promise of chill. She shook her head at the thought and headed towards the Hudson.

Ignoring everything and everyone around her until she got to the river. Looked out at the Statue of Liberty raising her torch to the air. Preparing to welcome immigrants, although it was true that they were not as welcome as they had once been. In another direction, the orange bulk of the Staten Island Ferry.

She did not understand why people left New York. Except, perhaps, for those who could not afford to stay. Sometimes it was a struggle on a cop's salary. She joked that she needed a rich husband.

Or, with the laws changing, a rich wife. That might be considerably preferable. She tended to lean towards women if all else was equal.

Beyond statue and ferry lay New Jersey. The New York part of New Jersey, the state line arbitrary, running through the river between her and the statue.

That was proof of how arbitrary it was. Liberty Island was in New Jersey and New York at the same time, a state line drawn around it for no reason other than to make it technically in New York when it should have been in Jersey, but New York wanted it. Claimed it.

Borders were drawn on a map to divide people. The bridges and the subway united them. The ferry.

She walked towards the ferry, drawn to it for reasons she could not explain. The back of her neck was pricking with the same peculiar sensation she'd experienced when she saw the skinny black man.

But *not* what she had felt around Victor Prince. Not that sense of predatory threat. Prince, she decided, would kill her without any hesitation, except to make sure there weren't any witnesses. Whatever this was it pulled at her, tugged at her. Niggled and nudged.

She headed for the ferry dock. Given the time of day, most of the traffic was Manhattan workers heading for Staten Island. The Whitehall Terminal buzzed, noisy. But whatever it was wasn't in the terminal.

She hesitated.

Somebody got off the ferry.

It was the skinny black guy. Their eyes met through the crowd. That was how clichéd romance novels started.

But there was nothing sexual about what flowed between them. Instead that hint of a scent, the scent of trees and forest and dirt.

She stood frozen.

"WE NEED TO TALK," she said, approaching him. She didn't pull out her badge. Somehow, this didn't feel like a badge moment.

"Apparently. Help a visitor out here."

"You don't know where to go?" She hesitated. "Let's just take a walk."

Cafes and restaurants could be wired for sound. Public parks were a lot harder. She turned to walk along the water front. "What's your name?"

"Tag."

"That's..."

"Don't even ask. I don't use my real name." There was the particular dryness in his tone that she had associated with people who never wanted to hear their real legal name again.

She couldn't help but laugh a bit. "Judy," she said in response. "I suppose I got lucky."

"As Bible names go..."

She turned her head slightly. "It's not a Bible name. It's a Hebrew name."

He blushed very slightly under the deep brown of his skin. "Got it."

"Not so many Jews where you're from originally?" she asked.

"Atlanta," he said.

She could hear the trace of the accent, but he'd done his best to get rid of it.

Then he added, "Amongst other places. Most recently DC."

But he wasn't familiar with New York. "Plenty of Jews in DC," she pointed out. Then, amused, she added, "Let me guess, you took the ferry for the free views."

He laughed. "I did. I suppose that's a thing."

"It is, although the actual harbor tours will give you better."

"I'd rather have tips on less touristy stuff." Then he turned slightly towards her. "Detective."

"Busted," she said, wryly. "There's something very odd going on." She couldn't talk about the case, no matter how much she wanted to. No matter how much, for that matter, she felt that she needed to.

This guy knew something. "And you know something about it."

"I might," he admitted as they approached the Seaglass Carousel. "But what do *you* know about it."

"I have a case. I can't talk about it. But I've already had one..." Had that been an attempt on her life? Did it count?

The hairs on the back of her neck perked up again. The faintest scent of something unidentifiable.

Tag shook his head. "Is there somebody involved with this case who's been suspected of an entire bunch of stuff but never caught, perhaps?" He lifted a hand. "I know you can't answer me. But somebody who gives you the worst vibes, somebody you don't want to meet in a dark alley."

"He says he didn't do it," she blurted.

"Maybe he didn't. This time." Tag turned towards her. "Do your job, Detective, but remember this: If this is who I think it is he won't feel any remorse about killing you."

She laughed harshly. "I'm a cop. Plenty of people...unless you're saying he's a true actual sociopath."

"No," Tag said. "He's a lot worse."

JUDY LEFT THE ENCOUNTER SHAKEN. She had never blurted anything about a case before, but there was something about this skinny, vaguely twitchy man that made her want to trust him.

Which meant he was really dangerous, perhaps more dangerous than Victor Prince. Worse than that, she suspected the two were on a collision course and woe betide anyone caught in the middle. Or anything.

She knew she should report Tag, but what could she say? He hadn't given her his name, he wasn't from New York. Maybe one day they'd have facial recognition databases.

Oh, who was she kidding? They'd all be programmed by white people and wouldn't be able to tell black folk apart.

And would probably think any picture of a black person was a mug shot.

She knew better. Not all of her colleagues did. So, there was no way of tracking Tag other than whatever force had drawn them together.

Which was what she really needed to understand. Why was she getting these feelings? Why these faint scents, drifting above the overall smell of the city? Her nose tuned that out, as did the noses of every city dweller. People who came from farms would notice, just as she would notice the smell of manure in a cow barn while the workers would tune it out. The human brain ignored scents until they changed. Yet, there were scents.

If she didn't walk away she would never be able to. What if it hadn't been a threat at all? What if it had been a mere statement of fact?

She headed back towards the precinct, stopping on the way to get pizza. Darrell was already there.

She handed him a slice of four cheese, his favorite. And nicely kosher, unlike too many kinds of pizza.

He looked at it quizzically for a moment, then smiled a bit. "Any progress? I know you went out to back brain it."

Judy frowned. Then, "I think there's more to this case than just a random killing."

"You think? You're the one who nearly got blown up."

"Exactly." She elected not to mention Tag for now. "I think we might be about to get caught up in criminal politics if we aren't careful. Or even if we are."

"Do you think this Prince guy did it?"

"Honestly? No, I don't." What if Tag was the killer? He didn't seem the type, but they only seldom did. "I think he's telling the truth and was being framed."

"He's definitely a piece of work, though. Look at these file photos."

She did. "Yeah. I could see it in his eyes. I think he's a clinical sociopath."

"I don't know. But we can't arrest him just because a terrorist said he did it." Darrell was younger, from Upstate. Naive.

"In fact, that's very much a reason *not* to arrest him. I told him not to leave town, and I suspect he'll stick around." If only because leaving town would make him look guilty. "He's a professional."

"Indeed. So maybe we need to work out who he pissed off."

And whether, Judy thought, they had killed the girl or just taken advantage of her death. Diabla. That name wasn't in the databanks, which he must have known. He had been hinting at something. But what? She did not know.

10

"LET ME GUESS..."

"I got something I have to do," Victor informed Richard, setting down the Chinese.

"And that's the bribe for me to leave you alone."

Victor grinned. "Yup, let me do my research in peace."

"I don't suppose..."

"Not this time." Often, Victor was glad Richard was as bloodthirsty as he was, but he had a feeling this one was going to take a finer touch than the pyromaniac could manage.

"Aww." Richard pouted, but took the Chinese food. It was easy enough to distract him with food.

Victor headed into the office with the other bag, and munched on fried rice while looking up Mr. Hodges. There were a lot of Christian Hodges around to worry about, but the right one wasn't hard to find.

Christian Hodges, partner in Hodges and Crinion. High flying lawyer, specialized in defending fraudsters. Which didn't make him automatically corrupt, but it was pretty clear that he was.

Absolutely and utterly corrupt. So why not leave him in place?

Answer: His wife.

They had been married for five years and she was, it seemed, a good influence on him. Victor smiled inwardly. She was a trophy wife, far younger than he. A model by her looks, or at least a woman who should be a model. Just the kind of woman a corrupt lawyer would choose to relive his youth. But a good influence, no doubt. If it wasn't her, then he wasn't sure who or what it was.

Maybe he could find an excuse to deal with her too. It would make him less frustrated about not being able to or wanting to touch that cop.

Or maybe he could deal with her another way.

Oh, yes. There was more than one way to skin a cat, and while he knew this had to end with Hodges' death, it didn't have to *start* there.

In fact, if he played his cards right he could have a lot of fun with this one. Yes, this definitely wasn't one in which he could involve Richard. However, he was worried by the long game it implied.

Time to pull out something he hadn't used in a while. His old private investigator's license. And yes, it was legitimate. He should have pulled it on the cop, now he was thinking about it.

He hadn't really done that stuff since he met Richard. It was time to do it again; or at least to pretend to.

First things first, was there any truth he could use to start the fire that would smoke this all out?

Yes, that was what he needed to find.

Some truth. Something he could use.

If not, then he would have to weave an appropriate lie. But if he could pull this off then he would win two souls for his master, not just one.

And if not he could always just shoot the guy.

OF COURSE, the problem was that he still had to worry about whoever had killed a Guardian and framed him for it.

The obvious answer was somebody who hated both sides. And the first thought on *that* was Faerie.

The fae were notoriously neutral, although specific individuals often took sides. And changed sides, fickle as the wind. He knew about some of the more famous ones. The attack on the dojo had not used fae magic, but he rather suspected that the explosion had not been the fault of the attackers at all. No, he suspected that had been backlash from a sorcerous defense.

He'd blown himself up that way a few times. Not in this life, mind, but in a previous one. He had it down now.

Or rather he hoped he did. One could never be sure. Fae tended to be more subtle. But wandering around in suits acting like mobsters?

Not at all out of character for the Unseelie Court. People mistakenly thought they were the evil ones.

People who thought there was such a thing as a nice fairy. No, he suspected the Unseelie Court of this. The Seelie Court would just have tried to kill him. It wasn't good versus evil. It was honor versus trickery.

So, why did the courts want him gone? He couldn't be sure, would never be sure in fact. You couldn't expect fae to tell you what their beef was.

Maybe he'd killed somebody they liked.

But the fae killing a Guardian seemed unlikely.

Infernal politics was the other obvious answer. He'd rather the fae. He'd *much* rather the fae.

So, after having set certain things in motion and got some rest, he helped Richard with the bomb for a bit in the morning. It was a tacit apology for deserting him with Chinese food the previous night.

Besides, sometimes you needed the extra hands. "Can we delay a little?"

"Your job or..."

"The cop is what I'm worried about. She's already suspicious of us for one thing, it won't take much..."

"And I suppose we really can't just kill her."

"Not yet." A pause. "Especially as I think she's touched."

"Oh *joy*. Fairy blood."

"I don't think so." No, it was something else. Something not from Europe, perhaps. Something... He couldn't work out what yet, it wasn't something he'd encountered before.

Not fae blood, though. He was pretty sure it was not that, not this time. Sure, it was the most common explanation for weird abilities showing up without training.

It wasn't the only one.

VICTOR INSISTED, given the circumstances, on getting food delivered that evening. Subs. He was kind of tired of delivery and takeout, but the more he showed his nose in public, especially in places where he would be there for a while, the more likely it was that something would happen.

He smelled a rat as the delivery guy came across the parking lot. He was dressed correctly, but there was something about the way he moved that clued Victor in.

He stepped behind the door, took the sidearm that was hanging there. The pistol was cool in his grip, heavy but not too heavy. Comfortable like an extension of his arm. Bloodlust rose deep within him. He fought to keep it down. This wasn't the time when a lilin could go on a rampage and vanish, only to reappear in the next town.

It wasn't as easy as it had once been. No, he could not lose it.

The knock on the door. The gun behind his back as he opened it, making sure Richard saw the weapon.

He trusted him to look after himself with that clue.

The door opened and bullets sprayed into the room. Yes, the gun had been in the bag that should have held their subs. Richard was behind the table immediately, but a yelp showed it might not have been immediately enough.

Normally, Victor would have emptied his own gun into the newcomer. Instead, he ducked into cover himself. Waited for the man to run out of ammunition.

He couldn't afford any dead bodies to show up, no matter how provable self-defense was. He couldn't afford anything like that.

The cop would come back and she would have sharp questions for him, ones he might not be able to answer to her satisfaction. He could smell the faint hint of gunsmoke in the air. His nostrils twitched, but he managed to resist a sneeze.

The shooter was a mundane. No aura at all. A hireling, then. Who, no doubt, had no idea what he was getting himself into. Which led him back to option four on Martin's death. Not good.

Victor smirked. Then he reached within himself and casually threw a sorcerous blast. The purple fire landed at the man's feet. Intentional, of course. Had he wanted to kill him, he would have, but a burned body was no more acceptable than one riddled with bullets.

The man froze.

Victor stepped out of cover. "Gentleman, I suggest you go home. Leave town. Forget this ever happened."

With luck he would do just that, his mind scrambling to rationalize what he had just seen. Purple and black energy crackled around Victor's form...he couldn't see it himself, but he knew it was there. He knew what other people saw, his eyes glowing with hellfire.

He hoped it would be too much for the man's mind. Mundanes rationalized it away. He'd explain it somehow.

The man ran.

Richard reemerged. "You're so hot when you do that."

Victor smiled and let his aura fade away. "You going to do something about that?"

Richard reached into the desk, pulled out a bottle of lube, and held it up meaningfully.

11

FORENSICS HAD STILL FOUND nothing hugely useful for the case. Dani Martin had struggled, but there was no match on the DNA under her fingernails.

Whoever it was didn't have a record, or not one recent enough to have DNA. Or local enough. When they found them...most likely him, from the DNA...they could use it. Not on its own, but it would help. Victor Prince's DNA should have been on file. It wasn't. DNA evidence was expensive to obtain and tour.

No, old-fashioned police work was how they were going to find him, and so far old-fashioned police work...

She idly wondered if Prince would be willing to hand over a sample so he could be exonerated.

No, there was no way he was going to be convinced of that. He would be convinced it would be used to nail him for something.

He wouldn't even be wrong. She couldn't blame him at all. Heck, she wouldn't be comfortable handling over samples herself, in his place.

Without a warrant...and she couldn't even call him a suspect. Except that when you've been told somebody did it, it's real hard to actually get that out of your head. No matter how much she told herself it was probably a frame up.

It didn't help that he was seriously hot.

And undoubtedly with the plump guy she'd seen at the warehouse. The body language was there.

Or maybe the plump guy just *wanted* to be with him.

And he was on the edge of being a suspect. "I need to get laid," she said under her breath.

"I know some great lesbian clubs."

Darrell's voice. She mock-threatened to throw something at him.

"Less STD risk!" he said, cheerfully.

"Oh..." She tailed off. Nope, she was not going to curse at him, not because he didn't deserve it, but because the rather strong word that came to mind was also going to be ammo. "You're shameless."

"Shameless queer," he agreed. "So, I think I found something useful."

"Good."

She was pretty sure that the Martin case was going to be one of New York's unsolved murders. Of course, despite the city's reputation, there weren't that many. Crime was trending downwards, and you were much more likely to have your pocket picked or something else stupid. New York wasn't the urban jungle it had once been.

But that didn't mean there weren't unsolved murders. And this was bidding fair to be one of them. "Go on," she prompted.

"Our victim did have a sexual partner. In fact, she had two."

"Oh." Now, that was a lead. The boyfriend did it might be a truism...

If she was cheating, it became almost infinitely more likely. And the sodam had said she had at least one...implying this was a habit of hers.

It was definitely a lead. One of the boyfriends might well have done it.

BOYFRIEND NUMBER one lived in a basement apartment in the Bronx. Boyfriend number two lived in New Jersey.

"You take Bronx, I'll take New Jersey?" Darrell asked.

She considered that. "New Jersey's more annoying. You take it. I'll take Bronx guy. First thing we need to establish is whether they knew about each other."

And if so, how they had found out. "Assume they'll lie."

They had to both know they were lead suspects. Ah, bigamy.

Well, technically not bigamy, but. Cheating. It lay at the root of so many problems. Most people just couldn't keep it in their pants.

Judy had had enough casual relationships that she couldn't talk about that, but she was proud of the fact that she had never cheated on anyone. If she was exclusive with somebody, it stayed that way.

Not everyone seemed able to manage that, though. Of course, if this came out there would be the victim blaming. It would be Martin's fault for being a slut.

She worked out quickly that Darrell had pulled one over on her. The basement apartment in the Bronx was so far out that the 5 line only ran there during rush hour. Thankfully, *she* had access to a car. She wasn't sure the boyfriend did.

His name was Mark Li. Asian or Asian mix, then, from the name.

The advantage of his location was that it was nicely close to the green spaces of Bronx Park and the Zoo.

The disadvantage was that it was right next to the train yards. That had to have a positive, from his perspective, impact on his rent.

The area was one of those weird mismatches geographers called "transitional." There were a few residences, a storefront church, a halal poultry plant...a hair salon offering to sell "100% Virgin Hair." She amused herself by wondering how you tested the virgin before cutting off their hair. Maybe they had a pet unicorn.

Li's basement apartment was tucked away behind the hair salon. There was no street parking left. Cursing, she hunted for a parking spot and then walked past. Knocking on the door.

No immediate answer. She would have to have them call his cellphone.

Then, finally, as if emerging from the depths, he opened the door. He smelled slightly, vaguely of alcohol and had not bothered to put on a shirt. Dark hair, sallow skin, mixed fatures. "Can I..."

She pulled out her badge.

He swore. "Come in. I'm..."

"I've seen worse, I promise."

"I should have called you, but this is about the first time I've been coherent since..."

She rather thought he wasn't yet coherent. "You should have called us."

It would have made him look less guilty. The alcohol haze could be guilt or grief or both. Plenty of people grieved for those they killed.

But she rather thought it was a man falling apart.

"I didn't do it."

"Does the name Carl Villain mean anything to you?"

Harshly, he laughed.

"YOU THINK Dani was cheating on me with Carl and that's why I killed her." The harsh laugh came again. "Look, the only thing I wish was that we weren't opposite ends of the city."

"I figured that was intentional to keep you from bumping into each other."

He pulled out his phone. Pictures. Lots of pictures. Him, Dani Martin, and a blonde guy who was presumably Carl.

She wasn't cheating.

She was just building a harem. Judy decided that was probably an unworthy thought. There was nothing wrong with a bit of healthy polyamory, but the world often thought there was. No wonder she'd kept it all secret.

It didn't let him or Carl off the hook, mind. The boyfriend still did it in far too many cases, singular or plural. But it made the lead a bit less solid.

"Do you have any idea who might have wanted to kill her?"

"I was just...I figured it was a mugging gone wrong."

His eye twitched.

That was a tell. "Don't lie to me."

"Detective..." He tailed off "I don't know who killed her. I know it wasn't me and I would swear in court it wasn't Carl."

"Somebody in her family who found out about her lifestyle and disapproved?"

"Maybe." He seemed hesitant.

"But you don't really believe it was just a mugging."

He looked away. "I..."

"I can get you police protection if needed. And nothing has to get back to *your* family."

Judy didn't know for sure whether this was one girl and her two boyfriends, one girl, her boyfriend and *his* boyfriend or, well, any other combination.

"My dad would cut me off," he admitted, right away.

"For sharing?"

"There was a lot of sharing. It..." He blushed.

Judy decided to try and make him relax. "I'm bisexual myself. You won't embarrass me."

He actually relaxed. "A lot of people are...but I don't think."

A pause.

"She was involved in things. I promised not to tell anyone, but now she's dead and maybe that promise isn't valid any more."

"What kind of things?"

"You..." A pause.

"Just say it. You might be surprised what I'll believe." Drugs. Or maybe the girl had fancied herself as a vigilante with her black belt and whatever else was going on.

"You won't believe it. Most people don't. They can't."

Her hair was starting to prick up. "Somebody blew up her dojang," she found herself saying.

"Did they?" Li said. He sighed a bit. "Monsters are real. Most of them, mind, take the form of men."

There was only one possible response.

"I know."

12

THERE WERE NO MORE HALF hearted, poorly-planned attempts on Victor's life that day. Despite that, he was being particularly cautious. No ordering delivery. That had proved more dangerous than going for takeout.

He was coming back with a bag full of Taco Bell. Not his first choice, but it was close, Richard liked it, and there was definitely worse to fuel your body with. Outside the warehouse, he hesitated for a moment. Something.

He could smell *something*. Or someone. Something vaguely nasty and vaguely fae-like.

Frowning, he entered the warehouse. Richard was not in the main room. He was upstairs, messing around with the computer. "Be careful, I think there's a pooka or worse around."

Richard wrinkled his nose. "*I* haven't stepped in any fairy rings lately."

That was laughable; they weren't exactly a common phenomenon in New York. But that didn't mean there weren't places the fae could sneak in, mostly in Central Park. The city wasn't warded or locked down against them.

And likely somebody had disturbed them and now the fairy was sniffing around. It was definitely not just somebody with fae blood. Victor sighed. He set down the tacos then went back downstairs. He had wards set against fae as best he could; warding magic wasn't his strong point. Really, you needed a witch for that, or a high magician, and Victor was neither.

But he had the best set he could put together, and he reinforced them now quickly with a few gestures, a few words, and a few drops of his own blood.

That should keep whatever it was out. If he was lucky, it would latch onto the cop and bother her.

Or if he was unlucky. Something like that could be the push she needed to awaken to whatever *she* had going on, and that was honestly the last thing he needed. Right now she thought he was a mercenary.

How would she react if she knew he was a demon? He didn't know and he didn't want to know. She might decide to find an excuse to shoot him while he was not trying to escape, as it were.

She didn't seem the type, but you never knew how somebody would react. If he was lucky she would react in ways that got her confined to Bellevue for a while.

That would definitely save him the trouble of getting rid of her. He enjoyed that pleasant fantasy for a few moments before wandering back upstairs and grabbing a quesarito from the bag.

RICHARD WAS DONE with the bomb and antsy to plant it. Victor, on the other hand, wanted to hold off.

He wanted to deal with the cop, one way or another. And killing her was moving further from his mind. If he didn't, he had two options.

Find somebody else and frame them.

Find the real killer and point her in the right direction.

And he preferred the second one. She couldn't see through a lie if it wasn't a lie, no matter how good she was. Of course, if she had too much pressure put on her to close the case now...

So, he was back to his original question. *Who* would kill a Guardian and frame him for it?

He ran through the possibilities in his head:

Option 1: It was the mob and they had no clue who Dani Martin actually was. Or they thought she was some crazy vigilante kid. This wasn't at all impossible. He had probably ticked off somebody over the last few years.

Option 2: It was the Unseelie Court. And he was in their way somehow. Which would also explain the pooka smell around.

Option 3: This was the one he didn't like and had feared from the start. It was a rival of his infernal master who wanted him taken off the board.

The best way to take a lilin off the board wasn't necessarily to kill him. Life in prison would take him out of the game just as easily, and possibly for longer. Whoever had killed her had hired a mundane to do the hit.

He was honestly hoping it was option two. He could deal with the fae, one way or another. As long as they didn't think he was a threat to the world and a certain very powerful faeborn didn't show up to complicate matters, he could negotiate himself out of the situation.

Which wouldn't give the real killer to the cop, though. He frowned. "I'm going out," he told Richard.

"Hunting?"

He nodded. "Hunting." He was going to go investigate his target, which probably had a more straightforward resolution than the other. Even though he was mad about it.

Even though he'd rather concentrate on the actual problem. Of course, to Beelzebub, the body Victor wore was completely expendable.

Victor himself had become rather fond of it, and who knew what he would draw next time. Of course, he knew that was the normal feeling of being *in* a body. If everything went as it should it felt right, it felt like *you* and you forgot what it was like to be anyone or anything else.

It didn't always go as it should, of course. Just ask any trans person.

But no, Victor had no desire to die, even if his boss would send him to his death without a first thought, let alone a second.

He always tried to survive.

Out meant a preliminary check on Hodges' home, and Hodges' wife. Her name was Deirdre. They had no children. They had no need, thus, for the home they had. An Upper East Side town house, from the address it was probably worth at least fifty mil.

At least.

This was more than just the wealth of a high-flying lawyer. Maybe the wife was heir to something. Maybe they'd had a windfall that had allowed them to buy the place cash or close to.

Payments on this had to be more a month than most people made in a year. This was sell-your-soul money. Victor had money.

He didn't have money like this. Many of these houses were split into apartments. Not this one.

There was a motorbike parked in the little yard area out front. He suspected it was the wife's. Or a visitor's. He studied the bay windows that adorned the first three stories. He could easily visualize the floor plan from here.

If he wanted to be dramatic on his way out of town, he could get Richard to blow it up, but no.

This called for a more surgical approach. If his boss wanted explosions, there were ways to do explosions.

Sabotaging the bike? The thought honestly crossed his mind. Or just stealing it.

It was a *really* nice bike that was no doubt alarmed and had some kind of tracker on it.

He studied the building again. From the outside there was little in the way of personal touches. An inward-facing house.

A house, he suspected. Not a home.

Did Deirdre Hodges love her husband? Love could be used, but its absence, oh that was much easier to work with.

Destroying Christian Hodges might prove easy after all.

Like most townhouses, it had a main door and a "side" door, an approximation of a servants' entrance in a situation where one didn't have enough space to do it properly and a time when nobody had real servants any more. Five stories. No rear access. There might be a yard, there might not.

The building next to it was an art school. He made note of that. The students might easily be bribed or convinced to give word of comings and goings.

They might even hate the rich guy who lived next door, hogging what was a generous space for himself while they slept in garrets in Hell's Kitchen or whatever.

Maybe.

Then Deirdre Hodges came out of the building and Victor, for a moment, forgot every bit of professionalism he had.

13

JUDY WOULD NOT HAVE BELIEVED a word Li said if it hadn't been for what had happened at the Dojang.

That explosion hadn't been a bomb. It had been something else. Her brain kept trying to insist it had to be a bomb, but there was a part of her that knew better.

This was like some weird episode of *Buffy: The Vampire Slayer*. Victor Prince even looked slightly like David Boreanaz. Slightly. Same coloring, anyway.

Dani Martin, though, had looked nothing like Sarah Michelle Geller. And she was dead, and Judy still had to find her killer. Had to. It was what she did. The fact that there might be vampires or whatever didn't change that.

She did have to consider how to keep Darrell out of it, though. She would never forgive herself if he got eaten by a vampire or something.

Leaving Li's place, she leaned against a wall. Looked at the sky. Calmed her heart, which was racing a little. It felt for a moment as if she hadn't been told anything. Just reminded of it, of things she had always known but somehow forgotten. Or, perhaps, repressed. Memories that no longer had a place in a world in which magic didn't exist.

So, she wasn't asking who Victor Prince was any more. She was starting to ask *what* he was. And that was, perhaps, a dangerous thought process. Othering. The first step to genocide is to redefine the target group as not human.

She knew all about *that*. People still defined her as not human. She reached up to finger her magen David, which she kept tucked in most of the time. Because even in New York there was always that slight edge of fear. She knew about how other cops defined black people.

No.

It didn't matter *what* Victor Prince was. She'd seen him in daylight, so he wasn't a traditional vampire. If he was a monster it would be based off of what he did, not whether he had some kind of supernatural abilities.

Maybe he was a werewolf.

No, they were gone, and he couldn't be one anyway.

Wait.

How did she *know* that? Or rather think she knew it. She shook her head a little. Maybe the mafia had been right and he *was* a descendant of Lilith, but it seemed unlikely. The person who knew the most, that she could think of?

Victor Prince.

And she certainly wasn't going to ask him about anything. He was the opposition. He hadn't killed Dani Martin, she was sure of that. But he had killed before and would again and perhaps in a place where she would know.

She couldn't imagine trying to arrest him.

She couldn't even imagine asking the uniforms. And she couldn't call in SWAT.

She shook her head a little bit and walked back to the car. Everything was coming together and falling apart, all at the same time.

Everything was shifting like a California earthquake, the ground unsteady under her feet.

She got in the car.

Li was not off the suspect list, but he was down in priority.

You never took the boyfriend off the suspect list. No, not until you knew for sure who did it.

Never.

IN THE OFFICE, Darrell, who had got back faster, handed her a cup of coffee.

"Apparently they were a threesome."

"Apparently. Doesn't let either of them off the hook, though."

Darrell shook his head. "There's healthy polyamory. And then there's...ya know."

"I do." Judy's lips quirked. "Mr. Li claimed that there was action along all sides of the triangle."

Darrell laughed. "That tends to help make it healthier. The real key is if they stay together without her." He stopped laughing. "I..."

"Look, that's a normal reaction. To talk around the victim like that," Judy said. "To stop using their name. To refer to them as the body. The corpse. The case. It's how we stay sane. It's how we don't waste all of our time weeping for them."

She knew she was telling the truth. She knew it was how detectives coped. This was New York, and with the best will in the world there would always be bodies. *Cases.*

Always. You could do all you could, your very best, but this many people would always rub up against each other in ways which ultimately resulted in violence. There would always be murders, as long as people were people.

She'd read science fiction in which everyone had brain implants that would knock them out if they had the impulse to hurt somebody.

She didn't see that as a utopia.

Darrell just nodded. "I know, but I still feel..."

"Cold."

He nodded again. "I guess we have to be."

"You never had to deal with this directly before." He'd been in uniform, but he'd never been called in on an actual murder.

Maybe that had made him a poor choice. "A little. Not as bad as paramedics, though."

"Oh boy. Paramedic stories."

"Vacuums on penises," she said, wryly. She'd heard enough variations on that one that she suspected it of being an urban legend, but some of them did claim to be first hand reports.

And men could be real stupid.

"Drunk guy backed into his tailgating grill, I hear. Third degree burns."

Judy winced. "Drinking and grilling."

"Well, that is kind of what tailgating *is*. Just because you don't like sportsball."

"I like sports."

"But not *those* sports. You like watching people try to go fast."

Which was true. It really didn't matter what was going fast, either. "Would be a boring world if we were all the same. So, we'll keep monitoring on the boyfriends."

Darrell nodded. "What other leads do we have? What about the mercenary?"

"I don't think he did it," Judy said, with a sigh. "I don't trust tips given to me by the bad guys."

"You should wear a vest," he said, finally, after a moment.

"Don't worry. I am."

JUDY DIDN'T REALISTICALLY THINK a vest would help her at this point, but it certainly wouldn't hurt.

She found herself watching the shadows, and she was looking for one of two specific people. Tag, and Victor Prince.

But this was New York. You couldn't randomly find people, and she certainly wasn't going to find a guy who had only given her a stupid nickname. Likely his real birth name was even more stupid, to prefer to be called that.

Finally, she just went home and tried to put everything into her back brain. She watched a stupid movie then went to sleep.

At least, she had the intent of going to sleep. When she opened her eyes she was in a wooded, slightly swampy valley that seemed oddly familiar, but which she could not place. As if she had been here before but not at the same time. Like some bizarre déja vu.

A dark gray wolf lay in the middle of the clearing, head on paws. Not quite a timber wolf, but bigger than a Mexican wolf. Yellowstone-sized maybe.

Her head was definitely clear enough to make those comparisons, but she was not afraid of the wolf. The beast seemed, in any case, indifferent to her. She reached for her magen David, found it wasn't tucked into her clothes the way it normally was.

Also, there were no wooded valleys in Manhattan, not real ones. Central Park had a few places that did a good approximation, but this was old growth forest, deep and dark. And certainly no wolves.

Slowly, she realized she was, in fact, dreaming, but it was a peculiarly vivid dream. For one thing, it was in full color. She nodded to the wolf and then started to walk down a trail, determined to find out what her subconscious was trying to tell her.

She hadn't ever really had a lucid dream before, at least not to remember. She had the feeling she could wake up any time she chose, but also the feeling that she would regret it if she did.

Following the trail led to a lake. A deer was drinking in the lake, but it started at her approach and ran off into the trees. Definitely not as indifferent as the wolf.

Prey and predator. But of course she was a cop, which should mean neither. A sheepdog would be closer.

Or perhaps the deer had really spooked at the figure that stood, hooded and cloaked on the far side of the lake.

"Who are you?" she asked.

The figure said nothing. It only pointed towards a stone that rested in a clearing. The stone was marked in Hebrew lettering.

She tried to read it.

She woke up.

But she woke up with a sure and certain feeling that *something* had been imparted and that she would get it when she needed it.

And the weaker, but still certain feeling that it would be a really good idea to talk to Tag.

14

VICTOR DID MANAGE to pull himself together after a moment. But the plain truth was that Deirdre Hodges was one of the most beautiful women he had ever seen. She tugged on a helmet and he regretted the lost view as she hopped onto the bike and rode off.

Much more sensible than a car for getting around Manhattan, and despite their money he'd seen her husband use the subway.

No doubt they both hated the traffic and hired a driver when they needed one. But that was a sweet ride, and it gave him an angle. An unexpected angle.

How, he wondered, would Christian Hodges react to a handsome man flirting with his younger trophy wife.

First, he needed to get his hands on a bike. He'd never been a biker per se, but he was competent on two wheels and could handle the lingo if needed. Besides, she was classy.

Or perhaps she was just the kind of classy who would go for a rough Hell's Angel type. Some women did, they liked imagined rough treatment. They liked to imagine they had cured a man, made him honest. It made them feel powerful.

Some gay men were like that too.

He'd dated more than one on both sides. He gave off a predatory air that attracted that type and he had never minded pretending to be tamed for good sex.

Maybe one day somebody actually *would* tame him, but her image, the image of the woman he had loved and destroyed came into his mind.

He couldn't imagine ever being committed to anyone like that again. He loved Richard in a sense, but it wasn't the over-consuming love, the one which turned to hatred so easily.

He'd never loved sanely.

He shook his head. A bike. He needed to get his hands on a bike. He thought through their current finances; he could swing it, easily enough, but Hell wasn't going to pay for this job and he had to get it past Richard, who tended to cling to the purse strings.

It wouldn't be useful for getting out of town. But it would be useful for getting close to Deirdre Hodges.

And in bed with her.

And then Christian Hodges would play right into his hands. Men always did when that particular existential threat hit. When they had a beautiful, young trophy wife and there was a hot young guy.

This wasn't just going to be easy.

It was going to be fun.

VICTOR SPENT the rest of the day out in Jersey looking at bikes. Looking to see what he could afford. Kicking tires. Part of him felt like a teenager again, poor but longing. Longing for the open road and then for the canyons of Manhattan, the city always calling him home.

But he knew it would not be home for much longer. He was not sure where he would go. Maybe he would let Richard decide, go with the flow of a relationship he knew in his heart would not last forever.

They both knew that.

He stopped to look at the last bike in the row. It was second hand, because he could get a better ride that way. The previous owner had painted flames on it. It looked like Ghost Rider's possessed motorcycle.

His lips quirked. He ran a hand across the decorated fuel tank. "Somebody loved you," he murmured to the bike.

Yes, there was sign of that. He could even feel the way it had sunk into the object.

This one, then. This one, because once he corrupted that love, it would...it wasn't like corrupting a horse, but there was an energy potential there. The darkness would claim it and that would help.

He wasn't sure how much help he would need seducing Deirdre Hodges. He also needed a backup plan.

Just in case their marriage was a beard and she turned out to be a lesbian. It could happen. He was sure the marriage was loveless, was a more formal form of contract dating.

Almost sure, anyway. She *could* love him, stranger things had happened. And he had sensed that she was not corrupt, that she was reasonably innocent. Just desperate, perhaps? But there was something else, something he couldn't put his finger on.

That was part of why he wanted to target her. Sending Christian Hodges to his reward would be far less satisfying than the fall of a soul which had yet to be tainted.

But he had to be honest. He looked at the price on the bike. Turned to the dealer. "Do you offer a cash discount?"

The haggling began. He beat the guy down by quite a bit, and rode out on the bike. He also bought a helmet. He had one at home and wasn't too worried, but there were risks you didn't take. Getting pulled over for riding without a helmet would cause him all kinds of problems right now. Problems he couldn't afford and didn't need. It was a cheap helmet, he pulled down the visor and rode.

RIDING through Manhattan was always a challenge. Victor avoided it as much as possible. He rode south through Hoboken, took the Holland Tunnel to Lower Manhattan, then turned right onto West Street towards the gaping wound that had been the World Trade Center. The miasma of death had yet to lift from the place, and likely wouldn't for years more. He drank it in, thought about it, and stopped by the memorial, just past One World Trade Center. The pools that had been the foundations of the building.

The work of Shetan done in the name of Allah, he thought darkly and wryly. There had been a Christian writer who had made that point. Ah, right, it was C.S. Lewis. *The Last Battle*. That evil done in the name of God served Satan...and vice versa. Maybe there was a point to that. The faint purple of infernal light still flickered around the pools.

It was cleansing out, slowly, it mingled with the sorrow of those who had come to pay respect, but there were spikes of hatred too.

The evil had not just been the murder.

The evil had been the hatred it had sparked, so many souls darkened by it. Darkened by "The only good Muslim is a dead Muslim."

By "Islam is evil."

By "Islam is not like other religions."

It had led to a war. It had been one of the best evil acts of recent times. Victor smiled at the thought, but something within him wasn't entirely sure.

Of course it wasn't. It had been ten years ago. He had still been a boy. But he remembered the smoke and the collapses.

He remembered how people had come together afterwards and at the same time pushed each other apart.

There was, perhaps, a part of him that was still human, that regretted the act. And the fires of hatred it had lit.

But he knew how he was supposed to feel. He pushed that side deep down within him and hit the road again. Down towards Battery Park, and then he hesitated.

Did he take the tunnel, pay the toll, and get his ass off the island, or did he continue to the Brooklyn Bridge. He chose the latter, but as he rode through Battery Park, he saw a figure watching him. Actually watching. Hooded eyes followed him.

It was a skinny young black man, but Victor also saw something else.

A wolf. The wolf. The wolf was following him, and *that* was not good at all.

15

FINDING a guy whom she only knew by a nickname. In New York. She couldn't do it, by any means she knew of.

Wryly, she wondered if she could somehow try magic. Not that she would know how at any level, or anything resembling how. Which assumed it was real and she was not insane.

But it was as good an idea as any. The only alternative was Li, and he was involved in the case. Tag wasn't. Tag wasn't a suspect, although she suspected he had a connection, some kind of...she wasn't even sure.

Maybe this was all personal. She should go home and get dinner. She really *should* go home and get dinner. She certainly couldn't afford to eat out again, not today.

But instead of home, she somehow found herself in Battery Park, heading towards the Statue of Liberty viewpoint. It was full, as it always was, of tourists who couldn't quite budget a harbor cruise.

She walked away, heading north, and contemplating dinner. Maybe fast food was the answer to not wanting to cook and not having the budget for anything sit down. As it always was. It wasn't good for her, but she was certainly not the only one to feel that way. It wouldn't hurt her just this once, until just this once became a habit.

No.

She shook her head, and virtuously turned towards the nearest subway station. She had frozen chicken at home. She had the fixings to make herself a better meal than any she could get here.

She slowed down. There was something. The hairs on the back of her neck were pricking again. An odd smell entered her nostrils, the smell of...

...wet dog. Distinctly the smell of wet dog, so much so that she looked around for a large canine that had jumped in the harbor recently. She didn't see any wet dogs. She did see somebody being taken for a walk by a brace of Dalmatians that looked so much like her personal image of Pongo and Missy that she had to smile.

But no wet dogs.

Narrowing her eyes, she looked around again.

Sitting on a low wall was a thin young man with close-cropped red hair. Seeing her, he winked. The wet dog smell radiated from him. Flowed out from him.

But she saw no dog. There were all kinds of people, all ages. Whatever he was up to he probably wasn't going to cause real trouble here in Battery Park.

But that he was going to cause some kind of trouble she was abruptly certain.

HE GOT up as she approached.

No, that was not what he did. He sprung to his feet like some kind of gymnast, or as if he literally had springs in his ankles. He twisted towards her lithely, a wry grin crossing his features. "Why, *there* you are," he declared, as if he had known her for years.

Mystified, about all she could do was stand there. She even contemplated just showing him that she still had her piece. Not that she would shoot the guy, but maybe he would back down?

"Uh..."

"Oh, right! We haven't met yet." He did a little bit of a dance. "Don't worry, I'm not your enemy."

"You're only my enemy if you break the law."

He stepped towards her. "Oh, how little does she know." And then he reached out and attempted to boop her on the nose.

She saw it coming and leapt backwards, windmilling her arms a little. She felt like a total fool, but also this guy was harassing her. "You're harassing me," she said out loud.

"Oh, what, you don't want to have a bit of fun?"

Her hands started to drift to her hips. With a scowl, she forced them back down to her side. No, she didn't want to look like that. She didn't want to show her indignation. "Maybe I have a different idea of fun."

He reached out a hand to her. This time it stopped a distance away. "Don't you want to know what's really going on?"

The yes caught in her throat on the way up. Yes, she did want to know. But this guy could also be a murderer. Or a madman.

More likely the latter. Or he was a street performer and thought all of this was hilarious. This being New York, that was the most likely of all. After all, this was the city where superheroes in costume wandered around accosting tourists.

"Try the out of town tourists with your routine," she said. She turned to walk away, very proud of herself for *not* pulling her gun on him, slapping him, or otherwise acting in a ridiculous and unprofessional manner. Anyone who saw the encounter would have seen her being completely cool about it.

Or at least cool enough. She frowned a bit.

Don't you want to know what's really going on?

That was a temptation, and it was why she was here, and abruptly she decided going home was a bad idea after all.

Going home would ultimately put her alone and she didn't want to risk being alone. Instead of heading for the Whitehall Street subway, she just kept going down State Street. Through crowds which felt protective and supportive. A sense of the city itself enveloping her. She knew where she wanted to go. She couldn't afford it, but maybe.

She stepped into the tavern. For a moment she felt as if everyone in the place was made of cardboard. As if none of them were real.

Including her.

Especially her.

A BURGER and a beer made her feel better. More grounded. But she still could not work out why she was afraid to go home.

Yes, afraid. Afraid to be on her own. Afraid to lock the door of her little apartment and sleep. She had to, though.

She had no other place to go, after all. Not for the first time she considered a dog, but she felt it a little unfair to leave one in a crate in her apartment while she did all the work she did. She didn't exactly get to live the nine to five life.

And she certainly didn't have space for *two* dogs. Maybe what she actually needed was a partner. But one mental look over her dating history reminded her how well she had done at *that* in the past.

She didn't have any confidence that she had, in fact, got any better at it. And the longer she stalled, the more dangerous the streets between here and home would become.

Should she call Darrell? It would be embarrassing to call her junior partner and ask him to walk her home. She was supposed to be the experienced and tough one.

And also the smart one.

She tugged out her phone to call him. Maybe he could help, or find somebody else who could. It wasn't cowardice. It was intelligence.

He didn't respond.

She frowned. Stood up and walked to the door. It was raining now, water streaming down the buildings and into the streets. Flowing into the gutters. She hesitated in the doorway, glad for the excuse to do so. Looked out at the street.

Still felt as if it wasn't safe, as if she needed to stay put or else get out of here. Shaking her head, she forced herself out into the rain, turned towards the subway station. Stupid feelings or not she had to go home and sleep or she would be good for nothing in the morning.

Then, like a rubber band snapping, the feelings were gone. She hurried past the glass that covered old foundations, sure for a moment that it glowed. Ducked into Whitehall Street, shaking the rain off herself. The train rattled across the East River, into Brooklyn where she belonged, where she had always belonged. Where she could hear Yiddish on the streets.

It should have made her relax. It didn't any more.

She smelled smoke as she left the station. Turned towards her building.

It wasn't there any more. It was a gaping hole in the skyline of Brooklyn. All kinds of thoughts went through her mind; the realization that she would have been there if she hadn't stayed for dinner, the realization she was homeless.

She was also relieved she had never got a dog.

16

"I CAN'T BELIEVE you did that!" Victor didn't raise his voice. Much.

Maybe a few decibels, but it was more his tone that spoke, or should have spoke, the story.

"You weren't exactly doing anything about her."

"That's because she didn't think I did it. When this is traced to you, what do you think she'll think?"

Victor turned, picked up his coat, and stormed from the warehouse. Outside, he hopped onto his bike and turned east, away from the city. He hit the Northern State Parkway and stayed on it, the road beneath his wheels.

Richard was good. The explosion would probably be put down to a gas explosion. But he had stepped over a line, trying to kill the cop without talking to Victor first.

Or had he?

After all, Victor did plenty of things without consulting Richard. But that was different!

As he left the anger in his exhaust, he slowly realized that he was being hypocritical. But not entirely unreasonable, because he knew he was right and this had been a bad move.

A stupid, dumb move.

He hit Long Island golf club country. Without really thinking about it, he realized he was heading for Oyster Bay. He knew why his subconscious was taking him there. Associations. His parents, the parents who thought he was an ordinary child, taking him to the beach at Theodore Roosevelt Park. Or to the Oyster Festival. He'd only years later realized that their choice had something to do with a certain brewpub in Oyster Bay that sold his dad's favorite beer in all the world.

As a child he had looked out over the water, and thought this was what it meant to be out of a city. Had stared at the sailboats, both the ones moored and the ones sailing across Oyster Bay harbor to and from Centre Island. He rode past that brewpub, across the light rail, and pulled the bike up in the parking lot.

With eyes far older and more cynical than those parents had ever imagined, he looked out at the sea. It was not raining as it had the night before but was, rather, a good day for sailing; despite it being a weekday the water was well-occupied. He was jealous of them for a moment.

People wealthy enough to afford sailboats and free enough to simply enjoy the water. Perhaps they had their worries, but they didn't have the kind of worries he did.

They weren't about to be arrested for a crime they hadn't committed.

His anger turned back to Richard. And he knew he could not go back to the warehouse.

Not now.

He might not even be able to go back to New York. Except that like a fool he'd headed into Long Island. He couldn't get out without going that way.

Or hiring a boat. Yes, that would be a reasonable escape. Charter a boat to go across to New Haven. Head north into New England.

But he also had a job to do.

Damn Richard anyway.

THE COMPROMISE, after a drink at the brewpub his father had so loved, was that he would not go near the warehouse. The thought of tipping the cops off to Richard to save his own ass occurred to him.

He did not do it because no matter how angry he was you didn't sell out your partner, sexual or otherwise.

Even if they hadn't thought things through.

He wasn't going to *rescue* him this time, but he wasn't going to sell him out either.

So, instead of returning on the Northern State Parkway, he cut across to the Southern. It was starting to get dark, but he didn't care. He stopped for gas then rode back to New York.

Just a biker heading out to Long Island to escape the city for a bit. The downside to this route was that it took him past the airport, mingling with jetlagged Europeans, some of them driving on the wrong side of the road. Through East New York as the sun set all the way. Into Brooklyn.

Which was where the cop had lived. She was presumably still alive. The headline hadn't mentioned anyone being dead.

Just a gas explosion, but the address had flagged his suspicion. He was glad he'd looked it up and sad he'd looked it up. Unsure why he was so mad with Richard.

Not knowing would have been something of a defense. He didn't even have a personal alibi. Along Linden Boulevard, he stopped at a cheap hotel and booked a room.

He had no choice in terms of plans now. Deal with Christian Hodges as quickly as possible, deal with the cop if he had to.

Then get out of New York for good. The hotel wasn't really much more than a boarding house, but it would serve.

He knew the cop would be looking for him. She would have no choice. He stood in the window, looking out at Linden Boulevard and the traffic. This wasn't Manhattan.

That didn't mean it was quiet, it was still New York, still the spreading tendrils of the City that Never Sleeps.

Still home.

He was going to miss it. Well, he would be back. In a few years, perhaps under a different name.

Or he would not. But he planned to return.

He had a sudden odd sensation of something akin to déja vu. A memory of what had not been, of being in a hotel room in Manhattan.

There was a woman in the room.

He shook his head and looked outside.

There, on the other side of the street, he was. Not unexpected at this point.

The wolf.

OBVIOUSLY, he wasn't a werewolf, and not just because they were extinct.

He was one of those who wore the cloak of the spirit world in real life. Call them shamans, medicine men, whatever.

And that meant, Victor knew, that he knew *exactly* what Victor was. And had sniffed him out, perhaps literally. The wolf was not the dominant form right now, but it was there. Victor considered what to do.

He saw only one option. He had to deal with this guy before he told the cop where he was or worse.

Letting the curtains close, he descended to the street, taking the stairs easily. He had a gun in his pocket, but he didn't plan on using it.

Shooting people was remembered. Magic drifted back out of the witness' minds as easily as it entered.

He stepped out of the building. A couple of cars passed before he could cross the street. For a moment, he was worried the man would disappear behind them.

No, he had no intention, Victor suspected, of leaving. The horrible realization that he was falling into a trap came over him, that he was confronting this man on his own terms.

He crossed the street. He could feel energy flowing through him. He was ready to fight, ready to defend himself.

He was not ready for the man's smile, bright against the dark of his skin.

"We finally meet," the man said. He had the slight southern accent of somebody who had been raised in the south but drifted further north.

"Did you kill her?' were the first words out of Victor's mind.

"'Course not. Did you?"

"No," Victor admitted. "Although some would like you to think I did." He kept his hands ready.

The man didn't attack. Yet. He didn't reach for a weapon. "I know about that. Maybe for once we're on the same side."

Victor shook his head. "Never."

The man smiled again. "Call me Tag."

Not his real name. He knew better than to give his real name to even a lilin. Or he hated his real name and nobody got it.

It was hard to tell. "Victor, but you already know that. Who sent you?"

"A ghost," Tag admitted, with his lips quirking.

"Or did a ghost call you?"

"I haven't been able to *find* her ghost, but then, I'm not a medium."

Victor inwardly kicked himself for a fool. He hadn't thought of finding a medium. Of paying somebody to talk to Martin's ghost. Except that Martin's ghost wouldn't want to talk to him and could be dangerous. "Neither am I."

Tag shrugged. He leaned against the wall. "Here's the thing. Some-body's hunting Guardians. And I'd like to know who."

"And I care why?"

Tag shrugged again. "Because we all know who's going to get the blame. You. Your boss."

He couldn't say the man wasn't right.

He also couldn't help but want to see more of him. In both senses of the word. It was probably rebound from his anger with Richard.

Probably.

17

JUDY WAS EXHAUSTED. She had spent the night crashed in her office, for want of a better immediate idea, and all day talking. Or what felt like all day.

Insurance would cover her stuff, but how was she going to find a new place? Where was she going to go? She couldn't afford much; a detective's salary was reasonable, but this was New York, where people joked you paid $2,000 a month for a closet...without that much exaggeration.

She knew it would only get worse.

And insurance wouldn't get her a new place.

She still had a case to work, but when exhaustion finally hit, she booked into a hotel in East New York. It was further than she liked, but it was cheap and reasonably convenient, and...

And it would have to serve until she worked out what to do. Thankfully, she hadn't owned that much. She wasn't the kind of person who needed to be counseled by a personal organizer.

But what she had had was gone, all of it. Anything that couldn't be pulled out of the ashes. Her mother's jewelry, gone.

Her photos, gone, the ones she didn't have digital copies of.

She was exhausted and on the verge of tears as she walked up to the hotel. She'd bought a change of clothes and fresh underwear, she'd eaten, but she didn't know how she was going to last the month.

It wasn't raining, at least. But it was dark, because everything had taken so long. The explosion hadn't been gas. Forensics had found something.

It had been a bomb. A crime. Possibly even terrorism. Possibly aimed at her. More likely not. She had only been one of the people in the building. Her neighbors.

She tried to think if any of them had done something to warrant this. If any of them had committed a crime, had pissed off the mob.

Maybe it was all her after all. Maybe it was even a compliment, somebody thinking she was dangerous enough to warrant being taken out of the game. It hurt, though. You didn't want to be complimented in this way.

One of her neighbors had had a cat. No humans had died. Everyone had been out.

But she wasn't sure about the cat.

She wasn't sure about the cat and she felt tears prick at the back of her eyes. She had to get into her hotel room. Then she could collapse. Cry herself to sleep as she so badly wanted to.

She saw the sign for the place. Started to approach.

Two men stood opposite.

Slow realization, near horror dawned.

One of them was Victor Prince.

———

THE OTHER...WAS Tag. This was enough to make her believe, not in the Christian concept of God, or even quite the Jewish one, but in the trickster archetype that was Loki or Coyote.

She didn't know whether to laugh, ignore them, run away or go over. Her feet took over and she found herself doing the last, her pitiful backpack slung over her shoulder.

She swallowed back what she wanted to say courtesy of many years of threats involving soap. Instead, what came out was, "What are you momzers doing here?" Which honestly wasn't any better, really.

It was a more direct insult.

Tag laughed. He might or might not have understood the word, but he understood how to defuse an insult when one was presented to him.

Victor rolled his eyes. "I'm sorry, by the way."

"Sorry?"

He smiled. It wasn't a very nice smile, even if it did reach his eyes. It was the smile of somebody who was taking pleasure in what he was saying even if he knew he really shouldn't."

"I know who blew up your apartment," he said simply. "I can't *prove* it for you, but I know."

"And you'll take great pleasure in turning this individual over to me." She watched him, almost thoughtfully. "How is that any different from people telling me you killed Dani Martin?"

"He's guilty." There was doubt in Victor's eyes, though. She knew to read people. He didn't want to do it.

Tag was watching the pair of them. He lifted a hand. "Maybe the public street isn't the place to talk about this."

She felt chagrin come over her face and saw something matching it on Victor's. "Okay. Let me drop this off, and there's a 24-hour diner down the road?"

Restaurants were remarkably safe places to talk, unless they took reservations. The place she was thinking of was the kind of place you went when you knew you had drunk too much and were hoping to soak it up with greasy food.

It didn't work, but people tried it anyway. She was surprised to find both men still there when she returned and set off down the street. It probably wasn't very smart of them.

Or perhaps Victor really did feel something resembling remorse. More likely he was still trying to convince her he didn't kill Martin.

That *had* to be his motivation. She'd heard of professional respect developing between cops and criminals, but she'd never been part of it.

The diner was down the street. The three of them went inside and she claimed a booth totally at random. "So, who did it?"

"Somebody who was trying to protect me," Victor said, finally.

"That can be a bitch." Tag leaned back in his chair, hands behind his head.

Judy nodded. "But you can't actually prove it without me having to bring *you* in too. That's it, isn't it?"

Slowly, he nodded. "Not to mention the fact that I don't know I want to turn them in."

"I get that." She actually did. But at least knowing it was connected, connected like the New York Subway, a complicated web in which you would get lost until you worked out exactly where you were going.

At least that.

THEY FELL silent until the waitress came over and dropped off their food. Once she was gone, Judy considered.

Victor was right there.

He was involved in this. She turned to Tag. "I was harassed yesterday by a guy who smelled like a wet dog." Of course, he'd been a big part of making sure she wasn't home when the explosion happened.

Tag frowned.

Victor looked up from his food. "Smelled like a wet dog, seemed to know stuff about you without being told, lousy sense of humor?"

"Yes."

He grumbled. "Pooka. They're a kind of fairy."

Tag looked at him.

"Dude, if she can smell them she can know what they are."

"Good point."

She looked between the two. "Aren't you guys enemies?"

"Absolutely," Victor said. "The only reason we're not trying to kill each other is that there's a lady present."

She managed a laugh, then realized that he was quite possibly serious. That she'd stopped a fight by walking up when she did.

"You need to know," Tag said seriously. "He's a kind of demon. A very *minor* kind of demon, but still a kind of demon."

Victor scowled at him. "You had to tell her, wolf."

So, maybe he *was* a lilin and she had heard it right, but then she glanced between him and Tag.

"Wait, he's..." She looked at Tag. "You are *not* a werewolf."

"I'm not a werewolf."

She took a deep breath. "So, let me guess, the hidden world of the supernatural is right there but most people never see or...smell...any of it."

"Or they do and it gets rationalized away. But sometimes...sometimes somebody's exposed to something they can't rationalize away." That was Victor, his tone serious. "That's you now."

The dojo explosion. Maybe. "And I suppose I'm lucky you aren't trying to kill me."

Victor shrugged. "Cop killing causes trouble. A lot of trouble. I was hoping to find the real killer."

There was a cold knot in her stomach. "Who's probably a vampire or something."

"Not likely a vampire," Tag said. "There aren't many of them...they're very territorial and tend to fight to the death. I'm sure there are two or three in New York. And before you ask, definitely not a werewolf. Nobody's seen a werewolf in over fifty years."

She nodded. "But there was a fairy in Battery Park."

There was a dark look in Victor's face that said he probably wanted to throw the fairy right back into Fairyland.

Or kill it, if fairies could die.

"Fairies aren't comfortable in cities, except for gremlins and goblins," Tag explained. "So of course he'd be in the park."

She nodded. "Okay. I suppose that makes sense. So what's your theory on who killed Dani Martin?"

"I'm *hoping* it was the Fae," Victor said.

From his tone of voice, she decided she didn't want to know what he was hoping it wasn't.

She had suspects, multiple. She had the obvious suspect that they would want her to choose. She had the boyfriends.

And she knew that there would be some who would look for something to get Tag on too, simply by virtue of the color of his skin.

She had to find the real killer fast. It was the only way to protect them.

18

So, the cop was...well. It was too late for her now. He might still have to kill her. Victor studied her across the table. She was probably forty, late to come into anything, but later had been known.

She was no Guardian and likely no witch; these days *somebody* usually found young people with that much talent and got them training before anything bad happened as a result of lack of training. Always a concern that.

She probably had some sensitivity, a talent which had manifested as luck or, more likely, as hunches that tended to be far more accurate than most.

She was his enemy. He had to remember that. So was the young man who wore lightly the cloak of the wolf. Him even more so. The young man was almost as dangerous, Victor suspected, as he was.

"You're not going to ask."

She admitted, her lips turning wry, "I don't know that I want to know."

"Smart woman."

"But I have a feeling you're going to tell me anyway."

"It could be demons," Victor said, finally. "And not your regular little imps either."

She glanced at Tag. "Didn't you say he *is* a demon?"

Tag shrugged. "One of the characteristics of demons: They don't get on. If it's a different prince from his boss..."

Victor felt his own lips twist into a smirk. "I'm not *exactly* a demon. But close enough. And, exactly. The wolf has it right."

She shuddered a bit, but he saw some realization in her eyes.

"And that's not the sort of thing you want to get caught up in."

Her eyes hardened. "It's my case."

"Then if it's your funeral as well, I have no sympathy." Victor studied her for a long moment.

"I've almost died twice," she admitted.

"But you won't back down." If Victor was honest with himself, he felt a certain admiration for the woman. He could also feel her faith, centered a little around the symbol she wore. Her soul likely had some protection. But it wouldn't stop a bullet or a sorcerous blast. It wouldn't save her.

"I can't." There was steel in her tone. "I know, I probably can't arrest a denizen of Hell, but..."

"But said denizen of Hell has more mundane minions, almost certainly."

Or she could arrest him. The fact that she hadn't called SWAT said, though, that she had at least some feeling that he didn't deserve to be arrested.

He was glad of that.

"So," she added after a moment. "You know who blew up the tenement. They're lucky. Nobody was in there."

Victor considered. "I won't tell you who it is just yet, but if you agree to not jump to the conclusion it was me, I'll make sure they stay off your back."

He didn't want to send Richard up the river yet. Well, he did, but he knew it was his anger thinking for him. He might not ever want to touch him again, after this, but that didn't mean he was going to turn him in.

She hesitated. Took a deep sharp breath. "Alright. But I am *not* agreeing it *wasn't* you."

"Smart woman," he said again.

If he could corrupt this one, he'd have a valuable ally, but he sensed it would be a difficult, perhaps impossible, task. She had faith, she had conviction.

She was the kind of person that Hell could never get its talons into and he felt something at that thought, a stirring of an emotion that should not be in this context.

He ignored it. After all, it was only a feeling, and it wasn't even the right feeling; it wasn't one somebody like him was allowed.

She turned to Tag. "So, where do you fit in?"

The man considered. He rested his slender, dark hands on the table. Victor found it hard to keep his eyes off of those hands.

"I'm here to investigate the death of Dani Martin. Who was..." A pause.

"A demon hunter," Victor said, finally.

For a moment it felt as if they had finished each other's sentences before. Victor thought of a memory. Shook his head.

"I was starting to wonder. So, maybe she hunted the wrong prey." Judy's lips quirked again.

"That was my assumption, but we have to be sure. She was, despite her age, quite powerful," Tag explained. "Victor here would have been struggling to take her out on his own."

Victor tilted his head. "I'd say try me, wolf, but you might take me up on it and I suspect it would be a tie that involved a lot of bleeding."

Judy actually laughed.

"I don't intend to fight you right now." A slight emphasis on right now. "As we all have the goal of finding out who killed her."

"Something more powerful."

Victor shook his head at that. "No. More likely something *less* powerful. I'm suspecting the killer was mundane."

Tag shot him a look.

"She might not have sensed a mundane with murder on his mind."

Judy was counting to five. "Okay, so supernaturals can sense each..." She tailed off.

"Depends on what suite of enhancements you got. And sensing things is the most common talent." For some reason he felt the desire to reassure her.

"Like smelling pookas."

"Like smelling pookas. It's a talent, that's all. You've always had it. You just haven't *noticed* it before." He felt mean, but at the same time? It was too late to save her from this.

"Why are you explaining things to me?"

"Because," Victor said finally, "we *are* all trying to find out who killed Dani Martin."

THIS WAS NOT a situation Victor liked, he thought as he went to his room. He had no choice, if he wanted to clear his name, but to work with a cop who clearly had the Sight and, worse, an entirely-too-attractive shapeshifter.

He was pretty sure the young wolf man was a full shapeshifter, even though he hadn't seen evidence yet. Shapeshifters were not easy to deal with or to trust; although at least Tag's second form would stand out in the city. Or would it?

Most people couldn't tell a wolf from a husky or vice versa. He stood at the window of his hotel room. Too much to deal with. Find out who killed Dani Martin, work out what to do about Richard, and kill Christian Hodges.

If he didn't manage that last one, then he would be in trouble. If he didn't find out who killed Martin, then the pressure on Detective Eidelman would eventually reach the point where she would arrest him because she had nobody else.

And if he didn't do something about Richard, it would come back to haunt him. He was still fond of the man, but he couldn't trust him any more. Heck, he rather thought he could trust the cop more, even the shapeshifter.

He knew where he stood with them. Allies of circumstance and enemies of nature. Once they'd found the real killer, he would get out of town and never see either of them again.

He found he didn't want to never see Tag again. Lust, no doubt. The young man did seem like the type to prefer other men, although Victor's 'gaydar' was not as accurate as it might be. He had been wrong before.

He certainly had no such feelings for the cop; she was a reasonably attractive woman, but he didn't feel drawn to her. He often found matters of attraction hard to predict.

And then there was the delicious Deirdre Hodges, but *that* was a different thing. That was business, even if he could hope that the business would lead him into her bed.

Okay.

So.

Priorities.

If he wasn't immediately going to be arrested, then he could start cultivating Deirdre Hodges. He had the physical tools to do so. He needed to find out where she might hang out without her husband.

But at the same time he had to try and at least think about who might have been behind Martin's death. He was sure the actual killer was nobody, a mundane.

But he feared he knew who was truly behind it. And that this could tear the city apart.

19

JUDY HAD her suspicion now as to who the bomber was. The overweight man in the warehouse with Victor.

Did she bring him in? Did she tip somebody off? It wasn't her case and wouldn't be; it would have been a massive conflict of interest. She wanted revenge, as anyone would under the circumstances. She wanted whoever it was to go down.

She wasn't sure she could trust herself not to shoot them. So, it was right for her to stay out of it.

Except that she couldn't, hort of handing over the Martin case and going out of town for a bit, taking all of her saved up leave. She couldn't do that either. Running away wasn't her style. Besides, she had nothing to run towards. The fact that it was all linked was as clear to her as the sky outside the hotel room window, well, wasn't.

She had no idea how to put together the jigsaw puzzle of what was going on. What connected the apartment to the dojo to Dani Martin to Victor Prince? It was all tied together somehow.

And if they were to be believed, tied to politics in Hell. Judy had never believed in the Christian concept of Hell. Heck, she wasn't sure she believed in souls at all, in any kind of an afterlife. This world was what there was; this world was of vital importance and to be protected.

Too many Christians forgot this world in favor of the net. Some rabbis disagreed with her, but that was okay.

You were supposed to disagree. Walking in lockstep was not how you found God. For a moment, she turned her thoughts that way. Prayed, although she was not praying *for* anything. Rather, she was just kind of acknowledging God. She was not one of those who denied his existence.

She acknowledged it, and she put her issues and problems on the table. She laid them out. She didn't ask for anything to be done about them.

Just put them out like one of those memory layouts, with her eyes closed. A thought exercise she'd done with cases before, although none this complex.

Item #1: Victor Prince claimed innocence of Dani Martin's death.

Item #2: Tag believed him.

Item #3: Magic was real or, alternatively, they were telling her that in the hope of driving her crazy.

Item #4: Her apartment had been blown up.

Item #5: Victor wasn't hanging out at the warehouse with his boyfriend any more.

Item #6: Victor had been eyeing Tag like a gay man on the rebound.

So, a breakup then. A breakup in nasty proximity to the explosion.

She opened her eyes, sure the man had tried to kill her. Sure Victor was trying to protect him. He hated him. He didn't hate him that much.

So. What did she do about it? The answer was keep her eyes open. Move when, and only when she had evidence that wasn't as circumstantial as a cobweb.

The sky outside darkened.

The hair on the back of her neck pricked.

SHE DID NOT SLEEP that night. Not that she did not sleep well; she did not sleep at all. She rose in the morning exhausted, with scratchy eyes and no breakfast. She returned to the diner, not sure what else to do.

Pulled out her phone and went through rental listings. Finding a new place to live was top of the list. She had a good credit score. She would find something, although it would be hard.

She started to look through. Studios at $2,000...prices were only going up and she had no doubt it would be $2,500 a month in a few years.

She finally found something for $1,300, available immediately. Not very big, but she didn't need it to be very big. She didn't even want it to be. It was in Brooklyn, that was good enough. She sent off a query on it and a couple of others, then finished her breakfast. Her greasy breakfast. Diner breakfast, not even really a treat and way too many calories.

Not that it mattered if she fit into her old clothes any more. She didn't have any old clothes.

Realizing she was wallowing, she headed outside and towards the subway. The sky was dark again, that faint hint of purple marking the clouds as it had the night before. Then, she had dismissed it as a weird effect of the street lights.

Now she wasn't so sure. She wasn't even sure anyone else could see it. It was just kind of there, and she smelled wet dog again.

The pooka, they had called it. Quickening her pace, she ducked into the subway. The fairy didn't follow.

Neither did her cellphone signal, so the urge to look up pookas on the internet would have to wait. The train rattled into the station then rattled her towards Manhattan.

Somebody had drawn a swastika on the window in sharpie. She didn't have rubbing alcohol to get rid of it.

Somebody else did. They took care of it as she sat there studiously not looking in that direction. Somehow, everyday anti-Semitism didn't seem like so much of a concern with everything else that was going on. It was impersonal where what she was going through was personal. The personal was always more of a threat. Always harder to deal with. She had so much to think about right now.

So, she ignored it, even as it made some part of her shudder deep inside. People who would do that would graduate to firebombing synagogues.

She somehow made it to the office before Darrell did. She pulled out everything on the Martin case so far.

Laid it on her desk.

Stared at it as if it would give her answers. It held none. There was a shadow in her doorway.

She turned.

"You *still* working on that? We know who did it. Bring him in and close it."

Her boss.

"I disagree."

"You're wasting police resources."

Her lips quirked. "Give me another week."

"Three days. Then I want to see this Prince guy booked."

She'd been on the receiving end of pressure before. This felt different.

This felt like a threat.

DARRELL CAME in as soon as the captain left. "Are you alright?"

She brushed back a stray hair; it needed cutting. "I'll live."

"Any idea who did it?"

"Somebody who thought they were protecting a suspect is my guess," Judy said, quietly. "But somebody definitely did it. They were good, too." And they had made it look for sure that Prince was guilty. Did she really know he wasn't?

It would be so easy. Bring him in. Satisfy the Captain. Work for her next promotion. Not worry about who ended up in prison.

They all had it coming, after all.

Darrell nodded. "So, how many demolitions experts are there on the black market in New York?"

She made a face. "Too many." He was right there. "But I have to assume this is connected to the Martin case."

"Because it's the only murder you're investigating right now. Are you sure it isn't somebody you put away that just got out?"

"No." She let out a breath. "I have other, highly circumstantial, evidence that it's connected to the Martin case. Nothing I can act on."

Darrell looked over the papers. Over the case. "Am I in danger?"

"I wouldn't go anywhere on your own or sleep with anyone you don't know."

"I'm not a slut!"

She grinned. "I'm giving the same advice to myself. Okay, I took the subway this morning on my own. I shouldn't have."

She did know she was perhaps a bit more likely than Darrell, a hopeless romantic, to sleep with a honeytrap. Maybe Victor was a honeytrap in his own way.

No, he definitely was. Or could be, if he turned on the charm lying behind those eyes. He would be hard for anyone who wasn't a 0 or a 6 on the Kinsey scale, in the wrong direction, to resist if he really wanted to seduce you.

Thankfully, she was fairly confident he didn't actually want to seduce her. He wasn't using that tactic, for whatever reason. Instead, he was treating her with the kind of grudging respect...

...that a criminal treats a straight cop with. When there were those. When there were any left. Sometimes it seemed they had always been an endangered species, nigh mythical.

"Penny for them?" Darrell asked.

"I was just thinking that I'm surprised the merc hasn't tried to seduce me as a distraction."

"Is he hot?"

She grinned. "Very. But I know better."

And he wasn't really trying to.

"I stand warned. Unless..."

"If anything he's going to go for you before me." That might be another explanation, but she didn't think so.

No.

He respected her. And she could leverage that.

Unless, of course, he turned out to be the killer after all.

20

THE DIVE BAR wasn't exactly the kind of place he would have expected to find Deirdre Hodges.

Once he found her there, it became exactly the kind of place one expected to find Deirdre Hodges. It wasn't that hard to track her movements. Her bike, parked and chained outside, confirmed her presence. He hoped it was her presence alone.

But no, Christian Hodges would never come to a place like this. So, why would somebody like Deirdre?

He found the answer as he walked in and was hit by a blast of good, old-fashioned punk rock. This wasn't the kind of music you listened to in a classy joint.

It was the kind of music that belonged in a trashy bar with beer and pub grub and X off rail drinks. He wandered over to the bar, glancing around for her. Not at the bar. Not at a table.

Playing pool against some girl in a purple and orange mohawk as the punk rock blasted. There was that sense of something akin to purity about her. Something solid and real and something which inexorably belonged here.

People mistook dive bars for evil. They mistook bikers for evil.

Some of them hadn't done anything to avoid that impression at all. Hells Angels had always amused Victor.

Those who wore the trappings of Hell but would never harm anyone, would protect children with their lives. That was always amusing to him.

Even more amusing were the fools who couldn't tell the difference.

He watched the game. Deirdre was winning. She was kicking mohawk girl's butt casually, without even breaking a sweat. It gave him an in. He wandered over, put the kind of grin on his face that didn't approach shit-eating (which might have scared her off), but had just enough lecherous in it. "I'd like to challenge the winner." He let his Queens accent shine through.

The mohawk girl turned to him. "I'm sure you'd like to do other things with her too." A smirk. "You ain't *my* type, mind. I don't do dicks."

"Fair enough," he said, then glanced at Deirdre. "But I was just hoping to get a game faster than hunting through the bar for a partner."

It was an insult to mohawk girl, but he didn't care.

She smiled sweetly at him. "Yeah, yeah. You sure you want to do this? She's got fins and teeth."

"I noticed. So do I." He would probably lose, but the confidence was an essential part of the act, as vital as anything else he was doing.

From what he was seeing, Deirdre Hodges wasn't just a pool shark.

She was a full-grown Great White.

THE TWO CIRCLED the table and each other. "I'm married," Deirdre said.

"Happily?" Victor asked, chalking his cue.

"I don't know," Deirdre admitted. "Mostly," she said, finally. "Is any marriage truly happy?"

Victor considered that, letting her break. "Depends. I think every marriage that isn't a dysfunctional mess is both happy and unhappy, sometimes at the same time."

She didn't manage to get any balls down off the break. He

suspected that was deliberate. It bothered him a little. He didn't like the feeling *she* was the one playing with *him*. "Likely so."

"So, did you marry him for his looks, his personality, or his money?" Victor asked, taking his own turn.

"His looks and his money," she said, finally. "He's not a bad guy, though."

He could hear the regret that laced her tone. It was the chink in her armor, it was his way in, but he found himself hesitating.

Because in amongst the regret was a hint of dishonesty; not the type which lets in Hell, but the type which is well meaning and has its own power.

She was lying to protect either herself, Christian, or both. And if she was fully loyal to him, this wasn't going to work. She wouldn't budge, she wouldn't move.

He wouldn't be able to seduce her.

And that meant she would have to die. "Not a bad guy? You deserve better than not a bad guy."

She peered at him through wisps of blonde hair. "Better like you?"

"Okay, so it was a line. A guy has to try."

"If you were trying hard..." She lined up a shot. "...you would have pretended not to know how to play pool."

Victor laughed. "That would have fooled you for about five seconds. You aren't hiding a pro certificate anywhere, right?"

She turned. Grinned at him. "Not pro, no. World Youth Champion, though, some years ago."

"I knew you weren't just a shark."

And he was getting his butt kicked. He didn't mind. It wasn't like it was an actual fight, one in which somebody might have gotten hurt. It was for fun and at the same time deadly serious.

She made a big mock grin at him. "Okay, you have no chance, either beating me at pool or getting in my pants. But I think I like you."

That was something. It was a chink in *her* armor. The back of his neck, though, was developing the odd sensation that indicated that he was being watched.

And not by a mundane.

HE TURNED SLOWLY. So, he noticed, did Deirdre.

He hadn't noticed anything odd about her, but now he did. The woman had cloaked herself with an expertise that said only one thing: Faeborn. High generation or high power.

She was *good*.

The man who had just walked in was very definitely not good, at least in terms of his morality. In terms of his skill? That was yet to be determined.

Victor thought of putting himself between Deirdre and the other. Then he thought again. If she was faeborn...which didn't explain why she liked him.

No, it did.

She was lying, expertly so. She didn't trust him, and she planned on finding out what he wanted. That made far more sense.

Right now, though, he had this other problem. He narrowed his eyes. Regarded the other.

Demonic. Lilin.

Not a servant of Beelzebub.

The pooka, then, had been a red herring. This was as he had feared; a conflict in Hell.

The other strode towards not him, but Deirdre.

"Leave the lady alone," Victor said.

"Why?"

"Because I haven't finished my game of pool yet." He studied the other. The lilin wore a male form, as he did. More wore male than female, it didn't necessarily relate to their *original* gender.

Victor had always been male. But had he been born a woman he would be one. Souls have no gender.

This one was a little larger than him, with a darker skin that indicated some unspecified non-white ancestry. Dark-skinned Hispanic, he decided.

"Forget the game of pool, Victor. We need to talk."

"You have me at a disadvantage."

A major one. Not only did this other lilin appear to know something of who he was, but he knew his current form-name. Which wasn't even the name this body had been born with.

He was very up-to-date. Victor wasn't.

Behind him, Deirdre was watching them both with narrowed eyes. The faeborn made no move to attack.

Likely she intended to let the boys sort things out between them. She had no dog in this fight, nothing except protecting her husband.

Protecting her husband from the forces of Hell. Victor began to see that something was going on here. And the other was not here to seduce Deirdre. It was in his eyes.

"Finish your game," he said.

Victor glanced at Deirdre. He mouthed 'kill you' at her, hoping she would get the hint. Her death would help his cause.

But he was not going to let it be at the hands of a rival.

21

THE WET DOG smell was back as Judy stepped outside. She was finally done with this. Majorly, completely *done* with it.

"Show yourself," she hissed.

The red-haired fairy stepped out of a doorway. "As you wish. May I have your name?"

"No."

She knew better. She'd read fairy tales in which giving a fairy your name caused you to forget it. The fairy could look her up in the directory.

"I had to try." He moved to lean against the outside of the precinct. "Victor Prince is going to kill you, you know."

"Possibly. He hasn't threatened me yet."

"It isn't about threats, it's about his nature. He's a lilin, a damned soul restored to walk the Earth as a servant of Hell. There is absolutely nothing good about him."

"I don't believe in that eternal damnation crock." Some Jews did. Judy didn't.

"You'd better start. If you keep dealing with Victor Prince, you'll find yourself in Sheol."

Judy managed not to laugh. Apparently, fairies didn't understand that Sheol and Hell were not, remotely, synonyms. "You're looking for Gehenna," she said, simply.

"Whatever. He'll kill you and he'll send your soul to Hell if he can."

"If he *can*." She meant him killing her. She meant him taking her soul. She was fairly sure he couldn't do the latter.

A few days ago she would have thought there was nobody who could do that, would have questioned the existence of demons.

But now? "What do you want?" she finally asked the pooka, trying to meet his eyes with her own.

"Well, a roll in the hay would be fun."

She rolled her eyes.

"But I want you not to end up...dead."

"Why?" She wasn't sure why a fairy would care.

"Do I need a reason?"

"Bluntly, yes. I know what you are." She studied him. She could see the hint of the fox about him, the hint of ears, of brush. Nothing real or solid, nothing that she could prove.

But it was there, it was something that she knew was real.

"You see."

"Actually, it's the fact that you smell." She knew it was insulting. She didn't particularly care.

"Eh, same thing. So, maybe you should be asking yourself why." He grinned, detached himself from the wall, and padded off down the street.

———

A MOMENT LATER, Darrell called her. "We have another issue."

She sighed. "I'll be at the precinct." No, she wasn't going to talk about it over the cellular network.

She knew better.

Maybe she shouldn't talk about it at all. The paranoid part of her was wondering if she had, in fact, had a tracker put on her by the fairy.

He wanted to keep her alive. Probably because he found her hot, reading between the lines. And he was right. Victor Prince was a threat.

She didn't trust a guy who smelled of wet fox either, though. It was definitely wet fox, not the wet dog she had initially thought.

She didn't trust him at all, not one iota. Who did she trust? She asked herself that as she walked to the precinct.

Darrell.

Possibly Tag, there was something about him that made her want to trust him. Which meant she had to be careful. She had known many guys with that aura of trust who turned out to be mob enforcers or worse. So, no, she was wary of Tag. Wary even of her own judgment. Certainly nobody at the precinct. The captain wanted her to wrap the case. Everyone else wanted what they always wanted. Keep things simple, keep things easy.

Whatever was happening to her made *her* less trustworthy, not because she thought she was evil. No, if she was sensing things that might be magic or whatever, then either she was going insane *or* she had a new ability she had to learn how to properly interpret.

Without Victor's help she would not have known what the wet dog smell meant. Of course, she also sensed that dark purple around him. She would know what *that* meant next time she ran into it.

If she did.

She reached the precinct and slipped inside. "What's the problem?" she asked as she reached her office.

"Bar fight at a dive bar in Queens. Wouldn't mean anything, except one of the involved parties was Victor Prince."

A headache immediately started behind her left eye. "Did he win?"

"Let's just say you should see the other guy. He didn't kill him. But he was apparently protecting a woman."

The headache reached her right eye. "A woman."

"Deirdre Hodges, trophy wife of a Manhattan lawyer. Not quite your regular bimbo. Pool champion."

Which explained her presence in a dive bar. "Let me guess, she was kicking the butt of all comers at the table."

"Yup. In any case, Victor and this other guy kind of did a number on each other. He ran off. The other guy didn't, mostly because of a broken leg."

Judy sighed. "So now we have to arrest him for assault."

"Maybe. The eye witness accounts say the other guy started it."

Judy thought, uncharitably but in her mind likely accurately, that Victor had probably done something to deserve it.

Like breathing.

———

THE VICTIM HAD the same purple aura as Victor, flickering around him and bringing with it the odd scent of a sickly-sweet flower.

Then he was the same thing. Lilin.

That was right. A descendant of Lilith. Or rather, something which looked human, wore human form, walked as human but was a demon.

How they had become associated with her, Judy didn't know. She had thought them something else, but with more than one person using the term she had to have been wrong.

He was sitting up in a hospital bed, a cast on his left leg. Otherwise, he didn't seem particularly harmed, but Judy wouldn't be surprised if they had fast healing or, well, something.

Something. "So, what was the brawl over?"

"Hot broad."

"Hot *married* broad," Judy said dryly. "Who probably wasn't interested in you anyway."

She would have picked up tells that he was lying even if she wasn't already sure of that. This could be Dani Martin's killer.

He had said infernal politics.

It all wanted to wrap up neatly with a bow on it, but Judy knew better. She had, besides, no reason to even put him on the suspect list except intuition. And she was never going to be that cop. She had fought for years not to be that cop. "Word has it," she added, "That you started it."

He shrugged, then winced as if he regretted it. That too seemed dishonest. As if he was faking being more hurt than he was.

"He called me a bitch."

Judy's lips quirked. "I've been called worse and not thrown a punch." But she could honestly just see Victor's smirk.

That shit-eating face.

Yeah, she might have punched him too. "Can we call this one just your regular bar brawl?" she asked the uniform.

"Works for me, although I thought you might use it as an excuse to bring the other one in."

Judy shook her head. She made sure the guy wasn't looking then made fish reeling motions.

The uniform laughed. "We'll let this one go when the hospital does, then. Save the paperwork."

Judy turned back to the man. "One moment." Then she walked over, leaned down and whispered to him. "You guys can take your politics out of my city and back where it belongs." She straightened and walked out, not looking back to see his reaction.

It felt like something out of a not particularly good cop show.

It also felt very, very good.

But once she was outside, she saw the shadow of the Captain. Not there, but leaning on her.

This guy was a sideshow.

Victor Prince was the one they wanted.

It was her job to bring him in.

Just as it had always been her job to bring in the usual, the most convenient suspect. This time she couldn't do that.

Next time, she couldn't do that either.

Maybe there couldn't be a next time.

22

VICTOR FINALLY GOT his breath back. Deidre Hodges was turning towards him, her eyes laughing.

"Thank you. I hadn't expected such courtesy from one of your kind."

Victor shrugged. "Don't expect it. He had already pissed me off."

"Ah, infernal politics. Now, I'm going to have to say it, aren't I?" She drifted her hands to her hips. "Hands off my husband."

This was putting a different face on the mission. Had Victor not been on the outs with Richard, he would have simply had his boyfriend do it.

Richard would blow the guy up, enjoy it, and take payment in tacos. Victor missed him.

He wanted to go and make up, but he couldn't. He would certainly blow everything to the cop.

And he didn't want to go and make up. "You know..."

"I know. Your kind only follow orders and have a *very* limited sense of self preservation." She blew on her fingers and a bit of fire appeared.

Not much spell behind it. A specialist fire mage with a lot of practice, not to mention the glamor. She was probably direct-lined to

Oberon or Titania or, worse, Gwyn...although he had only ever heard of one faeborn from *that* line.

Thank Lucifer that one was off the board.

The fire affinity suggested Titania. He shrugged. "I do have to follow orders."

"I know I can't save him," she said, quietly. "But I can hold back the darkness for a little while."

"He made his choice."

"He was *fifteen*," she fired back, a bit of that same energy glinting in her eyes.

"That's..." Victor opened his mouth to say it wasn't his problem, because it wasn't. He was ordered to collect the soul, and he would. And he was, he knew, going to have to kill Deirdre too. Or take her off the board temporarily some other way. Yet, part of him was unable to finish that sentence.

"I'm going to give you a fair chance." She blew the fire towards him, but it dissipated on the wind. "You can walk away now. If your boss will let you."

She sounded almost sad as she turned to walk back towards the bar and her bike. There were cops there now, but he knew she wouldn't be seen by them, wouldn't be noticed as anything but a random person.

An easy trick for a faeborn, that hint of glamor. He envied it.

He was going to have to wait for a while to retrieve his bike.

***

WALK AWAY.

He felt the binding close around him as he considered those words. He couldn't walk away. A lilin never could from their prey.

The difference this had made was that now he was going to have to kill Deirdre Hodges. Nastily. In a way that made it look like her husband did it, just to tie off the knot good. Unless he could buy her off, which seemed unlikely.

But he would have to be careful. He should have known, should have suspected that Deirdre was her husband's protector. Sometimes the other side fantasized that they could save somebody.

Very rarely, they actually did. The more time they bought, the more chance there was for the one thing that could preserve a damned soul; genuine remorse.

For whatever he had done when he was fifteen.

It had to be before he died. Afterwards...well. He had sold his soul, if he was very lucky he would be bound as a lilin.

More likely he would wander the halls of Hell forever.

Deirdre would...most likely be reborn. Pissed at Victor.

Maybe there was a way he could take her off the board for longer. Sometimes there was, but he would need a necromancer.

The thought stopped in his mind. Turned over in his mind. New York was a big city, no doubt there was one, but most necromancers, despite the obvious reputation of the art, wanted nothing to do with an agent of Hell.

Most people thought necromancy was a dark art about raising zombies.

It wasn't.

But the thought was going somewhere. He let it turn around in his head.

He could turn things around. He could try his best to kill Christian and make it look like *Deirdre* did it. Then feed her to...

...a cop who had the Sight. He'd have to find a different detective to do his dirty work. Or would he?

Judy didn't have any reason to like or trust fairies and Tag probably wouldn't deny the fact that faeborn were no more inherently good than mortals.

Perhaps he could use her after all...

RICHARD CALLED him as he headed back to the hotel. His first instinct was not to answer. His second instinct was to answer rudely.

He quelled both of them. "Richard," he said.

"Are you coming back?"

He could hear all kinds of emotions in his partner's voice. Hope.

Resignation. Anger. And he was not sure whether the hope was for his return or not.

"Do your thing. Get out of town. I'll find you."

He wasn't sure whether he was telling the truth or not. At all. Richard was a loose cannon. He loved him. He loved him not.

He wished for a daisy. Pulling the petals off and counting, a schoolgirl thing, think about your crush. So many girls had done that.

So many had found the wrong answer in the flower, the one they wanted to hear or the one they didn't. Not the one which was actually true, which often lay well within that boundary.

He loved him. He loved him not.

He wouldn't find him. He kept walking towards the hotel, hoping Richard would do as he suggested. The cop wasn't stupid. She'd work it out soon and fast enough and whatever hesitation she had towards arresting Victor likely wouldn't apply to the pyromaniac.

Odd that the mundane human was the more dangerous of the two. Or, rather, the less predictable. That was what it was really about, being predictable. Being predictable meant people trusted you. They might trust you to be evil, but they knew where they stood.

Judy struck him as a woman who liked to know where she stood with people, who liked that basic honesty.

He never wanted to see Richard again, because he hadn't been predictable, he hadn't thought things through.

He didn't hate him enough to want to see him in jail or worse.

He didn't hate anyone that much. Hatred required the capacity for true, absolute love, and while what he felt for Richard had been a bond, it had not been true love.

He was not capable of that any more.

The Sibyl had said...but she spoke in riddles and confusion. He would love and he would know love.

But he could not.

No lilin could. He loved him not.

Shoving his phone into his pocket, Victor quickened his pace to shelter as the faintest hints of rain started in the glowering sky.

23

It was raining.

Not just little dribs and drabs of rain, but the kind of full-blown downpour that streaked down windows, pooled in the street, threatened to flood the subway. Judy hid from the rain in the lobby of the precinct.

She had nothing to go home to anyway, nothing but a hotel room and waiting on approval for that apartment and the growing relief that she had never acquired a pet.

She wanted to go out drinking, to go to a bar, to find somebody else equally willing to lose themselves in a moment of hedonism and passion.

She couldn't do that, of course. It would be irresponsible and stupid, it wasn't something you did while investigating an active murder case.

She saw reflections in the rain and her imagination formed them into images. Victor Prince, hand extended towards her, asking her to dance.

He wasn't interested in her, she was fairly sure of that. But that hand was still extended, that request was still open and real.

A request to be drawn into his world.

But of course somebody like him would want to corrupt a cop, she realized. Would want her on the take. She could neutralize that easily enough.

There was the world of police, of cases and paperwork and getting away with murder.

There was the world of the monsters. Victor called her to the latter. Victor was a monster. Yet, was *she* any better? Was she really any better than those she worked with?

And if he was a demon, he would want her soul.

The pooka was right and wrong. Victor Prince wanted her soul. But he likely had no intention of *killing* her.

He likely had every intention, instead, of corrupting her. That welcoming smile and hand hid not knives or poison but the slow fall from good cop to bent cop. The fall she had seen so many others take before her. The fall almost everyone took eventually.

It wasn't easy to turn down the bribes, they came small to start with. The minor requests to look the other way at some small crime. (Judy was, mind, inclined to look the other way at marijuana possession and a few things she thought shouldn't even be small crimes). The easy wrap up of the case, the blaming of the person who already had a record, or of the black guy. It was always so easy to blame the black guy, because everyone assumed it was them anyway.

Then they grew and you were on the take and you were a bad cop, without even understanding quite how or when it had happened.

You didn't let it start. You didn't take that first bribe. Yet, she knew how good cops ended, how she would end. Why was she still a cop?

Why wasn't she bringing in Victor Prince?

Because she believed him not guilty. Not guilty of this particular crime.

But was she rationalizing this to herself?

The rain eased off and she braved it, stepping out into the streets in which rivulets ran. Water, washing the city's gunk and dirt into the Hudson, into the harbor, where the ocean would dilute it.

Where the pollution would only spread.

Only one drop of corruption was needed.

She knew that.

SHE'D HAD the uniforms keep a quiet eye on the other demon, the other lilin. But she couldn't ask for much.

It was a hunch, and while her hunches tended to be good, they weren't that good. Nobody's hunches were evidence. She wanted evidence. She was still trying to be a good cop.

Not even if she was seeing and, well, smelling auras. The smell part convinced her, was strong evidence that this was real.

In all of the occult literature you saw auras. You didn't smell them. She saw something around Victor too, but that might be specific to his nature.

She needed more data points to truly understand what was happening to her, what was going on in her own mind. More different kinds of fairies, perhaps.

Were there any angels wandering around New York, or were they less inclined...

...perhaps they didn't use things like Victor as agents of Heaven because they had more than enough priests and rabbis and imams to do it. At that thought, she knew where she was going to go.

She headed for the subway, the rain dripping from her coat. Escaping it down into the dark. The station had not flooded.

The subway needed better flood defenses, but she suspected it wouldn't be a priority until something major happened and shut down half of Manhattan.

That tended to be how things worked.

She got off at Marcy Avenue in Williamsburg. The streets of Brooklyn were as they had always been. She turned through a kind of park area around an apartment complex, the fading rain dripping from the trees. The light was also fading, drifting away from her, drifting around her.

She didn't like that. She didn't like that at all. She hurried through the park, down a street lined with brick buildings, across the street.

The building she was approaching smelled of something fresh and clean, kind of like cucumber water.

Something that would quench your thirst and restore your soul.

She smiled, standing outside, drinking that in. Heading for the main entrance.

She could sense places as well as people. And holy ground smelled like cucumber water; because of course it did, because she associated that with purity and cleanliness and cool rest on a hot day.

She hesitated at the entrance. Perhaps she had learned all she needed to know.

Perhaps she had something else she needed to do here, but no. There was no need. God was watching over her.

She might have a few words for Him, but that was, after all, normal.

He was still there.

THE NEXT DAY she was going over case files, letting the Martin case drift into the back of her mind.

"There's a lady here who wants to talk to you, Detective," came the desk sergeant's voice over the intercom.

When he said lady he meant that the woman was classy. Or he would have said "woman" or perhaps even "dame." He sometimes liked to make that joke.

"Somebody show her in."

A uniform did after a moment. An elegant young blonde.

"Detective." A pause. "I'm Deirdre Hodges."

She smelled of roses and ash.

Judy nodded. So, Deirdre Hodges...was another of them. This city was too big and at the same time too small. There was just no way this was a coincidence. "Why are you here?"

"I have a reason to believe my husband's life is in danger."

Judy nodded. "Then you should..."

Deidre rested her hand on the desk, a ring glinting on it. "I'm talking to *you* for a reason."

She swallowed, then nodded again. "I know you are." What did *she* smell like?

She didn't know if she wanted to know.

"Victor Prince," the woman said, finally. "He's going to kill my husband."

There was part of her that wanted to ask the, perhaps, obvious. What had her husband done to attract unwanted attention? Because no doubt there was a reason why somebody like Victor Prince had been hired to take him out.

No doubt there was.

But one didn't ask. "Then you need to..."

"I *intend* to file a report. But there's only one cop in this precinct who stands a prayer of understanding that any officer who goes up against Prince in a direct fight is dead."

Judy nodded. "You trust me to take a subtle approach."

"I don't care what happens as long as my husband is safe."

Those words sounded like words with a meaning. They sounded like this woman cared about nothing else in all the world.

Judy knew how to tell when somebody was lying.

Deirdre Hodges was lying through her pretty, straight, white teeth.

24

If he couldn't seduce or otherwise work on Deirdre Hodges, then Victor knew he had only one real choice.

Go after Christian directly, and do it fast before the faeborn woman had a chance to set up, say, a bevy of cops. Take her out if he could, but Christian was the priority.

Not that he couldn't deal with a bevy of cops, but he really didn't fancy spending the next few decades in prison. Prison was, of course, not meant to be fun. For somebody like him it could be a fiefdom. Just not a pleasant one.

More to the point, it would be embarrassing and possibly get him into trouble with his boss. He wasn't much use in prison, and even for a lilin, breaking out was hard. Not impossible, but hard.

There was a window of opportunity, but it wasn't a big one. Christian Hodges was at an after-work networking event, the kind of mixer where lawyers hung out with people who might need lawyers (insert other professions here as needed) at a bar in Midtown. It was the kind of event where nobody really cared if you snuck in without an invite as long as you looked like somebody who might hire one of the strutting professionals on offer.

The chosen location was a chic rooftop bar, the kind of place where you couldn't forget you were in New York for a second. And that was the point. It was at the edge of Midtown, with skyscrapers on one side and what might as well have been open space on the other, occupied only by shorter buildings, by tenements and low rises. Spangled by taller buildings that poked above them like broken teeth. Dressed in a reasonably nice suit, Victor mingled his way into the bar. There were gorgeous women and men; mere distractions to him right now.

Hodges was in the middle of a group of older men. Victor recognized a couple of them as mafioso, not top-ranking guys, but important enough to be a concern. If they decided Hodges belonged to them then he would have grave (possibly literally) difficulty dealing with the man as he needed to.

The thought of hiring somebody else to do it and take the fall came to his mind. Unfortunately, whatever happened to Christian Hodges, Deirdre would be right there to tell the police he had threatened the man.

Which was, after all, true. Her glamor had fooled him. And to be fair, her faeborn beauty had dazzled him.

Should have sent somebody with no interest in women, he thought as he circled his way through the room toward Hodges.

He couldn't do it here, of course. Unless he saw a remarkable opportunity. But this wasn't about doing it.

This was about setting it up.

"Mr. Hodges. I believe we need to talk."

THE TWO MEN stepped out onto a balcony.

"So, what do we need to talk about?"

"Your wife," Victor said. He wrapped his hands around the balcony railing. "You know she has a habit of going to less than savory bars."

"She's looking for people to beat at pool. I refuse to play her."

Victor laughed. "A wise decision. But that's not all she's looking for. Come on, you know the score. You're the old, rich model. But can you keep up with her."

"Deirdre is absolutely loyal to me."

Victor raised a hand. "Emotionally, maybe. Physically? Not hardly."

A seed of doubt, so when Deirdre warned him about Victor, he wouldn't necessarily believe it. Of course, he also hadn't given that name. He'd introduced himself blandly as David.

Lots of Davids and Daves around, he would blend into the sea of them. He was not going to be anything more than some guy who thought Deirdre was hot.

"So..." A pause. "What do you expect me to do about it?"

Victor shrugged. "I don't know. I just thought you should know."

"If Deirdre wants to pick up a younger guy because I go too far between rounds for her these days, I honestly don't care."

This was like pulling teeth. "Really?"

"As long as she uses a condom."

"What if she cuckolds you?"

Christian laughed. "That's not going to happen. Trust me."

If they had an open relationship, then he was denied another weapon. Had he been less concerned for his own fate afterwards, he would have tipped Christian over the railing then and there.

It would have been done.

But he was not that expendable. He had built skills in this life. More importantly, he had built connections, a useful network of criminal elements.

Throwing all that away just because it was the easy solution. "So, you trust her?"

"With my life," Christian said.

"Why? I mean, other than being a pool shark..."

"You figure I married her for her looks." He laughed. "I married her for...well...she married me for my money, and I don't care about that. I married her because, well..."

He looked up.

It was the tiniest tell that Victor couldn't ignore. It allowed him to drop behind the railing as Deirdre Hodges jumped from the roof of the bar to land between them.

SHE TURNED TO FACE HIM. "I told you to walk away."

"You know I can't." He considered the balcony. He probably wouldn't survive the fall.

Christian was backing towards the doorway.

"I had to give you the chance."

"I'd appreciate it more if it meant anything." He didn't have free will any more. He'd given that up when he'd...

...he pushed the memory back where it belonged.

"Perhaps you would." She lifted her hand. "Dear, please go inside."

"They'll get me eventually."

"It won't be today." It had the note of a promise. Christian Hodges fled into the building.

Victor let out a sigh, reached inward for his own power. "We're really doing this?"

"We're really doing it," she echoed, fire starting to form around her hands. It didn't burn her, of course. She was ordering it not to.

Purple flames leapt around him. The noise of the party within dimmed. The threat of rain would keep them inside. Its actuality would have no effect on the combatants.

Its actuality came a moment later, in sheets. It had no impact on Deirdre's fire, but it rapidly plastered her blonde head to her skull. She threw the first bolt.

He countered with purple flame, a shield that sprung up between them. Anyone who saw the sorcerous duel would not remember it.

Or they would and perhaps remember other things as well. It wasn't his problem. It wasn't her problem either.

Only one of them was walking away from this.

And that one would probably be going to jail. He countered with his own blast. Purple fire angled outward from his hands like vines.

Then he lowered one hand, keeping up the attack with the other. He reached into his pocket.

And hesitated.

It was an old trick, as old as firearms.

He had to kill her or she would kill him. Their energies contested, wrapped around each other. He could feel her will against his.

And with a snap they saw, as sometimes happened during such contests, each other's true intents.

Deirdre had been *paid* to marry Christian Hodges, protect him, and pretend to love him.

She wasn't his wife.

She was just his bodyguard.

He had no idea what Deidre saw in him. But suddenly her flames flared white. She was stronger than him in that moment, catching him off guard. If he had shot her things would be different.

His vision went white and then dark.

25

JUDY REALLY HATED people who acted like they were in a noir movie. Not that she didn't take Deirdre Hodges somewhat seriously.

But the entire dame in distress act was just that. An act. Without knowing what the woman was lying about, though, Judy could not be sure what to do.

She didn't *want* police protection. She was sure any cops who tried to help her would die. Judy was not sure exactly what would happen.

But she was obligated to report this.

Or was she?

She knew she was about to go off the rails, just a little. Become the very kind of loose cannon that annoyed her so much. But staying on the rails? That wasn't always the act of a good cop.

It wasn't hard to find out where Christian Hodges would be that evening. Presumably Deirdre Hodges would be with him. One of those stupid networking happy hour things for rich people and those who served them.

For those rarefied heights where those who might be called servants – lawyers, personal assistants, financial advisors – were making far more money in a year than a New York detective could imagine seeing in her life.

The people Hodges worked for could buy and sell her, if she was the kind of woman who could be bought and sold.

She liked to think that she wasn't, but she suspected she had a price somewhere and that one of these people could find it.

She knew she wasn't perfect. She donned her best suit and headed to the event. The price tag was beyond her normal reach.

Far beyond her reach right now when she was looking for a new home. Reluctantly, she prepared for her savings to take a hit, but she knew at some deep level that she needed to be here.

She needed to be in this place, but she eschewed the offered cocktail. Sobriety was important. Maybe if nothing happened she could get a drink before she left.

She didn't turn down the shrimp, nibbling on one as she worked the room. Looking for Christian Hodges, Deirdre Hodges or, well...

...Victor Prince, who was slipping through the crowd like a man on a mission. Judy was slightly disappointed, even annoyed. Whatever Deirdre Hodges was lying about, Victor Prince was here to cause a problem for *somebody*.

Possibly her.

No. He had spotted Hodges, was approaching him. She could not get close enough to hear their conversation and wished Deirdre had been more cooperative with standard police methods.

Like having her husband wear a wire.

The two men drifted towards the door to the outside balcony, which was notably empty right now. Likely due to the grey skies.

She did not see Deirdre Hodges anywhere. She only saw the two men go outside. She moved to the doorway, watching them.

Through the windows, she saw somebody drop from the roof above. And then, mere moments later, purple flame, and a moment later red responding to it.

Nobody else seemed to see.

———

SHE MOVED OUT THE DOOR. She dared not rush. It was like she was between this time and some other time, between reality and magic.

Between the sacred and the profane. As she moved, Christian Hodges ran in through the door, terror on his face. She ignored him, for now.

Victor Prince was on the ground, charred and bleeding. Deirdre Hodges stood over him, flames wreathing her hands.

"Ms. Hodges."

"Stay out of this, Detective. I'm sending him back where he belongs."

"I can't let you do that." It might already be too late.

"You know what he is."

Judy reached up. Touched her magen David. "I know what he is. I also know what murder is. And it's wrong. It's wrong no matter *who* the victim is. Because it's not just about what it does to them, but what it does to you."

Deirdre laughed. "You really think this is my first rodeo?"

It gave Judy an opportunity. She moved to stand between the woman and the fallen lilin. "No, I don't."

Now she knew what Deirdre was lying about.

Loving Christian Hodges. Whatever their arrangment was, it wasn't that.

"You think I care about the state of my soul?"

"I question whether you have one." The words came out without any thought.

"Oh, I have one, but it's bound to neither Heaven nor Hell. I can't be damned or saved."

Judy wondered if that was true, or if she just believed it. "In any case, you made a fatal mistake. *I* saw who fired first."

Deirdre hissed, more like an angry cat than anything else.

"So, how about this? You take your husband home, leave Victor Prince to me, and I don't make your life difficult."

"You can't prove I did anything. None of them saw anything." She lazily indicated the inside of the bar.

"I can still make your life difficult."

Deirdre shook her head. "*You* can be damned, Judy Eisenberg. Be careful." And then she swept into the bar.

Judy looked at Victor.

The burns over his body were already, visibly, starting to heal.

JUDY BELIEVED Victor when he said he didn't need a doctor or a hospital.

She took him to his hotel room.

"Why did you save me?"

"Because I didn't want the paperwork of arresting Deirdre Hodges." She paused.

He laughed. "You know she's a pro, right?"

"I do *now*." There was, no doubt, audible irritation in her voice. She stepped over to the window, looked out at the night. It wasn't raining any more.

"She's good. Had me fooled briefly too."

"And Hodges is her..."

"Client, the marriage is a sham. I wouldn't be surprised to find out Hodges isn't even interested in women." Victor sighed. "I don't want you involved in this."

"Why are you after Hodges?"

"Because he sold his soul and the debt is due. Deirdre was hired by somebody to keep him out of our hands, perhaps because he hasn't finished something. It's all infernal politics. You should..."

"I can't, can I? I *can't* just walk away, Victor, until I've found out who killed Dani Martin. I'm suspecting the guy you brawled with."

"That was a setup," Victor grumbled. "Okay, here's the thing. Dani Martin wasn't killed by a lilin."

"Are you sure?"

"She was...an extremely powerful demon hunter. She would have sensed him coming, and if he could take her she would not have been where she could be taken."

Judy shook her head. "The *truth*, Victor."

"Okay. The world has been a battleground between three forces for its entire existence. Heaven, Hell, and Faerie. There are others, but those are the main ones."

"And Deirdre represents Faerie."

"She's faeborn. At a guess, first generation faeborn, what used to be called a changeling."

Judy nodded. "So, Heaven is good, Hell is evil, and Faerie is..."

"Life and death. Prey and predator. Things which are beyond and outside good and evil. Things which simply *are*." Victor shook his head. "Fae don't have free will. Changelings do, but I heard what she said..."

"About her soul being bound to faerie."

Victor nodded. "She has absolute certainty about what will happen to her when she dies, and thus neither fear nor any need for a conscience."

"Are all changelings like that?"

"Oh no. The most powerful we know of started out as an evil bitch, learned better, and was a major force for good until somebody took her off the board."

Judy elected not to ask right now beyond, "Okay, so any..."

"Any being with free will can align themselves with the three. And while you can't align yourself with Heaven *and* Hell, you can align yourself with either of the two and Faerie."

Judy nodded. "Or not..."

"Most people don't. They live, they die, they're reborn. The Christian Church did its best to align everyone with Heaven, but look at the history of the church."

She shuddered. "You can do stuff in the *name* of Heaven without..."

"Precisely. You're closer than any of them."

She reached for her magen David again. "I'm just a good cop." She could say it even if she wasn't sure she believed it.

"And I'm an agent of Hell. Forever."

"Which means you have to be evil." Her tone was flat.

"I was human once. I made my choices, detective."

She still didn't believe in eternal damnation.

The problem was, it was very clear that he *did*.

And he belonged in jail. Yet, somehow, she sensed something. Something shifting and changing within her.

Who really belonged in jail? Only people who did evil from choice. He had no choice. Ergo, he did not belong in jail. And that meant half the people she had put in jail? They didn't belong there.

She wasn't sure what to do anymore.

26

THE LAST WAY Victor had expected this day to end was in his hotel room, healing up while he explained cosmology to a newbie.

A woman he should kill.

A woman he didn't want to kill.

"So, where does Tag fit in?"

"He's a shaman, and thus aligned to Heaven and Faerie both."

Judy nodded. "And a wolf."

"Very definitely a wolf." Victor felt a certain hunger at the thought of the man. Rebound, he told himself.

"You think he's hot, don't you?"

He laughed harshly. "Detective." A slight emphasis on the word. "Yes, I do think he's hot. But I did just dump my boyfriend, so..."

"So it wouldn't be wise to jump into another relationship even if you weren't enemies." Then she repeated the question she had asked. "Do you have to be evil?"

He did.

It was in his nature now, deeply woven inside him, the purple flame, the healing, it all came with the package. He was damned and nothing, no force in the planet could change that. Not even the gods, not even the most powerful of the fae. Not even his boss.

It had never happened. He snapped back with, "Do you have to be a cop?" followed by "I have to kill Christian Hodges."

"Or what? Your boss will give you a turn of hellfire?" She was apparently ignoring the cop quip.

"Pretty much."

There might have been sympathy in her voice. There was not much in the way of understanding.

He didn't expect understanding. She was still mortal, and while he could sense the faith within her, she was still that and she wasn't on the verge of becoming a Guardian or a true agent of Heaven.

But perhaps in the future. He could interfere with her growth, he could do so so easily.

She liked him. He could tell that.

"So, is there any way out of this situation?"

There was steel in her tone. "No."

"So, there's only one thing we can do."

We.

Not I.

"Move Christian Hodges somewhere I can't find him," he finished for her. "Put him in witness protection. I'll have to look, and I can't promise..."

"I'm not asking you to promise. I'm asking..." She closed her eyes. Swore briefly in Yiddish.

He understood her words, of course. He'd heard enough of the language. They weren't nice words at all, but he'd heard worse. Fact is that if he cooperated with her attempts to prevent him from getting to Hodges, then he would be punished.

He might even be killed.

Then punished some more.

But there was something about her peculiar sincerity. "Why do you care about me?"

"I already said, it's about the paperwork."

"No." He stood, his skin already healed, the effects of the faefire going away. "It's not and you know it."

There came a knock on the door.

VICTOR STOOD and looked at the door. He knew who was outside, but he opened it anyway. "Looking for me?"

Tag stood in the entrance. He actually shuffled his feet. "Yes."

There was something in his face, his eyes, his voice. "I've got company."

"What hit you?"

"Changeling."

Tag rolled his eyes. "I'll stay right out of that one, thank you very much." Then he sniffed. "The cop's here."

"I have a name," Judy said from behind him, archly.

"And when we three meet again," Tag mused. "Can I come in?"

"Depends on whether you're here to talk or try to chew on me."

Tag laughed. "Talk. My word. No chewing for right now."

He didn't promise no chewing in the future. Victor didn't expect him to. But he suspected it wasn't business that drew the wolf to him.

No, it wasn't business at all, and it was opportunity. Opportunity to work on this man, to corrupt him. He was powerful and could be more so.

Do you have to be evil? Yes.

It was a question he hadn't asked himself since, well. Since his memories had come back the first time, since he'd remembered who he was.

He'd asked it of himself then. He'd gotten his answer. Yes, he had to be evil. There was no way out.

But there was a man in the doorway who might have feelings for him.

There was a woman sitting on the bed who refused to give up on him.

Nobody had ever refused to give up on him. He'd been condemned for his crime, he'd heard nothing since but that he deserved his fate.

And he'd bound himself with his own chains of guilt, as strong as any hellfire. The purple flame within him.

Lilin.

Demon.

Damned.

And standing between these two. "Go," he said finally. "Both of you. *Leave me.*"

He had aimed for fierce in his tone. He ended up with plaintive. He didn't want them to go. He didn't want them to leave.

He wanted them to stay but they had to go, because if they stayed he would destroy them.

Wordlessly, Judy got up. She murmured something to Tag. They left.

He had to kill Christian Hodges, he could feel the urge prickling within him. Barbed wire wrapped around his heart.

They said people like him didn't have hearts.

It wasn't true, because if you didn't have a heart you didn't have a place you could feel pain.

They were gone and he dropped back onto the bed, pulled his knees to his head and let the pain wash over him.

A foretaste of what would come if he didn't complete his mission.

———

THE PAIN LEFT HIM ALONE, but too hollow to sleep, too driven to do anything but find Mr. Hodges.

It wouldn't work. If they made Mr. Hodges disappear from him, he would go crazy until he found him. Beelzebub was shortening his leash. Tightening it around him.

It had a prong collar with spiked prongs. He panted with the effort.

The message was clear.

He wasn't to care about his own fate or his own survival. He was to find Christian Hodges and kill him right now, directly. If he got caught, it didn't matter. If he died, it didn't matter.

And then he'd still be in trouble.

Deep breaths.

He'd never tried to fight this before, not like this. And it wasn't for Deirdre Hodges. It was for those serious words.

Do you have to be evil?

Did she have to be good? Did Tag?

Beings with free will. He'd lost his. It wasn't his heart the barbed wire closed around, although that was how it felt.

It was his soul.

Which was no longer his own.

He *no longer had free will*. But he had the ability to fight. Ironic. Hell hadn't started with the intent to be evil.

It had started with the intent to be free. And become worse than what it fought against. Far worse.

But there would never be a place in Heaven for him anyway.

So.

He had to do it.

Well, he had one other choice. One other escape which wasn't an escape. It wouldn't even save Christian Hodges.

He dismissed it. He pulled out his gun. Checked it. It didn't matter that it was legally purchased and could be traced by the cops.

He wasn't allowed to let that matter.

He had to kill Christian Hodges. Likely Deirdre too, when she got in the way. He couldn't hesitate this time.

His vision dimmed for a moment, veiled.

He wouldn't be going to jail.

They weren't going to trust him with anything after this. He had defied Beelzebub, he was no longer a trusted agent.

He was going back to Hell and he wasn't going to get to leave again, ever. Over the life of a man who wasn't worth saving.

27

JUDY HADN'T EXPECTED to see Tag. He stood in the pool of light of a street lamp, smelling of dog and musk. Lifting a hand in signal to her.

She slowed. "Can we talk? In a Victor-free zone?"

He shrugged a bit. "Kind of what I wanted. Dinner." He held up a hand. "One, I'm paying. Two, I'm gay."

She laughed. "So, I'm safe and my partner isn't. Then again, he's single, not bad looking, and very gay."

Tag grinned. "I doubt he's gayer than I am. I found a Dominican place with good reviews not far from here."

Her mouth watered. "Okay." Restaurants, still the safest place to talk.

He was limping a little bit. She elected not to ask why. They stayed silent until they got to the restaurant. Despite being a Dominican place, one of the specialties was Mofongo, which was, of course Puerto Rican. Or maybe it was Dominican as well.

She ordered it with fried beef anyway, settling at the table. "So, who starts?"

"We're probably both thinking of the same thing. Or the same person."

"We removed his target from the city," Judy said, quietly.

"Then he'll take the planet apart looking for him."

Judy closed her eyes. "I like him. I don't know why, but I do."

"You're better off than I am."

She opened her eyes. "*You* want in his pants. And I'm pretty sure he's at least bisexual."

"I'm pretty sure he doesn't care one iota what equipment his partner has," Tad quipped. "And yes, I do. It's probably just that."

"You should..."

"Get out of the situation. But I was asked to find out who killed Martin by her mentor."

"You could tell them..."

"He's dead too."

Judy frowned. "Somebody's targeting demon hunters."

"Somebody's *always* targeting demon hunters. Thankfully, they come back. Once a Guardian, always a Guardian. Well, perhaps not always, but...they aren't the kind of people inclined to retire."

Judy digested that. "So, reincarnation."

"We all live a good number of lives. The difference is that Guardians...and some witches and shamans...*remember*."

For some reason, that made her shudder. "I think I'm glad I don't."

"You've got a gift, though. Fairy blood a good way back. Or, given your geographical origins, maybe something else. Djinn comes to mind."

"Some people think they're fairies."

"Insult to both sides, that. Djinn have souls and free will. Pure fae don't."

Judy nodded a bit. "So, what you're saying is one of my ancestors dallied with a genie."

"That's *exactly* what I'm saying." He grinned. "Unless you want to learn magic, it's not a big deal. And probably very useful to a detective."

She nodded. "Maybe I could get some training just in using it better. If Victor Prince doesn't kill me first."

"I don't think he wants to. I've never seen conflict in a lilin before." Tag finally admitted. "It scares me."

"Scares you?"

Tag nodded. "Scares me. I mean, I'm sure he gave you the overly simplistic there are three sides speech?"

"I'm assuming there are a lot more than three and that Hell isn't remotely united."

Tag laughed. "Pretty much. And Heaven includes a lot of things...not all *gods* get on. Bast and Mithras hate each other."

Judy's lips quirked. "I won't even ask how you know that."

"But here's the thing. A lilin is a damned soul that is trusted by Hell to be reborn as an agent. Or rather by some faction within Hell. Usually a Prince."

Judy nodded. "Hence why Victor and the other one were brawling."

"There was probably some more direct personal reason for that. In any case, lilin still have free will, but they're..." He paused. "...bound to their infernal master. They can do what they want as long as it doesn't go against whatever their orders are."

"And Victor's orders are to kill Hodges."

"Who's a piece of work," Tag said. "I did some research and I'm sure you did."

"He's a corrupt bastard," Judy agreed. "Victor implied he sold his soul."

"Probably. It's not as common as in the stories, but some people will make deals with other powers. It's not necessarily a bad thing. I met a woman once who sold her soul to Odin."

Judy tensed.

Tag put a hand on hers. "Not a white supremacist, I promise. But people can sell their soul to a god as easily as to a demon, and get perks in return for, well, errands."

"I'm trying to imagine what kind of errands Odin wanted running."

Tag grinned. "Punching people who use His name as an excuse for white supremacy."

Judy laughed a bit. "You're...no, you aren't kidding, are you."

"Of course, a lot of people claim to work for various deities and, well, don't."

"I suppose at some levels a priest or a rabbi..."

Tag nodded. "It's not always that open, though. And gods don't make that kind of commitment to people who aren't, well...worth it."

"What about you?"

"Me? I'm a trained spirit worker who's powerful enough to be able to shapeshift in the real world."

He'd already told her why he was here. And why he was worried about Victor Prince. "So, what you're saying is Prince can't defy his orders."

"To my knowledge, no. I have no idea what would happen if he tried. But the worst case scenario is a really, *really* angry Prince of Hell."

Judy decided that was a pretty bad scenario indeed. But she couldn't help but say, "So, how can we help him?"

Tag considered that. Then, quietly. "I don't know."

THE CONVERSATION with Tag hadn't helped her mood; and it certainly didn't help her ability to sleep.

In fact, she didn't get a wink that night. She gave up at about 2am and spent the night journaling. Sometimes that helped.

She wrote everything down, but she tried to use a loose code so anyone who found it wouldn't call the nice gentlemen in the white coats on her. That was a very real risk right now, and her lead contender for who would actually do it was Darrell.

Or no. He'd not tell people she was crazy. He'd either try to solve the case himself or get them taken off of it on the grounds that it was driving her nuts.

Which it was. Just this was not a symptom of that.

She looked at what she had written. At what her subconscious had flowed out onto the page.

Going to the synagogue appealed, but she didn't need a minyan to pray. She didn't need anything for that but herself.

It helped.

It made her feel a little more balanced. She was one of the chosen people. It would shield her some, she thought. Maybe not protect her per se. But keep her balanced in the whirlpool.

Besides, this was probably His fault anyway.

The fault of whatever powers governed the universe of which God was all or one or part, depending on how you viewed it.

Elohim. Majestic Ones. Plural. Some people forgot that, saw God as singular and indivisible like the Christians.

She forgot it herself sometimes, but now that was the sense she got. How could God be only one thing?

The answer was that She couldn't. For some reason it helped.

A damned soul, who had done something to deserve it. Who had, per what Tag had said, chosen to be loyal to Hell.

Who had no choice but to follow his orders; no choice but to take the city or the world apart until he found Christian Hodges.

Who was probably on the road with a gun now.

Which was the real reason why she couldn't sleep.

Because she had to stop him. If Tag was right there was only one way.

And the shaman wouldn't be able to do it.

28

THE TOWNHOUSE WAS EMPTY. No Christian and certainly no Deirdre.

They'd done the smart thing and left. Victor felt the barbed wire pulling on him again. Yes, his boss was pissed.

He wasn't going to be given any breathing space, any relaxing of expectations. He had to find his prey.

Give me a chance he thought as firmly as he could. The pressure eased.

It might take a long time to find Hodges. It might take years. Years feeling as if his heart was being periodically squeezed.

He directed a string of mental swear words at Deirdre and Judy both, even though they weren't the ones he was angry with.

He was no witch for the mental vitriol to have any weight, but it did make him feel momentarily better.

The temptation to rob the place just out of spite grew in his mind, but it would achieve precisely nothing. No, he was better off, much better off, just working towards the goal.

Of course, Judy Eisenburg was waiting for him to leave New York; just waiting for an excuse to arrest him.

He would have to kill her if she tried.

Do you have to be evil?

Why did those words haunt him so much?

He was evil. He had killed his wife, had killed her lover. A crime of passion they'd called it, but it was murder. It was death and destruction.

He was death and destruction.

There was a pooka across the street, in the form of a thin-faced redhead. The fairy was watching him.

Was laughing at him. It was a target.

He glanced around, then crossed the street while it was still quiet. The pooka took off running.

He pounded after him. Felt the pavement under his feet. He had no chance. Within moments he'd lost sight of the pooka.

A fae trick. Folding the road so the distance was shorter for the pooka than it was for Victor. Nobody but another fae could catch a running fae.

But the burst of energy had actually helped, and the pooka was at least *gone* now, not hanging around laughing at him.

Of course, maybe he'd wanted to be chased. No, he would have played with Victor more if so, would have run slowly enough for him to keep up.

Would have made a game out of it. Not that any of this was a game. Well.

Perhaps it was now.

HE WALKED AWAY from the house into the night. The barbed wire had eased off. Beelzebub knew he couldn't find the man immediately.

But he could still feel the anger, feel the link between the two of them throbbing. Spooking the prey was bad.

He did have an excuse. He hadn't known that Deirdre Hodges was a freaking changeling until he got close to her.

Even then, she was a glamor expert. Sometimes changelings were more powerful than their fae parents.

He thought it more likely that she was, as he had suspected, direct-lined to Titania. He hadn't been prepared for her.

Maybe because of that he would be, not forgiven, but accepted.

But for right now he had to work out where to start on finding Hodges.

Bribe somebody in witness protection? That assumed they'd gone into formal protection. Things were starting to get to the point where somebody could vanish on their own, go somewhere safe, and still use the internet to work.

Find a hacker who could track him down.

Neither of those things could be done right now. He took a few deep, experimental breaths, wondering if he could get some sleep.

If he went back to his hotel room, Judy was in the building. He didn't have anything there he cared about.

He didn't have anything he cared about. Or, at this point, anyone.

And, to make things even worse? He was horny.

No outlet for *that* right now except his own right hand. He shook his head a little. It was an effect of adrenalin and hormones and whatever else was going on with him.

Deep breath.

Going back to the hotel room made the most sense, but he just plain couldn't. He walked towards the edge of the island. He was considering options involving bullets or jumping.

But that would definitely result in the outcome he wanted to avoid.

Deep breath.

He started to head back towards the hotel. There was an odd churning sensation in his belly that might have been fear. Probably was fear. But it was something else too, something he couldn't put his finger on.

Do you have to be evil?

Yes.

He could do whatever he wanted until those orders came through. And then if he didn't do what was asked of him.

So, yes, he had to be evil.

But was that really what she was asking?

He was no longer sure.

No sign of Judy at the hotel, to his relief. But he could feel or smell something else.

Oh great.

"You," he said. "Here for a rematch?"

"Not hardly," the blond said, approaching him. "You beat me fair and square."

Victor nodded. "I sure did." He shifted into a cocky stance. "What were you even doing there?"

"Getting drunk."

Victor laughed ringingly. "Well, maybe *that* we can repeat." Alcohol had only so much effect on him. Distraction, however, would definitely help. A drinking partner. A reminder that he was part of something.

"Maybe. I don't think our principals get on well."

"Screw them," Victor said cheerfully. "Until and unless we're on the opposite site of something, I don't care."

The other laughed. "Call me Maurice."

"Space cowboy," Victor teased.

"I didn't pick it."

Victor shrugged. "Then change it. Easy enough." He hadn't been attached to his so-called parents. They'd left him latchkey most of the time.

Maybe Maurice felt differently. But they were a means to an end.

"I thought about it, but honestly? People underestimate a guy named Maurice. They think they can just tease me about my name. They don't expect me to be dangerous. Whilst Victor Prince, come on."

Victor blew on his fingers. "I like being intimidating."

"So, the changeling broad."

"Is in my way. I'll deal with her." He kept his tone firm; he wouldn't honestly care if Maurice did take her out, but there was an unspoken etiquette. You never admitted you needed help. You never let anyone else get in the way on the hunt.

Maurice would know to stay out of the way.

"Got it. I was going to try and seduce her."

"Don't bother. She's *married*. Doesn't even love the guy, but won't violate the vows."

"Changeling," Maurice pointed out. "She may have tangled herself so she can't."

Fairy vows went beyond this world. If she'd... "Oh, Hell."

He hadn't even thought about that, and now he was embarrassed by it.

Deirdre wasn't protecting Christian Hodges from choice. And she would never back down.

She had sworn a fairy vow to him. She could no more stop protecting him than Victor could stop trying to kill him. "Oh well. I was going to kill her anyway. How about that drink?"

So much for going back to his room.

Heck, he might even get laid.

29

CHRISTIAN HODGES HAD REFUSED to go far. Judy understood why. He was New York born and bred.

Hiding him in New Jersey was likely to be just as effective as sending him to the other side of the country anyway. One of the tricks of protecting people was that you could stick them under the nose of the threat and the threat would *assume* you had sent them further. They never looked that close.

So, he was in New Jersey. Of course, Judy couldn't go check on him, but people were. For right now, he was fine.

His wife was fine.

His wife was angry. Specifically, his wife was angry with *her*. She wasn't sure of her own safety from that quarter.

So, she elected not to worry about it. She was still convinced that the other man, the blond, was the killer. Maurice was the name he had given.

Except Tag thought she was wrong.

Dani would have sensed him coming.

So, the killer had to be somebody Dani would not have sensed coming. Judy didn't know enough about that to hazard a guess.

A normal person would be her first choice. Perhaps Dani was so worried about supernatural threats she'd been taken out by a mugger. It was plausible. Unlikely, but plausible. She'd heard of similar things happening to combat troops. Paying attention to the machine gun nest, missing the half-trained soldier sneaking up behind them.

It was a good theory, but it didn't feel quite right.

And then there was the other factor. Most murderers knew their victims. Her mind flicked back to the boyfriends. She hadn't been able to eliminate them.

Heck, she also hadn't pursued the tae kwon do angle, given the explosion. A rival? Somebody jealous of attention Dani might have been getting from the instructor. There were all kinds of possibilities she hadn't chased down because she was distracted by Victor Prince.

Darrell came into the room.

"Darrell, I think we need to put more heat on the boyfriends."

"Already working on it. I know you have had...well...other things to worry about. Find a place yet?"

She shook her head. "No. Not yet. I'm still working on it. " She offered him a grateful smile. "Thanks for taking the initiative."

He nodded. "And I have another idea too."

"I was going to check out former students of the dojang."

"That's good, but no." He pulled out his phone, pulled something up. "We got a message from somebody who claims to be an old friend of Ms Martin's. And they think they know who might have hated her enough to kill her."

Judy nodded. "And?"

"And that person is staying in a hotel in Midtown. Shall we?"

Judy smiled. Good old fashioned police work. "We shall." The captain would let her do this.

Afterwards, though?

She couldn't stall him much longer.

JUDY KNEW this was a false lead. She knew it had to be. Yet, despite that, she found herself much happier to be doing something that didn't involve fairies and shapeshifters and Victor Prince.

It was a window of normalcy. And it was a lead that had to be pursued. She let Darrell take the initiative this time, watching him intently.

Sooner or later he had to be the one in charge. As he'd found this lead, it was his job to deal with it. To establish whether it was real or not.

She rather thought it wasn't.

The rain that had plagued New York on and off for several days had finally blown out of town. It was a gorgeous day, not warm but clear and dry. A little hint of what remained of summer even as fall set in in earnest.

Because of that, they walked a few extra blocks by silent consensus. Narrow sidewalks, crowded with people. The ebb and flow of New York. The lights changing red to green as they approached felt like a stroke of luck, a lightening of the mood that Judy needed. The hotel was a typical Midtown hotel, probably over two hundred a night and occupied by business travelers and better off tourists, but probably not by honeymooners and CEOs.

Midtown had a lot of these hotels, what passed for mid-range on an island with permanent constraints of land and growth. They went up, and they kept going up, and Judy sometimes thought that the future would bring a New York which had buildings that braced against each other for strength. Perhaps skyways would run across those braces, perhaps tram type elevators would rise along the outside of buttresses.

Because there was no place to build *other* than up towards the sky. You couldn't even go down that far.

You could only go up and crowd together and there were so many people on the street. People living their own lives, oblivious to the travails of others. Cultivating that particular brand of New York introversion, where it was possible to completely ignore and dismiss other human beings until you reached the point where you had to pay attention. When somebody tripped, they would be helped up.

Literally and metaphorically.

People from outside thought New York was cold. Judy knew better.

The lobby of the hotel held a kind of faded we're-not-as-rich-as-we-used-to-be opulence. Luxurious but a couple of decades out of date.

Blues and golds surrounded her, but both had faded to denim and a dull yellow.

"Do you already know the room number?" she asked.

Darrell nodded. "They really wanted to do this face-to-face."

Judy frowned. Sometimes that meant a trap.

She hadn't even thought that this could be a trap.

SHE SMELLED ashes as they went upstairs. Frowning, she slipped a hand in her pocket, close to the gun.

It was a very faint smell and might not even have come from anywhere close to where they were going.

But it made her tense. Darrell knocked on the door. She stayed to one side of it.

"Come in," purred a female voice.

Yes, purred. Judy rolled her eyes. It was the kind of voice that contained cultivated sexuality; the voice of a phone sex operator. Practiced, not genuine.

The door opened. She half expected to see a sultry dame in an off the shoulder dress, but the owner of that voice wore plain jeans and a light sweater.

Maybe she had been a phone sex operator out of desperation and it had become habit. She drew in a breath.

No odd smell.

Maybe this was just what it seemed to be after all.

"You're the detectives?" she asked in that same voice.

Judy nodded. "We are."

The hotel room, typically, had only one chair. Darrell took it and the two women sat on the bed, albeit well away from each other.

"You said you knew something?" Judy prompted.

The woman frowned deeply, then nodded. "Okay, so, it's actually about Dani's family."

Bullshit, Judy thought, but she didn't say anything. "Some kind of feud?"

Darrell cut in. "Please, Wendy, get to the point."

The woman didn't look like a Wendy. But adult women didn't look like Wendies.

"Dani's father made some enemies. Mob type enemies."

It would have fit perfectly. "And they hired somebody to take her out to hurt him." Movie plot story.

It wasn't entirely infeasible. Not entirely. But Judy didn't buy it.

"A mercenary. Presumably he did it."

Darrell nodded. "Do you have a name?"

"Victor Prince."

Judy found herself nodding slowly. "We've heard that name. But do you have any evidence?"

The woman stood up, walked over to a drawer, and pulled out a laptop. Opening it, she took a couple of minutes to find what she was looking for.

"There. The payments were made to Richard Litton. Who is Victor Prince's, well..." The woman scowled. "Lover."

She managed to get several reams of homophobic rants into that one word, somehow.

The overweight guy. Richard.

This was a trap. But it wasn't Judy it was set for. Instead, she was the teeth. She couldn't ignore this. It was actual evidence.

She had to arrest Victor Prince. She *had* to. The captain would not give her any more time.

And perhaps he merely had her fooled.

30

HE DIDN'T GET LAID. Nor did he get much sleep. He spent the night trying to make reasonable predictions as to where the Hodges were. The hotel room was not conducive either. It had that faint smell that might indicate that the cleaners had not successfully dealt with, well. Something.

He came to the conclusion he needed a witch's help. There was no doubt at least one around unscrupulous enough to help an assassin find his target. And he knew where to look. He dove into the dark web to find certain bulletin boards, certain places the police either didn't know about or turned a blind eye to.

Found a target and sent him a quick, anonymous message. There. That was done until they responded, and the barbed wire had loosened.

He was trying. If he couldn't find them then it might be that Beelzebub would eventually find another way to deal with the situation.

He wouldn't be forgiven, because demons didn't forgive. Couldn't forgive. But he might work his way back into good graces faster than he had been expecting.

There was the other one, of course. Now he knew Christian Hodges was Victor's current target, he would probably back down.

Or Maurice would make his life difficult for the sheer Hell of it, pun intended. Not much Victor could do about that other than kick his butt if he needed to.

And next time he would be ready for the guy. Sleep was still not coming. He walked the streets of East New York, trusting in confidence and body language to keep anyone from messing with him. Casual fights right now would only get him into even more trouble with the police.

He thought of Richard.

Richard had decided to help him by betraying him. There were worse choices the man could have made; but he was glad he was out of the picture, at least as far as Victor knew.

The sky was shaded oddly. He could feel something building faintly, something that was going to unleash chaos on New York.

Hopefully right after he left.

Or he could use it.

There was a dog like shape in the night. But not a dog. "You too, huh?" he said in the wolf's direction.

He got no response, not that he was expecting one. He looked up at the sky. "You know, I can't get that cop out of my mind...no, not like that."

She'd wormed her way into him by one simple expedient.

She was the first person in a long time to believe he was telling the truth.

THE WOLF FOLLOWED HIM HOME. Back to his hotel room, shimmering into a man before they entered the building.

"She's a true believer," Tag said as they walked in. "But her beliefs don't include eternal damnation."

"She's Jewish. I saw the star."

"Progressive, but not one of those who..." Tag paused. "She knows what she is, she knows *exactly* what she is and she won't change."

He turned to face the man. "Unlike those of us who can't."

"You know she's going to end up having to arrest you."

Victor took a deep breath as he backed into the elevator. The doors closed, giving them privacy. "I'm going to end up having to kill her."

"I don't think I can let you do that."

"You know I don't have the choice. She's going to try and arrest me and I'm going to kill her. That's how this ends. It how it *always* ends."

"Do you love her?" There was something almost plaintive in Tag's tone.

"Hell no." A pause. "I *like* her, but she's not the type of woman I go for."

"Do you love her *not* romantically?"

"I'm not capable." He felt the barb wires tighten again. Don't love. It wasn't allowed. Above all. "And if I was, it's not *her*."

The elevator doors opened. He spun, backing out of them. Down the corridor. Keeping his voice low. "And if I was it wouldn't be a good idea because I *just* dumped my boyfriend."

"Boyfriend or guy you liked to have sex with?" Tag asked. Following.

Hell, *why was he following*. "Guy I liked to have sex with. But it's the same thing."

He was on the rebound and right now he wanted Tag to go away.

"It isn't."

"What do you want?" He fumbled for his key, feeling Tag's wolf breath behind him as he turned his back on the man.

"The impossible," Tag said. "To save you."

"You're right. That's impossible." The key was found, the door opene.d "Do *you* love *me*?"

"I *want* you."

Not quite love, but it was something, it was something he could easily take advantage with. Take care of the itch in his groin. "You know what I am. You can't save me. I'll drag you down with me."

"Maybe I'm willing to take that chance."

"Maybe I'm not."

They stood facing each other. "You don't love me," Victor said. "Like you said, you want me. And to be blunt, I have lube, I have condoms, and I am horny as a demon from hell."

Tag grinned.

"But if there's any risk of you falling for me, we can't."

"Because you care. I thought that wasn't allowed."

The barbed wire. It wasn't. But he wanted to.

He *wanted* to.

ALONE, Victor felt instant regret.

He could have had what would probably have been quite, quite acceptable sex. But he couldn't.

It wasn't allowed to care.

Heck, he should have done it, everything he was said he should have done it. To turn a shaman? It would have got him so much. It would more than make up for not getting Hodges.

But somehow he'd held himself back. Or she had held him back.

He still wanted Tag. He wanted him badly.

It's not her. It wasn't Judy he wanted to love after all. It was Tag. And he knew it was rebound and lust and all those tangled hormonal feelings that came from being in a body. The faint animal smell of the shapeshifter. Chemistry.

It *wasn't* love. It wasn't love at first sight, certainly. Not that near mythical crowded-room phenomenon that did indeed happen, but was vanishingly rare. A privilege for a tiny few.

But he'd felt something when he saw Tag. And something quite different when he saw Judy.

It was possible to love more than one person at the same time. Even healthy, if anything he did was healthy. But that wasn't what was going on.

He had to talk to the witch he was hiring. But he had to talk to somebody else too. He managed to nap, then as the sun came up over the city, he planned out a route.

To Hell's Kitchen.

He stopped for bagels on his way, walking up to New Lots Avenue.

The very end of the 3 Line. Boarded the train and felt it rattle all the way through Brooklyn, under the East River and then north through Manhattan. No view. Nothing but the weird variety of people. A lot of commuters. The freaks didn't generally come out during morning rush. But he felt as if he was in a rush. He had to talk to somebody.

He had to talk to a very special somebody who had, for whatever reason, taken an interest in him.

No, not for whatever reason. She had reasons, and those reasons scared him. He was a pawn in her game, of that he was sure. 50 Street and Broadway and he was finally in the open air again. West towards the water. Into Hell's Kitchen. A gentrifying Hell's Kitchen, people were starting to be forced out, although it still smelled of the cookfires of many cultures. It hadn't lost its character yet.

The restaurants would probably get to stay, it would be the clientele that changed. He ignored them. Turned right on ninth street, left again on fifty-first. Away from the restaurants. The tenements with the fire escapes on the front.

You didn't look at the street numbers to get where he was going.

You counted doors and you didn't worry about where you were.

You found the little house between houses and you stepped inside.

From within came a female voice, "I was expecting you."

"Of course you were."

31

WHAT SHE NEEDED WAS SWAT.

What she should do was tell them to get him. Stay here where it was safe.

What she wanted to do was ask him why.

Why he had lied to her.

Except she knew. She knew what was the truth. She had given a space, a breathing space, to something born of evil. Or at least bound to it. Of course that snake was going to bite her. She knew better.

It was anger that carried her down the stairs. Then she hesitated. She thought about it.

The hotel. She shouldn't go back there or she should.

She just wanted this case to be over. She wanted to be right after all, but the money transferred to the boyfriend's account said it all.

The boyfriend. She had suspected Prince was gay. Or bisexual. Her ovaries still wanted the latter, but she silenced them.

She had a way to put this off. She found a car, found a uniform and drove over to the warehouse.

It didn't look abandoned, at least. It didn't look like Richard had left yet. If he had any sense he would have.

The uniform went first as they approached. Cautiously. She wasn't sure exactly what Litton was capable of, but she knew he was some kind of criminal.

He reached for the door and knocked on it. The kind of firm knock they taught you in the academy. Not timid. Not banging on the door either.

You didn't bang on the door; that was a prime way to have somebody run out of whatever back door the building had. They did it in cop shows.

In reality you wanted them to think you were pizza delivery or a neighbor so they would open the door.

The door remained mutely closed.

"Do we kick it in?"

"Try and see if it's locked first."

She glanced around. It was a beautiful day. There was nobody around. It was so quiet she could actually hear birds. The faint roar of a highway.

Something felt wrong. "Don't!"

It was too late. He turned the handle. The door exploded outwards, shards and shrapnel tearing into the man's body.

Being further back, Judy was only thrown back by the shockwave. She landed on the ground, bruised and battered and pretty sure a rib had cracked from the impact.

She swore in Yiddish.

She used the worst words she knew.

SHE PUT an APB out on Richard Litton. She considered putting one out on Victor Prince. She didn't only because she knew what would happen if she did. He would kill a cop. They would kill him. It would escalate. And who knew who else they would shoot.

Had he been telling the truth when he said they had split up? The warehouse, once explored, proved to be empty.

The man had booby trapped it and run. Which was both cowardly and sensible. The worst kind of criminal. The hardest to catch.

She sat in the break room, her hand curled around a cup of coffee she desperately wished was more Irish. They'd checked her out, pronounced her bruised but not broken. If she hadn't hung so far back.

She'd gotten a man killed. She was going to have to live with that. Richard Litton was going down, if it lay at all within her power.

It probably didn't.

He'd probably already changed his name and got on a Greyhound out of New York.

She knew what he looked like, but that could be changed too. He was a cop killer and he was getting away.

She heard multiple swear words from outside her office, from multiple sources and in two or three languages.

She got up, stiffly, and stepped outside. She needed to stop getting blown up. "What's going on."

"There's a bomb in the Lexington."

An expensive hotel. Right in Midtown.

A bomb meant a bomber. "Do we know what the target is?"

"It was found in the penthouse suite. The target was undoubtedly the current occupant, one Mrs Levsky."

A corporate widow. A woman with a lot of money and probably more power than she admitted to. "What kind of bomb?"

"You don't think..." Darrell's voice.

"I do think that somebody leaving a warehouse and boobytrapping it on their way out *and* a bomb aimed at a high-profile target on the same day are unlikely to be a coincidence."

"Let's hope not," Darrell quipped. "We already have an APB out on him."

"How did they find the bomb?" In a moment, the captain would come out and shoo them all back to their desks.

"Housekeeping. Sheer luck. Whoever hid it managed to slightly disturb the furnishings. Levsky requested the same maid clean her room every day, so she knew *exactly* where everything was supposed to be."

That almost amused Judy. "Housekeeping. The furniture."

Nobody paid attention to housekeeping. Which meant many a criminal plot had been undone by them. Or by waitstaff.

By people who were treated as furniture.

Now they just had to catch Litton.

Which wasn't her concern unless it connected to her case. She went back to her office, wishing even more for something with which to improve her coffee.

"WE GOT RICHARD LITTON."

Judy let out a breath. "Good."

Darrell frowned. "So, what about Victor Prince?"

"You know if we put out an APB on him he'll just start killing cops."

And she wasn't convinced they were going to *keep* Richard Litton. They might have him for right now, and they probably had him dead to rights for cop killing.

Probably.

Depending on how good a lawyer he had. He might be able to make a case that just because he was renting the booby-trapped warehouse, didn't mean he had been the one that booby-trapped it.

Heck, he would make such a case. Unless he'd been careless enough to leave fingerprints at the Lexington or her apartment he'd walk. She knew that, depressingly. It was going to be one of those cases where everyone knew who did it but nothing could be proved. Where a bad cop would resort to faking a confession.

"I know," Darrell said. "SWAT him."

"I probably should," she mused. If she did people would die. But hopefully only combatants. "Let them deal with it. Probably save us the paperwork. Unless he didn't do it."

"That large payment to Richard Litton."

Judy smiled. "Proves nothing when we know he tried to blow up a rich woman in her penthouse."

Darrell let out a breath. "Crap. You're right. It could be the payment for *that* hit not for one on Martin."

"And I'm betting you didn't like that woman any more than I did."

"I sure didn't. I was honestly expecting her to pull a gun. I think it was the phone sex voice, though."

Judy laughed. "That's exactly the reaction I had to the way she talks." She was quite amused by that. That they'd both had the same thought.

"She probably *is* a phone sex girl."

"Which isn't a bad thing. From what I know most of the women who do that work are just, well. It pays better than most call center work."

"Yeah." Darrell shook his head. "But then sex work in general doesn't pay bad if you know what you're doing."

"You sound as if you know from experience."

"Not personal experience, and you know I can't say any more."

She nodded. She wouldn't want to have to arrest any of his friends for something that not everyone thought should be illegal. And if he kept pushing it she would have to do exactly that. "So. What we need is hard evidence."

"And it's all growing cold."

"Or a confession to tell us where to look. And we're not getting one of those. I'm starting to wish..."

"If this was a movie we'd get..."

"We already *did* get the out-of-the-blue clue and it turned out to be useless even if she was telling the truth."

Judy didn't believe that she was. But then, the truth was a very uncertain thing and not everyone's truth was the same.

But now she had no idea what to do.

32

THE WOMAN within the house that most could not see was severe in her visage. She had steel gray hair, drawn back into a tight ponytail.

"Victor," she said as he entered.

"I promise I will not violate the sanctity of this place."

She nodded. "And if you do you will hit the street hard."

His lips quirked. "I have no orders that relate to you. You're safe."

"Following the letter, I see, not the spirit."

Victor shrugged as she closed the door behind him, stepped into the almost English parlor beyond. "I don't particularly want to be smited all the way back to Hell by *your* boss."

She laughed.

"But I need a consult, Sibyl."

"You can pay?"

He nodded. "Money? Pizza?"

She laughed again. "How about you bring me a couple of six packs this evening."

It was a token payment, because that which was paid for was more highly valued.

"Also, I won't help you find your prey."

"It's not about that. I promise." He sat down on the leather couch, a little gingerly. It was old and it seemed fragile.

"So, what is it? Woman trouble? Man trouble?"

"Man trouble is definitely part of it." Victor took a deep breath. "Honestly, it's both."

"Nothing wrong with a bit of healthy polyamory."

He laughed. "No, it's not like that. It's..."

"It's that for a lilin, you are surprisingly concerned with hurting others."

"Honestly, I just don't want the drama of a rebound relationship. I broke up with my boyfriend last week."

"Ah, yeah. That gets all of us."

"How would *you* know?" As the current Oracle, she was not required to be a virgin per se, but she was absolutely required to avoid romance. Most, Victor assumed, avoided the entire kaboodle.

The Sibyl laughed. "I may have no *personal* experience with sex and romance, but you know how many people find my door when they need to. I've had to learn."

Victor nodded. "So, the woman asked me if I had to be evil, of all things. And the man...well, I almost ended up sleeping with him."

"The woman either doesn't understand or she understands more. Does she have..."

"A trace of the sight, and possible djinn blood."

"Ah. Arab?"

"Jewish," he explained. "Ashkenazic, but..."

"But who knows. So, a trace of the second sight. And...a cop." Sibyl narrowed her eyes. "Who did you kill?"

"Believe it or not, nobody. Believe it or not, this time I got framed."

She shrugged. "For the Guardian. And so it begins."

"What begins?"

She fell silent for a long moment, as if she was doing her best to process information. "The end of the world. Or just change." She reached under the table, pulled out a tarot card. Set it on the table between them. Death.

"You can spare the drama, I'm not a mundane looking for a "gypsy" fortune teller." Not that Sibyl was Romany...if she was he might have hesitated before using the slur.

"Do you see a crystal ball?"

"Just tell me what your boss wants me to know. I wouldn't be here if there wasn't something.

She told him.

VICTOR PRINCE RAN.

Sometimes that was all you could do. Sometimes you didn't want to think. He eschewed Central Park, because he wanted something...he wasn't sure what he wanted.

But his feet took him to the Hudson, to the Greenway. Running north past Locomotive Lawn. Along the river, the waters reflecting the fading blue of the sky and the knife grey of Midtown, the buildings that towered above all. That made this place what it was.

He ran because it kept him from doing anything else, from doing any of the things he wanted to do. Following the destructive impulses the Sibyl's words had put in his head.

If she had wanted to kill him, this would be a good way to do it. She didn't want to kill him. He didn't want, right now, to die.

In the future it might not matter. Right now it did.

So, he ran. He ran past the West 79th Street Boat Basin. He ran past the 96th Street tennis courts. His stamina was higher than a normal person's. He could run all day. While he ran there was no barbed wire. There was no thought of a certain slender man, who's hands he wanted on him so badly.

There was no echo of words which had struck something within him.

He was what he was. He couldn't change. He knew he couldn't change. She said if he didn't change Hell would win.

He was supposed to want Hell to win. He was supposed to want that. He wasn't *allowed* not to. Even the slightest bit of doubt would get him consigned back to the pit.

He finally ran out of energy at the Ten Mile River Playground. He ducked behind some trees, not even looking towards the sound of young voices. Instead, he looked at the river.

You are the one who can break the rules. You can stop following orders.

He knew that wasn't true. He knew the pain, the consequences. He knew his heart would burst if he ignored it.

But he wanted to.

But he was unforgivable.

But this wasn't about him. This wasn't about saving him. This was about the world and the things which needed to be done.

Things which would require a damned soul to do. Somebody who didn't, who couldn't, care about his own fate.

He could break his chains, but he could never be free. He could only serve and work.

And part of him did care enough. The trees. The river. The high voices of children who might not get to grow up.

He *did* care and he was surprised he didn't feel the squeeze on his soul at the thought.

His boss, perhaps, wasn't paying attention.

Or maybe it was something else...

HE KEPT RUNNING, getting ever further from any place he should be. From any place he wanted to be. To Riverside Park, which wasn't as big or as intriguing as Central. It was the park on the wrong side of the tracks.

But it felt like a good place to be right now. He wanted to jump into the river.

He wanted to push somebody else into the river.

He wanted to throw something into the river. Instead he found the traveling rings, launched himself to them. Flowed through them like a pulp hero. It helped. It made him feel a little bit better. It made him feel more as if he was centered and grounded.

He went through things in his mind.

First of all, he couldn't ever escape Hell. No matter what. He wasn't even supposed to be able to want to. Something had broken.

And if that was true, then some other power might have stepped in. If so, then why him? The Sybil had not answered that question.

But he could think of a few answers, some of them as simple as being in the right or wrong place at the right or wrong time. Some of them as complex as somebody thinking he didn't deserve to be damned in the first place.

He'd killed his Olivia.

He deserved to be damned. He could not argue with that. Perhaps he wasn't allowed to. But he truly believed he deserved his fate. If anyone disagreed, then they...were wrong.

So, he went back to being the convenient one. Expendable as he had always been.

Do you have to be evil?

Not all the time. Not entirely. But when it really mattered he did.

And when it really mattered, he didn't. An expendable agent. If he died it wasn't a huge deal. If he died it was annoying and unpleasant and painful.

But it wasn't an end to anything.

It wasn't an escape either, but he'd accepted that the only escape he had was those times when his boss wasn't paying attention. Was letting him be a man.

He crouched down. Touched the water of the river. It was cold. It wasn't very clean. Once Manhattan had been a wilderness. Once it had been the home to people who had lived lightly on the land. Who hadn't invited anything in other than the spirits of nature.

He found himself envying them. Those who had lived and died long before the white man came.

But he had all of the dilemmas of the twenty-first century. And he had this.

It could not be done.

But his feet started to lead him back into the city.

He had a shaman to find.

33

RICHARD LITTON SAT in the interview room, cuffed hands resting on the battered blue table in front of him. The room had the faint smell of stale sweat and fear. Of old beatings, of things which should not happen here and yet did.

Judy sat opposite. "Oh, I don't expect you to admit it. You're smarter than that. Besides, what I'm interested in is who killed Dani Martin."

"Which I don't know."

"Oh, come on. You blew up my apartment."

"I did not."

"You're the only one with a motive."

"I'm sure it was a gas line."

She smirked. "We already know it wasn't, although that's a nice try." It was a nice try. It was also the usual excuse, the thing they had already checked.

"And even if I did do it, you can't prove it."

"Like I said. I'm more interested in who killed Martin. You claim it wasn't Victor. Who was it?"

"How am I supposed to know? She must have pissed off the mob."

She leaned slightly forward across the table. "You and I both know it wasn't the mob. You and I both know who Victor is."

She was pleased to see him flinch back slightly. "What do *you* know, Cop?"

"Everything," she lied. It wasn't true. But she knew enough of the picture to fill in the rest without too many problems. Close enough to "everything."

He squirmed a little.

"And you know that or you wouldn't have tried to kill me." Satisfied, she sat back. "I probably can't hang it on you, you're right. But you're going to spend the rest of your life wondering about it. Wondering if I'm going to find that piece of evidence you're only ninety percent sure you didn't leave behind."

He squirmed more.

"Tell me who killed Dani Martin."

"I really don't know. Neither does Victor."

"If Victor knew he'd be jumping through hoops to prove it," Judy said, wryly. She felt this was information that could be shared.

"He would."

"Of course, he's going to go down for something sooner or later. But I'm sure he'd rather it was at least something he actually *did*." That definitely seemed part of his attitude. He didn't want to be arrested when he was actually, for once, innocent.

"But anything you know will help me make sure he doesn't go down for this."

"He dumped me."

She nodded. "I know. But I'm counting on the fact that you probably don't hate him *that* much."

"...you know."

For some reason that made him more uncomfortable than anything else she said.

Then, finally, "There were guys in suits. They told me that I would be well served if I testified against Victor, whether it was true or not."

"Well served as in bribery."

"As in." He shrugged. "Maybe it *is* the mob. But I don't think so."

No.

It was, she suspected, what Victor had said he feared.

Infernal politics.

ONE OF THE men had been one of the ones in the dojang. With the addition of a scar that appeared to have come from that occasion.

They had put the heat on her to blame Victor. They had put the heat on Litton to blame Victor.

It was a lead she had shied away from, the trauma of the occasion.

No, she had forgotten it. Forgotten them until reminded. But now they were clear in her mind. And Scarface shouldn't be that hard to find. Not with police resources. He'd been burned.

That would stand out.

And one of the others was the guy who had got into a brawl with Victor. Of course he was.

And he seemed to be the one ultimately in charge. The chief thug of a bunch of thugs. She was going to have to find him and Scarface again.

She headed out into the squad room, glancing around. At least she wasn't getting random expressions of sympathy anymore. Her apartment's destruction was old news.

Well, she'd also got some practical offers of help. And she had a lead on a new place. But it was the oh I'm so sorry from people who wouldn't normally give her the time of day that had become tiresome.

"I need to locate these two guys," she said to the sergeant, putting the pictures down on his desk, the grain of it harsh against her hands.

"That guy was in a fire."

"He was in an explosion. Should make him easy to pick out of the lineup."

"And didn't we bring the other one in for brawling?"

"Yeah. It was a drunken fight over a girl, I didn't think it was anything serious. Or connected."

"But now you do."

"I have a witness who claims this guy was involved in some, shall we say, professional intimidation."

"He looks the type."

"He does, doesn't he."

Unlike Victor Prince, who didn't look the type but was completely, thoroughly intimidating. He had to actively try not to be, she suspected.

"I'm guessing it's their employer you're really looking for."

"It is."

"This is the Martin case?"

"Yes. Yes it is." She let out a breath. "The guy with the burned face was there when the dojang she went to blew up. The other guy was beating up a possible suspect."

"Joy. I really hate when things get organized, as it were."

"So do I." She let out a breath. "So do I."

And she hated what she had to do.

What she could not do.

Redemption had to be possible. Even for somebody like Victor Prince.

———

A FEW WELL-PLACED questions led Judy to a pub. Darrell was sitting at the table with a pint of something dark in front of him, looking innocent and as un-cop-like as possible as Judy canvased the room.

He was very good at looking un-cop-like, she mused. Better than she was. She tended to radiate it. Sometimes she thought it was because she was a woman. Looking like a cop gave her a protection from street harassment she thoroughly appreciated. It also made it hard to make friends.

Street harassment was, of course, unavoidable in New York. For the most part. She knew some women who could walk through Times Square in a skimpy dress and not be bothered, but few had that kind of peculiar confidence and strength. She wasn't one of them, so the cop look was her best protection.

Leaning against the bar, she spotted the thug. "Maurice, right?"

He narrowed his eyes. "I'm not talking to the police. I don't have to."

"We can do this here or at the station. Your choice."

"Or we can not do it at all."

She smelled a rising scent of sulfur. "Oh come on. You're really going to start a fight here?"

"No, *you* are." He was on his feet, his eyes facing her. They were hard as onyx, almost black suddenly.

No, they were black, all the way into the whites, all the way into the corners. She wasn't sure whether it was some kind of strange illusion, some kind of intimidation trick, or whether it was real.

She tried to remember Victor Prince's eyes. Dark. But not like this. Not midnight orbs with no kind of variation.

She felt herself start to sink into them. Then felt something flare between the two. Something tugged and grabbed at her and abruptly she was pulled clear. "Naughty," she said.

"Ah. You *are* protected. But your partner, I doubt he's as secure."

His voice was low. It wasn't carrying.

She raised hers. "So, do you generally threaten black guys in pubs?"

Heads turned. "I mean, that's a very 1950s thing to do."

Darrell would be mortified, but it had the desired effect. The barkeep growled, "I suggest you either settle down or leave."

He elected to leave. Judy followed him out, leaving a tip on the bar. Stepped out into the night.

He turned to face her. "Ah, so that was your way of making sure we took it outside."

"Sure was."

"You don't have anything to back this up with."

"Try me."

It was probably a stupid thing to say.

But she couldn't quite keep herself from saying it.

34

When he had been trying to avoid Tag, the man had been everywhere. Now Victor was looking for him, he was impossible to find.

Completely, utterly, impossible. Shaking his head, Victor stood outside the hotel. He'd tried the diner. He'd tried the hotel Tag claimed he was staying in. Of course, without the man's legal name it was hard for anyone, even with his skills, to locate him.

He had probably not given his name on purpose. Well, maybe not his legal name. He certainly hadn't booked a hotel room as "Tag," however. That was not a name the clerk would take. It would be whatever name was on his credit card.

Which could be anything. On the other hand, it wasn't in Tag's interests to hide completely.

He pulled out the card Tag had given him. Turned it over. There was an email address on it. He slipped into the hotel's lobby, looked to see if the business center was empty.

There was somebody pulling a print off the printer, a woman in a smart pantsuit. She ignored him disdainfully as he went into the room and sat down at the computer.

Which was fine, he wasn't exactly paying any attention to her, even if she did have a rather nice butt, one which showed plenty of time spent in the gym.

He turned to the computer, glad he was still having thoughts like that. It probably meant he wasn't crazy in lust with Tag.

Probably.

He pulled up webmail, logged in. It took forever.

"Slow," the woman grumbled, finally looking at him. "Crappy hotel internet."

"Yeah."

She picked up her print, politely not looking at his screen beyond what she'd already glimpsed, which was a half-loaded webmail.

He refreshed, got it up a bit better. The note he sent to Tag was simple. An invitation to have breakfast.

It felt like he was asking him out on a date.

But it wasn't. It really wasn't. If anyone could help him, it was a shaman. And the man cared about him.

As did the cop.

People weren't supposed to care about him. They were supposed to find out what he was and then try to put bullets or swords in him.

That was how it was supposed to work. Why were they breaking all of the precious rules? He was a damned soul, a demon.

He wasn't somebody who deserved to be cared for.

He sent the email anyway.

He realized what the odd feeling he had for Judy Eisenberg was.

He wanted to be her friend.

People like him didn't have friends. He didn't even know how anymore. He didn't even want to.

———

THE OBVIOUS THING TO do was disappear, leave town. To spend the next however long hunting for Christian Hodges. He could feel the barbed wire again, wrapping around him, tugging on him.

It wanted him to go hunting, and he couldn't resist it much longer. He wasn't capable.

But he could perhaps manage this one last night. Get breakfast with Tag.

You don't have to be evil.

He couldn't tell himself that. He was by nature.

But did he have to be evil by deed? Had he ever done anything good? He thought of Richard smiling and laughing but, no, that wasn't evidence. Richard was as bad as he was.

No, Richard was worse than he was. Richard didn't kill because it was his nature or his orders. He chose to and he enjoyed the act. Gained pleasure out of it. Gained something that would make him come to Victor afterwards.

The best sex, that. It didn't bother him. It couldn't bother him.

Or did it? How could it *not* bother him?

Richard had tried to kill the cop for him, assuming he would be happy. No, not the cop.

Judy.

Richard had tried to kill Judy for him. Hadn't realized it wasn't in the plan. Or hadn't cared. Maybe he'd just wanted his own pleasure at the flames and destruction. He liked to watch.

He'd probably watched the penthouse, but now he was gone.

Or was he?

Victor idly thought of searching for him. Changed his mind. Thought of running again, thought of the rings. They had brought clarity to him, of a sort. He was not a good man. He was, by some measures, not even a man.

Deep breath. A deep breath he didn't really want to take. A measure of the pain that was growing within him.

He wasn't going to, he couldn't use this damned public hotel computer.

Yes he could.

He had to.

The barbed wire was tightening again. With a cry, he turned from the room and ran, the impulse to stay safe warring with the need to do his job.

It didn't matter if he got caught had gone into he was going to be caught, was going to be sacrificed. His punishment was that they wouldn't let him do it right.

He was going to go to jail or be shot by cops, and he ran into the night.

Ran east because he didn't want to run towards Manhattan. Ran past houses and delis, past the airport. Didn't stop running. Couldn't stop running.

There had to be somebody who could stop him running.

———

EVEN LILIN RUN out of energy eventually. By the time he did, he was somehow in Jones Beach State Park. He wasn't entirely sure how he had got there given there was no sidewalk on the bridge, no pedestrian access.

He must have run through traffic, in this realm of the car. He might have caused an accident. But he wasn't harmed himself.

He didn't care.

Did he?

He'd come to his senses on a dirt road not far from the Parkway. Hands on thighs, breathing hard.

For a long moment he didn't know where he was and suspected he would never know how he had got there.

It was all her fault.

But nobody harmed the Sibyl. It simply wasn't done. It wasn't even respect for or fear of the God she served.

It was that you just didn't. Even the forces of Hell acknowledged that.

But if she had wanted to take him briefly off the board she couldn't have done a better job. Her vaunted neutrality...

...fell apart if there was a genuine threat to the balance of the world. She might be neutral. She cared about the fate of humanity.

And perhaps that was it, that was the spark. The thing which allowed him this freedom was the existence of the world as it was.

If it was destroyed, well.

He was one of the fools that lived in it, and he might well be rewarded in the annals of Hell if he chose to help them destroy it.

He didn't want to be.

He wanted the touch of a man's or a woman's lips against his own. He wanted the clear skies that were above him now. The short grass.

The sounds of birds that knew nothing of the conflicts that might determine their fate.

Victor Prince, above all, wanted to live.

Perhaps it was enough. Perhaps it was not enough. It was not the best motivation to do something good.

It was, perhaps, enough.

35

SHE SAW it in his eyes.

She saw her death. He couldn't do whatever it was he had tried to do. The gun was pulled out, raised towards her.

It all happened in slow motion, before she could reach for her own service piece, as she knew she needed to. As she knew she *had* to.

Quick draw duels seldom went well in real life.

Slow motion.

And then he was falling towards her, hitting the ground hard under the weight of...was it a wolf or a man?

A wolf that was *becoming* a man before her eyes.

She kept the gun trained on him. "Why thank you."

Tag grinned up at her. "Hand me your cuffs would you?"

She unhooked them from the belt with one hand and tossed them over. It wasn't something she would normally have done.

But it would be much easier for him to cuff the guy he was sitting on. Who seemed to have been knocked silly by the impact.

He put the cuffs on surprising expertise, that made her wonder when and where he had learned the skill.

"Thank you. I wasn't sure..."

"You need a watcher to keep you out of trouble." He got up. "So, why were you..."

"I'm pretty sure he was involved in a case." She didn't say which one, not in public. It would look odd.

"Ah." Tag smiled at her. "Well, next time, don't take on lilin alone. That includes Victor, by the way."

She scowled at him.

"You're good. You're not that good. I wouldn't have been able to knock him down if you hadn't been distracting him so nicely."

On the ground, Maurice squirmed. Tag put a foot between his shoulder blades.

Was he striking a pose?

Yes.

He was striking a pose.

"Enough. I'm going to get him taken downtown for assaulting a police officer. That means we can keep him this time."

"You're going to need me to come too." A resigned sigh accompanied his words.

"Don't worry. I'll make sure you're the hero of the piece."

"That," Tag said wryly, "is exactly what I'm afraid of."

TAG GAVE HIS STATEMENT QUICKLY. Judy tried not to lay the gratitude on too thick. He seemed genuinely not to want a fuss made over him, and she could respect that. She could do her best to respect it, anyway.

Afterwards, she followed him out of the station, making sure none of her more prejudiced coworkers got any ideas. "I'm sorry."

"Don't be. You were only doing your job." He turned to face her.

"And my job is dangerous." A pause. "But not nearly as dangerous as that of a fisherman."

Tag laughed. "Is it fisherman or lumberjack that's actually the most dangerous?"

"I forget. But we aren't even in the top ten. Until we do stupid things." The excuse. The excuse they used to shoot black men and looking at Tag, thinking of Darrell, she was not sure she could tolerate that excuse any more. No, she knew she would not. And she...turned off her radio. It was a moment. She was going to solve the case, but she was going to do it on her own, calling for backup only if her life required it.

She was not listening to anything anyone said.

The man grinned. "Stupid or not, you can hold him now."

"And question him about intimidating Richard Litton." Which was all true, but she couldn't do it. She couldn't do it anymore.

Whom she couldn't hold much longer. There just wasn't the evidence. The DA knew he did it. She knew he did it.

There wasn't enough evidence to hold. The sad ending to too many cases.

"Was that what he was doing?" Tag frowned. "Who's Litton?"

"Victor Prince's partner in crime and, I suspect, bed."

Tag shrugged. "So they were Bonnie-and-Clyding."

"Seems that way." A pause. "You're too easy to talk to. In a moment I'm going to be spilling the entire case."

He laughed again. "I promise I'm not using any magic on you."

She mock-scowled. "How would I know if you were?"

"You'd probably smell it."

She probably would. "So..." A pause. "Maybe you can help me with that."

"Only to a point. Everyone with magic sensitivity perceives things a little bit differently," Tag explained. "Unfortunately, the only way to get really good is to find out what maps to what."

Judy nodded. "I was afraid of that."

"And if you want to learn actual magic, then you'll..I can get you information to help you make an educated choice."

"You mean as to what *kind* of magic to learn."

Tag nodded. "There's consequences."

"I'm Jewish," she said, finally. "If the kabalah's real."

Tag nodded. "It is. And there are definitely people who will teach it to a woman. But there's, like I said, consequences."

She smiled at him. "But it's the magic my people approve of. Which means..."

Tag broke into a grin. "I can't help you with it, but that's as good a reason as any. Of course, you might turn out to be bad at it."

"I won't know *that* until I try." And then she frowned. She wasn't sure why. There was something oddly crisp in the air for a moment.

Tag swore.

Clearly, he felt it too. Whatever it was.

———

"WHAT WAS THAT?" Judy asked.

"That," Tag said, "was somebody opening a hell gate. Which I don't need to tell you is bad."

"Demons in New York?" she asked.

"Demons in New York."

"Can you tell where?" she asked. "I...."

He sniffed the air, wolflike in his mannerisms and attitude. She could almost see it overlaid on him, could smell fur and pine needles and something of the wild. Something which did not belong in New York.

"Central Park."

"Great. Halfway down Manhattan." She checked her gun. "But..."

He looked at her.

"We *are* going to check it out, right?"

"You're crazy."

She grinned and flagged down a cab. "Columbus Circle."

Far from being an unusual request. The cabbie nodded as she hopped in. Tag followed a moment later.

"How do you like New York?" she asked him.

"Crowded as heck," Tag admitted. "And even more expensive than DC, with both of them heading for the sky."

They had a few minutes. Small talk seemed a good idea. "I fully expect to be priced out of Brooklyn soon. I'm struggling to find a new place."

"Where will you go?"

"I dunno. Probably Jersey City." She made a face. "I love my neighborhood. I don't want to leave. But when everyone leaves it's not a neighborhood any more."

"A white woman who understands gentrification," Tag quipped.

She flickered him a weak smile. "A *Jewish* woman," she pointed out.

"Still. A lot of people don't get what you just said. They don't get it at all. They think you can just move and it'll still be the same, but it's not just changed. It's destroyed."

She nodded a bit. "And pretty soon only the richest of the rich will be able to dream of a place in Manhattan proper. I'm surprised Chinatown is as vibrant as it is."

"DC's Chinatown is, well." Tag makes a face. "It has a Hooters in it. With the name in Chinese."

"You're...no, you aren't kidding. I'm not one to have something against Hooters, but..."

"Most women do."

She couldn't resist, "I like a good pair too."

"I *don't*," Tag said, making a face. "Definitely no breasts for me."

"You make me want to introduce you to my partner, but I know that wouldn't be right. Just because you're both gay and black..."

"Maybe there's somebody else I'd rather have." He looked away.

They rode on in silence.

36

It felt like a soft thwoosh in the air. His heart throbbed, barbed wire tightening. Something in Central Park, but there was the other thing too, pulling him from his reverie with a side of curse words.

The throbbing, the *knowledge*, the pulling. He knew where his target was. They hadn't taken him far enough away. Jersey City.

He also knew something else was going on in Manhattan.

Should he go back there?

He needed to, but he couldn't. It was like a physical impossibility, an invisible barrier, a peculiar fear of tempting fate.

He could steal a car.

Then he had a better idea. Something people were bizarrely less likely to secure properly.

He set off at a run. This was dangerous, because one of the things he passed was the police station, and the coast guard was right there.

But if he was lucky...

He looked over the boats in the basin. There. The one which looked like it needed a serious job of paint. He'd bet...

He leaned over, felt under the gunwale. Found the key. Idiots. But he was glad they were that stupid. Cops weren't looking. Coastguard wasn't looking. He eased the cheap wooden motorboat out of its berth.

The owners would probably eventually get it back. He had no intention of keeping it. He checked the fuel tank.

Full.

Idiots, he thought again as he roared along the coast. The barbed wire had eased off, which probably meant he was also heading in the vague direction of Christian Hodges. And this would give an opportunity, too.

Deirdre was no doubt as distracted by the gate forming in Central Park as he was. And the shaman would be distracted too, and maybe even removed from the board.

He could hope.

He could fear.

He could want. He could want so desperately. The wind was in his hair. He put on a set of sunglasses not so much because he needed them but because it worked.

They fit well.

The owners of the boat weren't getting *them* back. Past Long Beach and Arverne. The seagulls followed him briefly, then realized he wasn't going to eat lunch any time soon and went back to looking for fish.

He thought about it, then turned into Dead Horse Bay. He ran the boat aground on Glass Bottle Beach and set off at a run again.

But did he run for Jersey City or Central Park?

He didn't know.

He couldn't know. He just knew he had to keep running.

THE BUS RATTLED toward Manhattan and his inner battle had not eased. For right now, the two directions ran as one. He didn't have to make a decision until he got to Lower Manhattan. That was another bus and a subway trip away. It was a lifetime away. Stale tobacco filled his nostrils, and he ignored the cityscape as it went past. Over the bridge.

He wanted to jump in the river, but he wasn't going to, he wanted to live.

Live.

Live.

It was a beat in his ears, it was the blood in his brain. It was the fact that he knew he wasn't going to that made it so keen. He was going to kill Christian Hodges then make sure the cops took him down.

He had to.

What the Sibyl said was nonsense. Or she would find somebody else, because there was somebody else. He knew there was somebody else. He could not be the only one who fit parameters of prophecy.

It could not all be on him.

But at the same time it promised, not freedom, but a respite. A respite from the barbed wire and he swung himself off the bus. He didn't thank the driver, he was too absent for that, too caught up in his problems and his hopes and his fears.

He wanted to get blind, plastered drunk, even knowing how much booze that would take, how expensive it would be.

Half a block and waiting for the next bus. Somebody was smoking. It wasn't tobacco. He hesitated, then turned to them. "Can I bum a joint?"

"Sure," the young man said after a moment. "S'long as you aren't a cop."

"Ain't a cop," Victor agreed. He took the lighted blunt. Drew a deep breath from it. It wouldn't affect him much, but perhaps it would take the edge off. He couldn't get on the bus with it, of course. He didn't try to. He just kind of drew on it and looked at the sky.

He felt the portal was still open, it drew him. It tugged on him.

But duty tugged on him more.

"You okay, man?"

"Broke up with my boyfriend." First excuse he could think of, virtue of being true. "Worked out I couldn't trust him the way I thought I could."

"Sucks, man. Or doesn't suck."

Victor managed a laugh. "I take it you know about sucking."

"I prefer it from girls, but sure."

He laughed again. For a moment he could imagine he was normal.

For a moment, he could imagine he was free.

IT COULDN'T LAST. The bus came, finally, and he stubbed out the joint, handed the kid a five, and swung onto it. He'd never see that kid again.

He hadn't harassed him, he hadn't treated him unfairly, and that felt wrong and odd. He shouldn't have given him the five. It was like he was being pricked by the conscience he no longer possessed.

Except in reverse.

Little barb wire prickles that told him he did, indeed, have to be evil.

He couldn't fight them any more. He knew which route he was going to take. He could only hope and pray somebody would stop him.

He could hope and pray somebody would kill him and end this entire mess. He thought of Judy.

Hopefully not her. Hopefully some cop he didn't know, who would only know they had cornered a professional hitman. Who would do what was needed and call it saving paperwork.

A bent cop. A violent cop. That was what he needed, and the taint it would add to them would be points in his favor, would support him when he faced Beelzebub.

But it wouldn't be with failure.

It would be with doubt, though. Doubt was worse. You didn't doubt, you didn't question. You enjoyed the perks of being alive.

Didn't question. He was questioning, but he also knew what he was going to do.

Off this bus, across the street. Down into the subway station. A press of people. It was unusually crowded. A delay. The first train full to the gunwales. He got on the second that came, standing pressed like sardines, the warm breath of other people in his face, shared with his own exhalations.

It was claustrophobic, but he was a New Yorker. He knew it, he loved it. Another moment of normalcy and also of regret. He didn't want to leave this city.

He had been planning on leaving, for a while, to get rid of the heat. Now there was no guarantee he would ever be allowed to return to it, and if he did he wouldn't be the same person.

Did he love the city?

He wasn't capable of love. But he felt something for it, a sense of home.

He would leave it behind.

He would have to.

Even if he somehow survived this, he knew he was going to be going somewhere else. Eventually. Maybe now, maybe in a few years.

There was only so much space for him.

Lower Manhattan. Out of the subway. Onto a ferry, because there were no subway lines into Jersey City.

Of course there weren't.

Who would want to go there?

37

"SENECA VILLAGE," Tag said, grimly. "The portal."

"Great. Right up by the lake. We should have got that cab to take us to 86th street."

"We should." Tag looked at her. "I doubt you can keep up, no offense."

"None taken. I'm not a runner." She wasn't out of shape or anything, but she had no doubt that Tag was a better endurance runner than she was. Magic aside, he was built like one.

Maybe he was one. She hadn't asked.

"Let's go," he said, finally, and took off up Central Park West at an easy jog. He was staying on the sidewalk rather than going into the park itself, where winding paths would make the distance much greater.

It still wasn't flat, though. Judy set off after him. She managed to keep up, although she suspected he was slowing his pace for her. He almost had to be. She shook her head a little as she ran.

She wished she knew some kind of trick to go faster. But she didn't. They ran past the back of Tavern on the Green, past Strawberry Fields.

Central Park. Seneca Village. She knew the story, but it had never really resonated with her. Not the way it probably resonated with Tag.

Why would a portal to Hell...

...perhaps the anger of the people who had been displaced. Perhaps that attracted demons, perhaps it stayed as some kind of residue.

Tag slowed to a walk just as she needed to, as she couldn't run any more. As if he had sensed it. They kept going up the sidewalk. Most people seemed to be ignoring them.

"This is when I wish we had a faeborn."

"Why?"

"Because most of them can make it so nobody notices us and some of them can make the distance shorter."

"I was wishing for that kind of trick earlier."

And then she smelled it. "Ugh."

Tag sniffed the air. "Ugh." He kept walking. "Are you sure you're up for this? Your gun might not be much use."

"Who else is there?"

"We need a Guardian."

"But let me guess, this was Martin's beat and she hasn't been replaced yet."

Tag frowned. "There aren't as many as there used to be. We're not sure why."

There was something sinister about that. Maybe magic was fading slowly out of the world to be replaced by technology.

Somehow, Judy didn't think that trite explanation was it. "Or is it that there aren't as many new ones as the population needs?"

Tag shook his head. "No. Good thought, but no. Now..."

He stopped where the 79th St Transverse hit Central Park West.

He stepped into the park, taking one of the small trails, then ducked into the trees.

Judy followed.

Tag sat on the grass. "Hush, please."

He was going to meditate or something. Judy hushed, but moved into a position between him and that smell. That trite brimstone smell, yet oddly mixed with lavender.

Lavender?

Well, she'd work out what it meant soon enough.

Surely.

THE FIGURE STEPPED through the trees, looked at Tag, looked at her.

Lavender. And sex. This figure definitely smelled of sex. It seemed to shimmer and then settle into the form of a handsome young man. As if, for a moment, it had not known exactly how to appear.

Judy tensed. Tag still had his eyes closed. Vulnerable.

"Oh, what have we here?" the figure smiled. "A tired cop. You must want a break from your duties."

"Well, yes, but..." Judy gave a one-shouldered shrug. "I'm not buying what you're selling."

It was hard to speak the words, though. It was hard to take her eyes off the figure. It wasn't just a handsome young man, it was a handsome young man of her precise physical type.

"Come on." It extended slender figures. "We can go to Bermuda. The beach. Cocktails. You can leave this mess to the professionals."

"I *am* a professional."

The figure laughed, and the laugh was exactly her dream lover's laugh, but she'd seen that shimmer.

"You are out of your depth, Detective." The figure smiled at her. "I'm offering you an easy out. A brief vacation, a bit of fun, and by the time you get back everything will be resolved."

"I think I know what *you* are."

She wasn't sure, but she had seen it shimmer. And she suspected anyone else would have seen only their heart's desire.

"But can you resist me, even knowing?"

Their hands touched, and her groin stirred. It had been too long since she last got laid. Long enough that it was, indeed, hard to resist. She needed this, she needed it so badly.

And what would it hurt? They weren't asking for her soul, just a bit of fun.

Just her integrity.

With a huge effort she pulled back.

Tag's eyes snapped open. "Judy...back away..."

"I got it."

But the hand laced with hers...when had that happened...was now made of steel. She couldn't pull back. That moment of wanting had perhaps been enough. The desire for relief, for release.

The desire.

And something hit her from behind. It hurt.

The demon dropped her and she rolled to the ground, bruised.

A wolf stood growling at the being. Which no longer looked like her heart's desire simply because she wouldn't desire somebody with that much raw hatred on their face.

That was before the wolf leapt...

...and tore out the being's throat.

JUDY GASPED.

There was no body, only a rush of smell. The lavender scent was gone.

"Sorry," Tag said.

"Don't be." She rubbed the bruises from where he had knocked her out of the way. She hadn't seen him change back to human form. "That...was an incubus. Wasn't it?"

"Yes, and now you've met one of them you'll do better next time."

"He looked like he couldn't make up his mind what form to tempt me with for a moment."

Tag laughed. "You're bisexual, right?"

Judy blinked. "Oh..."

"Incubi and succubi are the same thing. They appear as the person's, well...their form is drawn from who you want to sleep with. Sometimes bisexual people confuse them a little bit. It's probably my presence that made them go male."

Judy took a deep breath. "What do they do if their target is asexual?"

"Buy them chocolate."

Judy laughed. "By which you mean..."

"Lust demons work on desire. Sex is just the easiest way for them to do it. They'll try something else if sex doesn't work. Usually food."

She nodded a little bit. "And they smell of lavender."

"To you," Tag said, wryly. "To me they smell of chocolate."

"Hence the chocolate joke." She frowned. "Was that the only thing that came through the portal?"

"Oh no. That was the distraction."

"Targeting me."

"I was in deep trance. You were right there. You were by *far* the easier target in that moment."

"It wanted to..."

"They wanted to take you off the board." Tag's tone was firm, but oddly calm, despite or perhaps because of the circumstances.

"But possibly not permanently."

"Oh, it would have led to permanently. They wanted your soul. And the chink in your armor would be to get you to abandon your duty. That would have been a step towards not being you any more."

Judy digested that, then nodded. Except that her duty wasn't what she thought it had been. Maybe she should abandon it. Would that...no. Not if she did it for the right reasons. "Whilst with somebody else..."

"With somebody else it might be getting them to cheat on their partner. With another it might, heck, be getting them to cheat on their *diet*."

She didn't ask what it would be for Tag. It seemed too personal a question.

"But now you know."

"And you let them tempt me," she accused.

"Honestly, I was deep enough in trance I didn't realize right away."

She believed him. "So, how about we find out what we were being distracted from?"

"I already know. It's not pretty."

38

JERSEY CITY. Where people priced out of New York City live. Perhaps that's not an accurate picture, but many believe it.

You can't get there by subway, only by ferry or through the one tunnel. To get there from Lower Manhattan without a vehicle, the easiest way is via the West 39th Street Ferry Terminal. That ferry lands at Lincoln Harbor.

Because, Victor thought again, who wants to go to Jersey City. It is and is not New York, it strives for its own identity, but all it succeeds in being is some place people live who can't get better.

Of couse nobody thought he would look for somebody like Christian Hodges *here*. Behind him, he could feel the open gateway. He wasn't sure who was behind it. His alies. His enemies. He didn't have friends.

Judy's face flashed into his mind.

He couldn't have friends. But maybe if this all went down in Jersey City she wouldn't have to know about it until it was over.

He was drawn north. And then he felt her. Deirdre Hodges. She was waiting for him. She was spreading her fae aura out, making *sure* he sensed her.

He knew, or suspected he knew, what she wanted.

Well, perhaps it was time for that, while the supernatural forces in New York slowly or rapidly converged on Seneca Village.

There was a darkness ahead too, something warm and welcoming and yet not.

He quickened his pace. Down Port Imperial Boulevard. Across the street was only the railroad tracks, and across them a depot with trucks parked outside it. On this side, a sports park. At the side of the road was a vehicle with its trunk open. A cop had stopped to help. He ignored them, walked past an apartment building.

Quick.

She was on the other side of the tracks. He could feel her, using dark energy to draw him in. Risking taint to herself to do so.

He frowned. Got further down where the cops wouldn't see him, wouldn't see him duck across the street at the light, as if going to the bus stop, and then duck across the railroad tracks. Over the fence on the other side and through bushes and trees. A mess of trees. The only paths here made by neighborhood children who, like children everywhere, would never confine themselves to marked trails.

She stood above him, by the street, and he knew where they were.

"This seemed an appropriate place."

He nodded. "Of course."

"Don't worry. I set wards. Nobody will see us. I think it's time to end this, don't you."

"Why are you willing to die for Christian Hodges? You don't love him."

"Money," she said. "For my daughter."

He almost saw it in that moment. But the barb wire tightened around his heart and he had no choice. "Don't tell me where she is."

He couldn't promise not to harm the child.

Except that part of him already had made that promise, that one he could never make.

VICTOR DIDN'T WAIT for her to fire first. Based off his previous experience with her, he couldn't. The purple magefire leapt from his fingers towards her.

Once she was dead, the wards would start to fade. Or more likely she had wove them to her life force to *ensure* they faded, quickly and immediately, so he wouldn't benefit if he won.

He couldn't tell.

She moved to the side smoothly, retaliated with soft green. The two bolts struck each other in the edges, giving off a smell of ozone.

He didn't follow up with another one, but rather launched himself at her. There were no rules in this.

It was a duel, but it wasn't a duel between gentlemen, with rules and seconds and paces counted. It was all out, it was knock down, it was drag out and he was determined to win.

He had to win, because she would kill him if he didn't. And he wanted to live.

She twisted out of his grasp, aimed a knee at his groin that struck his thigh. "I might have..."

"...a man uses his advantages." He threw a punch at her that was wreathed in purple fire.

She dodged again. "You aren't a man."

"I'm certainly not a woman," he quipped, then rolled to the side to evade a kick, followed by another blast.

She didn't know the trick of energizing her aura. He made note of that. She couldn't back down.

Wouldn't back down.

"How old is your daughter?" he asked.

"Seven," she responded. "You going to back down for her sake?"

"I can't." His entire aura was glowing now, counting on the wards and people's natural tendency to forget about the supernatural.

But he couldn't back down, he couldn't stop, he didn't want to kill her and he had to kill her.

He couldn't think more about anything else, because she had called shards of green that fell from the sky. He was bleeding now.

First blood to the changeling.

Last blood *had* to go to him. There was no choice. There was no other option.

She looked like her.

She *looked like her* and then he realized it was deliberate, fae trickery, pulling the person he would least want to hurt out of his mind.

He sent waves of fire towards her, followed by himself. Bearing her down in his anger.

"Damn you," he said to her. "That was too low a blow."

She was laughing. And then she wasn't there.

Curse her, she'd provoked him into attacking empty glamor.

He rolled to his feet, looking for the real woman. Sniffing for her.

She wasn't there.

He wasn't bleeding.

It had *all* been fae glamor. A distraction while she moved her husband.

She was good. He would give her that.

And he had left his bike in East New York.

SNARLING, Victor looked for something to throw.

Then he pulled himself together. She wasn't purebred, she had to be in the area somewhere. Even if she had folded the road, she couldn't have gotten that far.

He just had to work out in what direction. He wished for the wolf shaman's capabilities. For the ability to follow a scent, even if that scent went partly into faerie.

Lacking them, he narrowed his eyes.

Forget Deirdre.

Where was Christian Hodges?

Where *was* he? That way.

Victor set off at a run. Then he hesitated. There was an unattended bike. He looked around. Hotwired it quickly and hopped on. No helmet. Hopefully no cops. Being stopped for not wearing a helmet would suck.

Unlike the changeling, he couldn't glamor one up. And the road his senses led him along was heavily trafficked.

He could sense his target moving. And then *moving*. Folding the road, damn her. She'd turned west.

She was heading towards Hackensack Meadowlands. That was perhaps not the first place he'd look for a gate into faerie, and she couldn't take Hodges there anyway. But the only fairies in Manhattan or Jersey City were likely goblins and gremlins. Nobody trusted either of them. There was that one pooka, but nobody trusted *them* either. Not even other pookas. Clearly, she was going for help.

He forked inland, then turned down sixty-seventh street. Residential area, now. Less chance of traffic cops, not that he felt he could relax. Varied houses. White boxes painted around each driveway to discourage parking. For now it seemed to be working.

A stupid dog leg jag, a Hispanic market the sight of which made him hungry. When had he last eaten?

Too long ago and he couldn't now and it didn't matter.

Crap. A one-way street. He kept going.

A dead end.

This was ridiculous.

The next street was also a one way against him. What the...?

Had she cast some spell or was this just that bad a street layout?

He had to go clear down to 62nd Street. "I hate Jersey City," he said out loud.

Sped down 62nd until he reached the next cross street. Of course, this was a jag too. He tried to go back north.

Wove through the mess of streets, feeling that she'd beaten him to it. Knowing he was probably going to lose.

No, he was certainly going to lose, but the barb wire wasn't even wanting to let him get there without flying.

There was the bridge that crossed the railroad.

He skidded to a halt.

It was closed for construction.

If he *had* been wearing a helmet he would likely have thrown it across the road.

39

THE ONLY THING that physically remained of Seneca Village was a sign. Judy knew the story, but it was just that.

A story. A thing which happened in the past, which didn't impact her. A sad thing, but it still wasn't personal.

Tag had his eyes narrowed, and he sniffed the air.

"I don't *see* anything," Judy said, warily, one hand perhaps dangerously close to her service piece. Not that she expected whatever it was to be vulnerable to bullets, but it made her feel just that little bit better. Just that little bit safer.

That didn't say much good about her, to be honest. But it was true and she couldn't entirely deny it.

Then the smell of brimstone strengthened.

"Paydirt," Tag murmured. "I wouldn't recommend the gun as a weapon."

She nodded. She wished she had some other kind of weapon. Except prayer. She had that, and it was likely to work better than the gun.

There were trees in all directions, the paths winding through them, the Central Park attempt to create the illusion of not being in the city at all.

The illusion of escape for which people's homes had been razed. It didn't entirely work, but it helped those who needed that illusion.

Stepping out from behind the tree was a woman.

She was breathtakingly beautiful, not in the vaguely fake way the incubus had been, but in a way that said it was part of her nature. Judy would have expected a demon to be dark haired, but this woman was white blonde, so very white. Aryan as the northern Europeans misused it. The breeze seemed to twist around her, exaggerating her hair and features.

White blonde hair, blue grey eyes, skin that seemed bleached of all color, in stark contrast to the simple black jersey dress she wore.

It wasn't an outfit she would have expected of a demon.

"Is this all the welcome I get?" she inquired. "An untrained seeress and a dog."

Tag's metaphorical hackles were up, but he managed not to respond to the insult in any overt way.

Judy shook her head. "What were you expecting?"

"The baby Guardian. Oh, wait..."

"You know what happened to *her*." Judy knew she probably shouldn't engage in conversation. It was hard to take her eyes off that form.

Even Tag was watching, and he wasn't interested in women at all from what he had said. The demon's pale beauty transcended such things.

Which was what allowed her to break free of it. It was twisting against nature, against the way God had formed them.

For her, attraction to women was normal and acceptable. For Tag it wasn't.

She jabbed him with a sharp elbow. He shot her a grateful look, then murmured, "Keep her talking."

She wasn't sure what he was planning. But keeping the demon talking did not seem as if it would be hard...

AN OLD MAN wandered into the area. And around them. It was as if he could not see the demon.

Or Judy.

"I suppose you don't want to be disturbed?"

The demon smiled. "Maybe one day you'll learn that trick. Maybe I can even teach it to you."

Judy pretended to consider it. She felt an odd heat at the top of her chest and realized that her magen David was just slightly warm.

Holy object. Demon. "I think I'd rather find a different teacher."

"I think you would at that." The woman smiled. "But you are still going to help me, Detective."

Judy shook her head.

"You *do* realize that while we're having this oh-so-fun conversation, your friend Victor is busy murdering Christian Hodges."

She tensed. She had no reason to think it was true.

She had no reason to think it *wasn't* true.

Demons lied.

Victor Prince was also a demon. "If that's the case, then there really isn't anything I can do." She tried to sound nonchalant.

The demon shrugged. "No, you'll just have to send him to jail for a very long time."

"Which will weaken your rivals."

Judy frowned. The demon seemed just a little bit thin at the edges. She smelled of brimstone, yes, and also something spicy, something almost Chinese-food-like. If that wouldn't be a horrible insult to every Chinese person she knew.

"Well, yes. But what do you care about politics in Hell.'

Judy examined her nails. "I care about them when you bring them into my city."

"Oh, *your* city is it now, Batman?"

Judy actually laughed. "I suppose I'd be Batwoman, but no. I don't claim to be the sole protector. Still, I swore an oath." And she had held to it even though everyone else had failed, but she was not sure she could do it for much longer.

Or she had to find another way to keep it.

"Which you actually let bind you. Most don't."

The magen David became warm again.

"Well, *interesting*," the demon added. "But you will still help me. You'll just call it doing your job."

Whatever Tag was doing, Judy hoped he finished soon. She was ignoring him, keeping her attention entirely on the demon as a way of keeping the demon's attention entirely on her.

She could only pray it was working.

THE DEMON abruptly stepped towards her, reached a hand to her chin. Judy stepped back.

"Nope, not doing that cliché."

The demon laughed.

"Do you have a name?"

"Of course," the demon said. "We choose our own. One of the things people like you don't understand is that what we represent is freedom. The angels in their marching ranks, never breaking them. Singing what they're approved to sing. Or do you..."

Judy laughed. "I'm not Christian." The demon couldn't read everything in her mind. "You know what Israel means?" Her lips quirked. "He-who-wrestles-with-God."

Many Christians followed some interpretation of the Bible blindly.

That was...all but against the rules in Judaism. "We question. Because children are *supposed* to question their parents."

"When we question, we fall."

Her lips quirked again. "So, you're saying the choices are blind obedience or evil. You sound *just* like an evangelical Christian."

The demon actually looked insulted.

"Makes me wonder who they really follow," she added, thoughtfully. "So..."

"So. You are going to go to New Jersey. If you hurry, your case will be so nicely wrapped up for you. If you're really lucky, Deirdre Hodges will kill him. No more hassle. No more paperwork."

"And I'll have done your dirty work."

"Really. He's a demon."

Who clearly worked for this one's rivals. Judy noted no name had been given. No name was likely to be given. It gave the entire encounter a faint air of surrealism, she mused.

Or maybe out and out unreality. None of this was reality, anyway, none of it was the reality she grew up with.

Heck, maybe she'd died in the explosion at the dojang and all of this was a dying dream, a hallucination of a failing brain. However, to act as if it wasn't real was likely to be suicidal.

"I don't care what he is," she said, finally. "It's my job to find the real killer."

Who was probably, indirectly, standing in front of her.

Faded around the edges.

Did that mean she couldn't...

...and as Judy had that thought an explosion of blood red energy expanded from behind her.

The demon said something in what was perhaps the language of Hell or, perhaps, Sanskrit or something. It didn't need translation.

Then she vanished.

Judy turned. Tag was kneeling on the grass behind her. He was bleeding.

"You're hurt."

"A little bit of blood magic. Before you ask, it's perfectly fine if you use your *own* blood."

She sighed and rummaged in her purse for her first aid kit.

Shamans.

40

THERE WAS ANOTHER WAY ACROSS. It took him a moment to clear his mind enough to find it. He rode across the first set of tracks at level, not even looking to see if there was a train. Not even caring if there was a train.

He couldn't care whether there was a train, he didn't have that luxury. He was in a shabby industrial area, a place that just felt like every bad image of New Jersey. And again, he couldn't...

He cast his gaze, turned right. Huge power lines towered above him. He could feel the electricity in them, feel it crackle. The warehouses and power transformers were as good as a city wall. It was as if there was nothing beyond them, nothing to reach. He envisioned a fog, the end of the world, people never realizing that they couldn't leave.

He hit the gas, speeding up until it was all a blur, the clouds in the sky above, the warehouses, the power lines.

There was no left turn. There was no way to get there without flying until West Side Avenue curved, a single rail line next to it. The wrong side of the tracks, a place nobody would come who didn't work in one of these shabby units.

Green fields patchworked with more, and railroad tracks that ran through the road.

Dead end.

Dammit! He just kept going, through the railyards. He didn't care if he was trespassing.

He got off the bike. The railyards might come out up ahead, but he could see only one good way out.

He carried the bike up through the trees, hopped the railing and remounted on a road...that curved back around the railyards. She was there. He could feel her. She had positioned himself where he couldn't get to her.

Counting on his desperation. By the time he found a way through...

There! A ramp onto the New Jersey turnpike.

In the wrong direction.

He twisted around, found the right ramp. Powered across the bridge over the Hackensack River. Had he been thinking straight he would have known to come this way in the first place.

Had he been thinking straight.

Had he not had a history of avoiding Jersey City as if everyone there had bubonic plague.

Across the bridge, off to the right. She...they...were somewhere in the trackless and close to treeless brush beyond.

He abandoned the bike. The owner would probably get it back. He didn't think he was going to need it.

He walked into the brush. He kept walking.

AND HE STOOD on an empty plain.

Faeborn.

Changeling.

Bending the world with glamor. She was a threat, Victor sensed.

At the same time, she was only protecting her husband from the damnation he had earned.

No.

She was not a threat. She was so determined to protect him, for her daughter, that she was burning herself out. He could feel it. She was using more power than anyone could, more power than she could channel through her body. Changelings did that sometimes, tried to keep up with purebreds and died.

He felt relief. For a moment he had feared that she was, somehow, the kind of existential threat that could cause angels to work with demons.

She was a mother who felt she could do more for her daughter dead than alive.

"You're killing yourself," he called.

He sensed another presence. "She's being stupid."

He didn't look at the voice. Pooka, he knew. "I noticed."

"At least *you* have an excuse."

"She's doing it for love." If he had had a daughter, what would he have done for her? Anything. And women were supposed to be even more protective.

He would never have a daughter.

"Well, true. A foolish thing, love. But a powerful thing."

"I assume you're here to watch. Did you at least bring popcorn?"

"I'm here to make sure the two of you don't manage to hurt anyone *else*."

Victor nodded to the pooka. "I won't ask why you care. But I'm figuring it's because you care about the faerie veil even more than most of us."

"Got it in one."

He walked towards her. "Where is your husband?"

"Where nobody but me can get to him."

"A faerie howe. Clever. But when you die he won't be able to get out."

"I don't intend to die."

"You're burning out your body. You're going to die, win or lose, if you don't back down now."

"If I back down, I don't get paid."

"And your daughter's medical bills don't get covered. How much is it?"

"You think you can buy me out?"

"It's worth a try," Victor said. He wasn't confident he could beat her.

He was pretty sure, in fact, that this battle would end with both of them dead, and Hodges trapped in a faerie howe until he starved.

Which would, admittedly, be a reasonable punishment.

"I stay bought."

"Admirable. But we don't want to..."

"Why do you think I came out here?"

He narrowed his eyes. "You're real this time," he mused.

"I decided that I could only play with you for so long. It *was* funny when you got lost in Jersey City. Did you really not remember that there's only one bridge?"

"Who the heck comes to Jersey City?"

"The people who live here."

She had a point. He took a deep breath, building power. But he couldn't kill her.

If he did, she wouldn't be able to open the howe.

THE SKY TURNED RAINBOW.

They were no longer entirely in the material world. They were at the gateway to the howe.

"You realize now I might be able to get in."

"You realize now I can *destroy* you, Victor Prince."

She might be right. He turned it over in his mind.

He wanted to live.

He certainly didn't want to cease to exist.

But it was more appealing than going back to Hell, something he wanted to put off as long as possible.

"We have an audience," he pointed out.

"I don't particularly care what the fox sees."

"It's against the rules of faerie to seek final death against an opponent."

"I don't care. My daughter..."

"...needs her mother." Victor found a gentleness in his tone. "Go home, Deirdre. Go to your daughter. Find another way to help her.

One which won't end with you...and possibly her...being prey for the next Wild Hunt."

That was the real reason the pooka was here. To make sure she didn't tear his spirit into such small pieces there would be nothing left of him.

He was grateful for that. Of course, the pooka was also here to make sure he didn't do the same thing to her.

He didn't intend on it, but accidents happen.

"I can't."

"Did you swear a faerie oath?"

"Yes."

"So, neither of us has the choice, in the end." The pooka would not stop this. Christian Hodges might be able to if he let Victor take him.

But beyond that he knew of no force that could free a lilin and none that could free a changeling or faeborn from an oath true sworn.

At least the howe would keep the real world from being damaged.

"We don't, do we." She sounded sad.

"If you lose, I will find your daughter and I will do what I can."

"A lilin with honor."

"I have free will when it doesn't go against my orders. Just as you do. And I have no reason to harm a child."

He pulled his power together. He couldn't stall any more. Christian Hodges was in the howe, he could feel him.

All he had to do was get past her.

Think of it as a particularly morbid game of capture the flag, he told himself.

Then he broke into a run.

41

"So, now I suppose we have to go stop Victor Prince from killing that guy," Judy said, once she'd bandaged Tag's arm.

"We do. But that's not the biggest concern." He indicated where the portal was. "You just argued with a Duke of Hell. Somehow you did so successfully."

"My magen is warm." It still was, although it was fading slowly away, leaving only a peculiarly pleasant sense of something inside her that wasn't going away and that she didn't want to go away.

"Oh." Tag took a deep breath. "We'll talk about that later. For now, let it guide you if needed."

She nodded. "So, the biggest concern is what Hell is up to, but I'm pretty sure it's all connected."

"So am I." He frowned. Then he murmured something. "Give me a moment here."

He sounded tired. "Are we going to need a vehicle."

"Yes. Where did you stash Hodges?"

"A safe house in Jersey City. I can't say more."

"That's enough, I just needed a direction."

He lifted his hand and smoke appeared between them for a moment. "Get us a vehicle. Without a driver."

She nodded. She didn't think she should take orders from him, but she also didn't want to get another uniformed officer killed in the quest to deal with Victor Prince and whatever else might be going on. As annoying as they were, they didn't deserve that. She pulled out her phone, making a call. Stepping well away from Tag to do so. Whatever he was doing, it was probably best he was able to concentrate. She asked Darrell to bring her the car they used, leave it with her, and then go check on the boyfriends. Get them in one place if he could. She thought they might be in danger.

He said he'd get some protection on them.

She turned back to Tag.

"Tell him to hurry."

"I did. Where are we going?"

"Hackensack Meadowlands. And when we get there I'm going to need your help."

She nodded. "I'm driving."

"Wish there was a more direct route," Tag grumbled. "But if Victor Prince is in the mental state he's likely to be in, he'll probably try to cut through Jersey City and forget about the river."

Judy laughed. "I know people who've done similar."

Darrell pulled up. Got out. "Sure you..." He peered at Tag.

"He's a consultant. I'll explain later."

"Consultant. Right. Not your type, Judy." And then he headed for the nearest subway station at a good clip.

Judy got in the car quick, before they could be towed for illegal parking.

Tag was laughing.

"Darrell normally has better gaydar than *that*. It must be seriously malfunctioning."

"He's not my type, at least."

"Nor, as he pointed out, are you mine, even if I did have the right plumbing."

She drove onto Central Park West, speeding up as fast as the traffic and the law allowed. She didn't want to use the sirens; even in New York that drew attention.

The air was throbbing. It felt as if there wasn't much time.

The sky didn't look right. There was a lurid purple tint to the clouds, faint but visible.

She didn't ask Tag about any of it. She just drove.

GETTING off Manhattan was never fun. Getting from Manhattan to New Jersey when you were practically in Midtown?

You weren't "supposed" to do that. She drove through Upper Manhattan. "So..."

"So, what seems to be going on is that Deirdre Hodges who, by the way, is part fairy, used her husband as bait to draw Victor into the middle of nowhere. And is using fae magic. Extensively. Enough that she's probably going to be looking at a hospital stay if she's lucky."

"So, you can overstrain yourself with magic."

"Sometimes. It takes a lot, though. If you get a headache, though, back off some. That's usually the first sign that you're pushing it a little more than you should be."

Judy nodded. She took a diagonal street onto St. Nicholas Avenue. "I hate driving in Manhattan."

"It's worse than DC," Tag agreed. "A lot worse. Bigger, for one thing. In a pinch you can get out of the district on foot reasonably easily."

"I've walked back to Brooklyn before, but I know what you mean."

Through Washington Heights. She hated it.

She hated every block of it. It was taking forever, and she didn't think Tag was going to explain too much. He'd fallen silent. Was staring out of the window like a young child excited by a road trip.

Any moment now he was going to ask her if they were there yet. But it allowed her to concentrate on driving.

She slid onto Broadway, followed it to Mercado Market, under the underpass, turn left. Across the bridge into New Jersey.

She hated that bridge, with its multiple levels and, of course, its tolls. Tolls that she had to stop to pay. It made her impatient.

She could feel that there wasn't much time. Whether it was real or her imagination, it made her want to speed.

Onto the New Jersey Turnpike. Keep driving.

Just keep driving.

Tag reached over and handed her some change.

"Thanks." She didn't need it, but she appreciated the gesture. They stayed on 95 as it curved through and around the Palisades. Over the rivers, multiple.

"Okay, here."

She found a place she could park the car. It wasn't entirely legal, but nobody was going to tow a cop car. The meadowlands were barren, empty.

"Where are they?" she asked.

Tag made a face. "Here and not here. I did say I was going to need your help."

She nodded. "What do we need to do?"

"So, the problem is, they're in a howe. Which a half-breed shouldn't be able to create, but something's fueling it," Tag said. "The most likely thing is a faerie vow."

"A..."

"The fae *must* keep their promises. This literally means that they are more powerful when pursuing their promises. She's protecting her husband, to whom she has sworn a vow."

Judy nodded. "Okay. But that doesn't work for the rest of us."

Tag shook his head. "No. So, we need to get into the howe. And I'm already exhausted."

"And I wouldn't know where to start as to how."

"You know where it is."

As soon as he said that, she realized she did. She was drawn to it. It smelled like a rose garden. And she also smelled...

...wet dog.

"The pooka's here," she said.

"Don't count on him to help us."

"I wasn't. Just saying that he's here."

Tag nodded. "Okay. So you know where it is. I can talk you through this, but..."

"But?"

"But it might open your third eye further, as it were."

"If you do it, you'll pass out on me."

Tag made a face. "Likely."

"Then tell me what to do."

"You start by walking around the area counter-clockwise. Or widdershins as we call it."

She nodded. As she did, she felt warmth at her throat again. It felt like she was doing the right thing. The thing required and asked of her. The thing which would make a difference.

It was going to change her, but it wasn't going to damn her. Even if she believed in that, in truth, it wasn't. She was going to walk a different path.

One which would, she knew, make her a better detective.

The howe sprung into reality around her. The smell of rosebushes filled her nostrils.

"Through the gate *now*," Tag hissed, reaching to grab her arm.

She stepped through the gate. She felt the entire world shift, and she knew she was no longer in reality.

She knew she might never escape.

That was the thing Tag had not told her.

It changed nothing.

In front of her she saw two people throwing fire at each other.

What did she do now?

42

VICTOR WAS STARTING TO TIRE. Deirdre was starting to...crack. Crimson faefire flowed out of her orifices.

The wild hunt was watching. They were shadows in the smoke and fog beyond the howe.

She was going to die.

They were both going to die. Christian Hodges was going to die.

And the howe...was violated.

Deirdre turned, gave a startled cry. Almost went down as he took advantage of the moment. He didn't look to see who had arrived.

"You can't save him," he said, moving to pin her. To do so physically, seeing how her beautiful face was now ravaged by premature aging.

"I can't even save myself." It was pained, it was plaintive. "Save my daughter."

And somebody cleared their throat.

"Stand down," came a female voice.

It was the voice Victor both most and least wanted to hear.

Judy.

She had opened the howe. She had come here, as if bound by a faerie vow of her own.

"We can't," he said, looking down at Deirdre. "Neither of us can."

She probably had her gun out. He wasn't looking. If she shot him, then at least there was no risk of destruction.

Except he'd go back to Hell.

If she shot Deirdre. "Don't...shoot...Deirdre."

He didn't get any acknowledgment from her. "I just want this madness to stop. Victor, you don't want to do this."

"I don't get what I want."

He had her on the ground. The next thing to do was wrap his hands around her throat. Kill her in a mundane way which would not result in the Hunt coming after him. Her soul would slide into faerie.

Then he could take Hodges from this place.

And get arrested.

She hadn't said they were under arrest. Perhaps she recognized that she was not the one with jurisdiction here. That was the shapes of twisted hounds and horses, of beautiful and terrible riders.

They were the police here, not a no-nonsense Jewish detective from Brooklyn. The incongruity of her presence here got to Victor.

He laughed sharply and harshly. "I don't, she doesn't, you don't, he doesn't."

With that last he meant Christian Hodges.

Then Tag spoke. "While we're messing around over one guy who doesn't even deserve to be saved, Hell is getting into position to harvest a *lot* of souls in New York."

"Not allowed to care, sorry." Victor started to close his hands around Deirdre's throat. She was past fighting back. Wait. *Tag* was here?

"Right, you're supposed to help them." Tag's tone was flat. "Massive brownie points. Maybe even a bit of relief from torment. You're supposed to make more and more people *just like you.*"

He couldn't see either of them. He could only see Deirdre's shocked face.

Then there was a tired male voice, "I know. I know what..."

Christian Hodges. Stepping out of a rose bush that had not been there any more than he had.

"I know what they're planning."

Victor had to let go of her. The barbed wire curled so tightly around his soul that he screamed as he struggled backwards.

He had to get Christian's soul.

He had to.

But what he managed to say, through the torment that rose out of Hell was not that. It was "Help me."

Help me.

He wasn't sure how those words even came out of him. He wanted out. He wanted to *live*. And he didn't want to harvest a large number of souls.

He didn't want anyone to have to be him.

He didn't deserve freedom, but some of them did. Some of them were about to stumble for the first time. About to find that instead of some beautiful angel catching them, there was only the darkness.

He couldn't do it.

He would give himself to the Wild Hunt first. They could destroy him. They circled. All he had to do was destroy Deirdre Hodges and they would ensure he paid the penalty.

All he had to do was commit one more murder and he would face the freedom of the endless night.

He turned back towards her, started to build power. Saw the fear in her eyes.

The barb wire tightened. Not her. She wasn't the target. Agony exploded outwards into his limbs, and he thought for a moment he was going to die on the spot.

If he died he couldn't complete the mission.

"I know what they're planning. They're going to do something that will make 9/11 look like the *first* World Trade Center bombing. They're going to feed on the anger. And I'm going to be rich."

"Having second thoughts?" Judy asked him.

He nodded vigorously. "Yes. I want to stay alive a little longer."

"An honest man."

Victor was fighting to turn back to Deirdre.

"Please. Don't let him kill me. I'll tell you everything." Christian wasn't babbling. It sounded more like a promise, a promise he was determined to keep.

He felt something, very slightly, shift.

A faerie vow.

A faerie's *consort* could sometimes be so bound. It wouldn't be enough to stop him, but he could feel it.

It would be enough to let him do what he was going to do. He prepared the soul blast, felt it flow through him.

Turned back towards her. "I'm sorry, Deirdre. I think this is the only way."

"Do it," she said, softly. Then louder. "Anyone who lives. *Help my daughter.*"

The plea was almost painful. He prepared his attack. It would all be over soon. The howe was partially open. They could flee.

The pooka wasn't interfering after all.

The hounds howled.

TIME SLOWED. He didn't want to do this, it went against his orders, it went against his desire to survive.

She was willing to let him. There was a power in that, a power in all of this. In this place.

The hounds howled.

He prepared the soul blast. In this place it would do more than merely throw her soul from her body, killing her. Not something he did often.

To be blunt, guns and knives were more fun.

And he lifted his hand to cast it.

"STAND DOWN."

Her voice was louder than it had ever been, but he couldn't obey, no matter how much he wanted to. This was the only way to save Christian Hodges, the only way to foil whatever plan there was, and he couldn't then be used against it.

The blast streamed from him...

...and suddenly Judy Eisenberg was in the way. Somebody, some-where, a long way away was yelling "Don't."

It struck her, and it recoiled, it flew in all directions, it dissipated into the mess that was the Wild Hunt, the hounds dodging it.

Pure blue light around her for a moment.

He stopped.

He stood there for a moment. "Well, *damn*," he said, finally.

"I couldn't let you do that."

"If you hadn't been protected you wouldn't even exist right now."

The air still tingled with holy energy. She seemed as shocked as he was.

"I...think I know that."

"And now I have to...."

Tag, stepping forward. "Do you?"

He felt the agony start again. "They won't give me any choice. *He* won't give me any choice. I'm not a mortal man any more. I *do* have to be evil."

"You asked for our help," Tag said. "I don't know if this will work, but isn't it worth a try?"

A deep breath. Fighting the agony. Christian Hodges was checking on his wife. Judy was kind of staring at her own hand, or perhaps at something in her hand.

She was clearly even more shaken than he was. "You don't know if what will work?"

Tag smiled. "This."

And then he kissed him. His lips warm. His arms sliding around Victor, eliciting a response that he felt reciprocated.

It wasn't true love.

But it was something.

And it was spirit energy flowing around them, and they fell out of the howe or it ceased to exist, standing in the middle of Hackensack meadows.

There was a snap of energy and the agony was...no longer there. At a sense of remove.

"That's the best I can do."

It was still there.

"It will have to be enough."

43

JUDY WAS BREATHING HARD. She wasn't sure what had just happened, any of it. But she was next to Deirdre.

Who looked about sixty, but was slowly returning to her normal appearance. As if she'd had life drained out of her and then restored.

She had a strong pulse. "Is there anything we can do for her?"

"Chocolate," Tag said simply. "All round."

Victor was on the ground now, his knees drawn to his chest. Whatever Tag had done to him had clearly knocked him for at least three, if not a full six. He wasn't saying anything.

"I don't have any," Judy said, mournfully. She had the beginnings of a headache and whether there was some magical connotation to chocolate she didn't care. Chocolate just *sounded* good.

She turned to Victor. "Can I trust you not to kill him?"

His response was ragged, as if something had torn into his throat. "Not entirely. Don't leave us alone together."

"Then we're going to the safe house and afterwards we'll move him," Judy decided. The car would hold everyone. She kept Christian in the front, Tag between Victor and Deirdre. The best she could do.

She wasn't sure she should be driving, but she certainly wasn't letting anyone *else*. Hopefully there would be chocolate at the safe house. If it would help.

Booze. She could use that too, as bad an idea as she suspected it was. This was the kind of day to drive anyone to drink. "What did you hit me with?"

"Something you shouldn't have survived," Victor said. Then, "Thank you."

"For keeping you from killing Deirdre." She kept her tone flat. He was not in control of himself or he was. She wasn't sure which.

"You saved both of us."

Deirdre was still silent, head in hands. She looked like she had a migraine, conscious but distinctly out of it.

"Unlike most cops I'd rather prevent the crime than arrest people afterwards. Besides, a demon told me to arrest you. That makes me want to do the exact opposite."

A harsh, bitter laugh, "I'm..."

"I don't care. You aren't a demon Duke or Duchess or whatever up to something."

"Oh...crap."

Judy kept her eyes on the road. They had to get back across the river and then through the maze that was Jersey City. Finally she pulled up outside a battered townhouse.

"Let's get everyone inside."

Inside there was nobody. There should have been a plainclothes cop. There wasn't. Tag stumbled into the kitchen, found hot cocoa and started mixing it for everyone. Judy helped Deirdre onto the couch. Victor collapsed into an armchair opposite.

Christian sat as far from him as he could.

Judy remained standing, folded her arms. "Talk to me. *All* of you talk to me."

She had to take charge.

She had to find out the true depth of what was going on.

THERE WAS A MOMENT OF SILENCE. Tag handed out cocoa, first to Deirdre and Victor. Judy took her cup. "Talk to me," she repeated.

"Okay." It was Christian who spoke up. "Look. I've done many things I'm not proud of. And yes, I sold my soul. Years ago. For success."

Deirdre reached for his hand. He shook her off. "Last year or so, I was approached by a man who offered an extension on my contract in exchange for, well. Information about key movers and shakers."

"One of whom was Caroline Levsky," Judy said. It wasn't a question.

"Yes," he said. "Somebody try to kill her too?"

"Somebody blew up her penthouse. She wasn't in it at the time." Judy sighed. "So, they just wanted information."

"But I saw the pattern. Demons..." Christian paused. "Demons want people to be miserable and uncertain and poor. I think they're trying to crash Wall Street."

Victor laughed, "Again."

She turned to him. "I take it this is a common habit of some demons."

"Oh yes." His lips quirked into a bitter smile. "Recessions are awesome from the viewpoint of Hell. Like Christian said, people get miserable and uncertain and poor, they lose faith, they get desperate. It becomes a lot easier to harvest souls."

Judy nodded. "Except somebody else disagreed. That somebody hired your boyfriend to kill Caroline Levsky, and then tried to frame you for murder. Because..."

Victor swore. "*I* was never the target. I mean, getting me off the board. I need to make a phone call."

"Go on. Warn him. I'd bring him in, but I can't prove anything."

"He'd be safer in jail," Victor admitted. Then he got up and left the room. He took his cocoa with him.

"You're just going to let him call?" Deirdre's soft voice.

"If he believes his ex is in danger, then I'm going to let him do the warning. I doubt the guy would listen to anyone else." Judy let out a breath. "So. What do you think..." She turned to Tag.

"From what I know, Martin was investigating a crooked investment firm for possibly supernatural influence when she was killed. She'd already asked for help. An eighteen-year-old college student can't..."

"And you're that help."

Tag nodded. "I can wear a tux if I need to."

Judy laughed at the image. "But by the time you got here, she'd been murdered and Victor framed. I'm pretty sure I know who actually did it."

Tag shook his head. "The only person who could sneak up on her like that would be a mundane professional. They hired somebody."

"The question is. What do we do about it?" She could bring in the hireling, if she could find them.

"There's a we?" Deirdre asked. "I just need to take my husband out of here."

"I'm going to need that list from him."

She glanced towards the door.

Victor was taking a long time over his phone call.

EVENTUALLY, she stepped out into the kitchen, where he had gone. The back door was open.

Frowning, she moved outside. She expected to find him gone.

Instead, she found him standing in the yard. He seemed to be concentrating on his breathing. "I warned him," he said without turning round.

"We thought you'd done a runner."

"It's tempting. I could get over that fence easily." He turned to face her.

"What did Tag do to you?"

"A temporary ward to help me resist the urge to kill the Hodges. That's the best he can do."

"Meaning..."

"Meaning that when it wears off we're right back where we started. No matter what you do, as long as my orders are to kill Christian Hodges I'll keep looking for him, I'll take out anyone who gets in my way. And Deirdre Hodges is half faerie and oathbound to *not* let me kill Christian Hodges. There's no way out that isn't us killing each other. Which you stopped. And I'm glad you did, but..."

"But it's all a temporary band aid on a deep problem."

Victor nodded. "I can't..."

"You can't fight it."

Anger flared in his eyes. "You..." He took a deep breath. "I can't fight it. It's too late for me. You asked me if I have to be evil. I do."

"You have some choices, right?"

He nodded.

"From what I've seen, every time you've had the *choice* you've chosen the course of least damage. You're not evil, Victor."

"I killed the person I loved more than anything else."

"How long ago?" She knew she shouldn't be alone with him. "And look, if you were evil I'd be dead."

Something flickered in his eyes.

"I get it. You did something unforgivable and now you work for Hell, because....because that gives you some freedom, because it gets you *out* of Hell." She didn't know for sure, but from his face she'd hit at least something of a mark. "And when they tell you to kill somebody, you have to do it or you're going to be right back in Hell."

"There's a bit more to it than that. But yes. I don't expect to be allowed out again any time soon, because I questioned. I hesitated."

"You didn't want to hurt Deirdre Hodges."

"You realize she's a paid bodyguard, right, not *actually* his wife?"

"No, but I'm not surprised. Still..."

"I wanted to kill her." He turned away. "No, I wanted to destroy her so that the Wild Hunt would tear me apart and it would all be over."

"You tried to commit suicide by cop." It all made sense. "Because you don't want to be evil any more."

"It doesn't matter what I want."

"My people wrestle with God. It matters *absolutely* what you want."

He turned away. "Please. Leave me alone. I promise I won't leave."

With his target inside, she trusted him. She walked back inside, found her cooling cocoa.

Tag was right.

Chocolate helped.

44

JUDY WENT BACK INSIDE. Victor felt confined and at the same time...he finished his cocoa. Chocolate did help, even him.

He was exhausted, in any case. He could leave, probably should leave. Really, he should kill himself while he could. While whatever Tag had done to him lasted. He could still feel the compulsion.

The difference was that he could fight it.

You aren't evil, Victor. He was. He was, by his very nature. But she was right. Of late, he'd been making choices that led away from it. When had that started?

He thought of Richard. His choice to leave Richard rather than help him finish the job had been...something. He hadn't had orders. He had had free will. And he hadn't wanted Judy dead.

It should have been about the tactics. About the fact that if he killed a cop there would be consequences.

It wasn't. It was about her eyes and her hair. He didn't want to sleep with her, he wanted to sleep with Tag.

He wanted what she was willing to offer. Friendship.

A second chance.

She didn't know what he'd done. She wasn't forgiving him. Which he realized might be dangerous. He didn't know what would happen.

She didn't *care* about what he had done in the past. She cared about what he did in the future.

The door opened.

Tag stepped outside.

He didn't turn around. "Thank you. For the respite."

"What happens if somebody forgives a lilin?" Tag asked.

"I don't know." He turned to Tag. "You can't forgive me anyway. If you knew what I had done."

"I would hate you?" Their eyes met. "I don't want to know. I don't want or need to forgive. I only need to not know. I've wanted you from the moment I saw you." A pause. "You have some role to play. I don't know what it is yet, but it isn't the role of Hell, it isn't the role of destruction."

"Then what is it? I made all the choices that led me here."

"Knowingly."

"I killed people. Without hesitation. Knowing that it would damn me. Not caring." He didn't tell the truth. The story was starting to form.

He was afraid of forgiveness. Terrified of it. Then he added, "And I agreed to work for Hell so I could get out, for this. For the star above me, for the cool air on my face. To be *human* again. Except, of course, I'm not and never can be."

"No, you can't." Tag stepped around him slightly. "And what I did is a respite. Except that it's allowing you to choose. You are, right now, *choosing not to kill*."

"Until the pain comes back."

"There might be an answer."

"There..." Victor closed his eyes. The only way not to look at the other man. "There has never been an answer."

"I will find one for you. Even if it only gives you the rest of this life."

His eyes snapped open. "That's all anyone could give me. But..."

"But what would you do with it?"

There was no hesitation. "What good I could. What amends I can make."

"Then I *will* find a way." Tag stepped forward.

Before Victor could react in a way that wasn't dangerous, the man had his arms around him, his lips pressing up towards his.

This too was what he had agreed to this for.

But right now it was more than that.

Right now it was a taste of salt and sweat and freedom.

Perhaps even of love.

THEY SLIPPED INTO THE HOUSE, upstairs away from the others. Victor heard quiet conversation. Police type discussion.

The conspiracy might well be revealed, although he knew Judy cared far more about finding Martin's killer. Far more. Perhaps her single-minded stubbornness explained how she had resisted the attack.

No, he knew the truth. She probably didn't. Should he tell her? Nah, he decided.

Besides, he had other things on his mind. Tag drawing him into the room, dark hand on fair, pulling him towards the bed.

"Wait..."

"In my pocket," Tag said, wryly. And somehow, yes, the man had lube *and* condoms.

Of course he did. It was a sign of promiscuity, preparedness, or both. Victor didn't really care. He didn't have to worry about disease.

He had to worry about bad habits, because bad habits got passed on, and their lips were pulling together again as if of their own accord. His groin was telling him how much he wanted this man, and he didn't particularly care if those downstairs realized what was going on.

He didn't care at *all* because it wasn't their business. It was his and it was Tag's and there might only be this one night.

He might have to ask Tag to kill him. It might be the only way. And he couldn't think about that, hands drifting down pants, and then pants falling to the floor, shirts opened and cast aside, clothing twisting into a single pile that would be hard to sort out later.

The bed calling to them, drawing them inwards, and then there was only their bodies entwining and coming together, experimenting as one always did with a new lover. The awkward fumbling, not knowing the other's body, the inevitable laughter. It was that which told you it was going to work, the laughter.

Sex, never to be taken seriously, a bit of spilled lube, a condom that didn't want to go into place. Arousal that ebbed and flowed and grew and shrank again, and then climbed towards a shared climax that left them both sweating in the bed, entwined with each other, faint aches in various places.

He didn't know how much he had needed this, and for the first time in a long time he was relaxed.

The hellfire was still distant, threatening. But he had made this choice instead of the other and he heard the Sibyl's voice.

When you find her.

Her.

It wasn't Tag who was supposed to be here. But it was Tag who *was* here.

It would last and it would not last.

It would work and not work.

For now there was no space to worry about the future, no space to worry about anything but their feelings.

And sleep slowly claimed them, still wrapped together.

Victor woke alone.

BAREFOOT, he came downstairs into the kitchen. Judy was making breakfast.

He didn't ask where Christian and Deirdre were. Presumably still upstairs. "Where's Tag?"

"Convenience store run. There's no orange juice."

It was a logical explanation. He wondered if she knew, if she smelled it on them. He wondered if she cared.

He hoped she did and hoped she didn't. "Okay," he said, awkwardly.

"Are you..."

He frowned. He answered the question he guessed she was going to ask. "I'm not yet overcome with an overwhelming desire to kill Mr. Hodges."

"Good."

"What are you going to do?" he asked. "You'd be well within your rights and perfectly reasonable to arrest me. Or shoot me while trying to escape."

"I thought about it." She turned from the stove, stepping to the side so she could still see the eggs she was scrambling while looking at him. "But you haven't tried to kill anyone while *not* overcome with an overwhelming desire. We generally call that temporary insanity."

"Then I belong in a nice padded cell with a jacket that zips down the back."

She laughed. "Maybe we all do. I suppose what it boils down to is whether you can be trusted."

"And what about the letter of the law? I assaulted Deirdre Hodges, at the very least."

"She's a piece of work," Judy said, finally. "More mercenary than anyone I've ever met."

"She has a sick daughter."

"Which is the only..." A pause. "Really I should just arrest both of you and let the courts sort it out. But no jury's going to convict *her* of anything."

Between the sick daughter and, well, Deirdre's looks, Judy was right.

"So, the question is, if I make them go away, what do we need to do to keep you from going after them?"

"Tag's supposedly working on it. But I don't know. I think his hope that something can be done..." Victor tailed off. Let out a short huff of breath.

"I know exactly what you two were doing last night," Judy said, wryly. "So, yes, he's biased."

"I suppose..."

"You were *loud*," she said wryly.

Victor felt something unaccustomed rise to his cheeks. A blush. "Well, uh..."

"I'm a little bit jealous."

He felt himself blush even more, "I'm..."

"Don't be sorry. It wouldn't be any of my business if you hadn't made so much noise. I'll ask him if I can help." A pause. "But there's a question. Why didn't you kill me with that blast?"

Did he answer her?

He was saved from having to by Tag's return.

45

WHEN SHE ASKED THE QUESTION, Victor looked...like he didn't want to answer.

And he was saved by Tag. Judy could have killed him in that moment, except that he had unexpired orange juice.

This meant awkward breakfast happened, with Christian and Deirdre coming downstairs. Victor stayed between Tag and Judy, and she had no other opportunity to ask.

It was clear he'd intended to kill Deirdre. It was equally clear that *something* had prevented that attack from even fully hitting her.

She didn't know what. She wanted to know. Needed to know. She just didn't want to ask while people were eating and making the smallest of small talk.

Heck, Christian was literally complaining about the weather. It was clear this couldn't work.

"I think we're going to have to send you..."

"I have an idea for where to go," Deirdre said. "But obviously..."

"Obviously we're not discussing it here. But you also can't stay here."

Victor was very, very silent. Then, quietly, "I'm sorry."

Christian shook his head. "I made my decisions. I know you're just the instrument. And while you have the choice..."

He closed his eyes and looked away.

"Deirdre, can you take your husband back upstairs? There will be a car coming for you." She turned to Victor. "We'll keep you here as long as we can."

Tag shook his head. "No. We need to deal with a couple of things. One, we need to deal with the conspiracy. Two, we need to deal with Victor's problems, and we can't do that here. However, we'll definitely give those two a head start." He grinned.

Judy noticed his hand was slipping towards Victor's. She wasn't about to argue with that. "Okay. I'm going to trust your judgment, just remember who the cop is here." For what that was worth. Was she a cop any more?

Arrest Victor Prince. She was ignoring that order, that order to wrap the case. Bring in Prince and probably Tag too. She couldn't do it any more. She had turned off her phone. She was off the rails and heading to...to something she was not sure of.

Tag laughed. "I haven't forgotten. The cop who isn't arresting people."

She made a face. "Arresting people won't fix this. Well, except Litton if I could prove anything against him. No offense, Victor, but he needs to be off the street."

"None taken. It's what I saw in him. He's as crazily destructive as any demon."

"But I can't prove anything."

"Don't worry. He's so scared I think he's going to skip the country or something. He never wants to see me again, and he never wants to take any more jobs from demons. At least knowingly. He was talking about getting out of explosives and into drugs or something."

Judy rolled her eyes. "Depending on the drugs, that may or may not be an improvement."

They said nothing more until Christian and Deirdre had been removed by Darrell and a uniform.

She wondered if she'd damaged her relationship with her partner permanently.

She couldn't afford to care.

"Okay, now those two are out of the way, we can start planning."

"You don't trust the Hodges?" Judy couldn't help but ask Tag.

He shook his head. "Deirdre Hodges is the daughter of a high-ranking Sidhe. If you've got an oath on her, sure, you can trust her. But that's only her husband."

Judy nodded. "So, basically..."

"She has human free will, but just like you take after your parents, so she's going to be inclined towards being mischievous, even malicious. Think of them as flaws she has to work on. And she isn't." Tag glanced at Victor. "*You* are doing a better job of that."

Victor coughed.

"Okay, so we trust her to look after her husband, and nothing else."

"Also, the chances are that if we bring down the conspiracy, Christian Hodges will be in more danger," Tag said grimly. "*He* is fine with that. *She* isn't."

Judy decided he had a point. "Is there any way to get him his soul back?"

"It can be done," Victor said. "It would involve a lot of remorse, a priest or similar, and a certain amount of time he may not have."

"First things first," Tag said. "We need to sever the link between you and your boss."

"*That* can't be done."

Judy frowned. "You have remorse. Could a priest do something?"

Victor sighed. "No. Look, if somebody tried to exorcise me they'd kill me. An exorcism would help Christian. It can't help me because my soul is from Hell in...not the first place, but..."

Tag nodded. "If it was that simple we'd ask you to find us a rabbi."

Judy's lips quirked. "I don't know of any who would be up for something like this. Besides, rabbis aren't priests. They're teachers. They're people who know stuff rather than being like..." A pause. "We don't *have* priests any more."

"I suppose I sort of knew that."

"So, being a rabbi is more about knowledge," Victor mused. "Whilst what we would need would be..." He looked amused. "Somebody who was devout, somebody who had the favor of God."

She wasn't sure what was so funny. "So, what we'd probably really need would be a Catholic priest."

Tag was looking at Victor, then at her. Something was definitely funny, and it was a joke she wasn't in on, which annoyed her. They didn't seem about to spill it, though.

"But," Victor said finally, "that wouldn't be enough."

"What about confessing your sins and being absolved?"

Victor frowned. "No. I don't know why, but that doesn't feel right. We're in blind territory here. Nobody has ever tried to separate a lilin from his patron."

Tag suddenly smiled. "But...you put it that way and I have an idea." He turned to Judy. "And I *am* going to need your help."

"So, this has never been tried before," Tag said. "And none of us are witches."

"A witch," Victor explained, "might be able to come up with a spell for this."

Judy nodded. "Do we know any?"

"I know one who's very talented, but she's in DC. Even if she got on the next flight up, I don't know how much longer my...bandaid...is going to hold."

Judy nodded again. "So...we're going to improvise, aren't we?"

Victor gave another of those harsh laughs. "We're going to improvise. There are worse things we could be doing."

"So, the first thing we need is a place."

"I'm assuming somewhere where we won't be disturbed."

"That's honestly not as important as the symbolism."

Victor frowned, then. "I know where. I know where we need to go. But I still don't think this is going to work. And if it doesn't..." He turned to look at Tag and then her. "I need you to kill me."

Judy shook her head. "It will *not* come to that."

"I'm done," Victor said. "One way or another, I'm making the choice to be done. It won't last forever, but I might be able to do something, to achieve something. At the very least..."

"Somebody else will take your place," Judy said.

"But it'll take time. But I know where." He indicated the map. "Liberty Island."

Tag actually banged his head into his hand. "Duh."

"Duh?"

"We're looking at something integral to liberty. Free will. Lady Liberty is possibly the most powerful symbol of that on the *planet*. Of course, she's not pure or clean, but..."

Judy blinked. Then she nodded. "Okay. Which from here means we'll need to drive to Liberty State Park and take the ferry. How are we going to keep people from seeing what's going on?"

"The veil will help, but there's a spell we can do that will mimic fairy glamor for a while. It would be easier if we had a faeborn, but..."

"But I'm sure as heck not trusting Deirdre Hodges with this. Even if she is as tired of the mess as I am."

Judy recalled that the woman had been quite willing to let Victor kill her to stop the madness. Maybe it was a point in her favor. Maybe it wasn't.

If the Wild Hunt had been unleashed, Judy wondered if anyone there would have survived.

"So, what else do we need?" she asked Tag, her tone thoughtful.

"Something sacred," the spirit worker said. "Certain herbs, which I *do* have access to. I'll have to go get them too."

Judy reached up for her magen David. "Will this do?"

"No. I think you need that for yourself. Something more expendable"

Judy nodded a bit. "Then maybe we need that Catholic priest after all. Jews don't do holy water."

Victor laughed. "You're *good* at this."

She took it as a compliment. A higher one than she had ever expected from him.

46

THIS COULDN'T WORK. They seemed to think it would. Did they care about him?

Judy cared about justice. Tag probably cared about the sex. He couldn't quite find that place where he acknowledged that they cared about him. It was a black hole in his mind that he could only see by the Hawking radiation that spilled from it, the radiation of doubt, uncertainty and, above all, guilt.

Caring for him could only lead them, surely, to their own destruction. He could not return the favor.

There had been that moment when he thought he was going to kill Judy. A moment of something indescribable, of a feeling he had forgotten the name for.

His mind shied away from that too. They were putting together a spell.

That could not work. They could not change his basic nature. Nothing could.

No. There was, perhaps, one entity that could, but she was not just dead but missing, imprisoned somehow. All but forgotten.

And even that was, well. A legend. She was a myth to him at this point.

But he couldn't bring himself to refuse to let them try. What did that say about him?

That he wanted out. Or rather, he wanted as far out as he could get. Even if all they could do was make him forget the order to kill Christian Hodges.

Even that would be, he thought, enough.

Tag left. To get spell components.

Judy turned back towards him. "Victor..."

"It won't work."

"Then we'll have wasted an afternoon."

He half-smiled. "That's at least a positive way of looking at it." Put that way it wasn't like they were spending a lot of effort on this.

Except the effort of actually caring.

"So. The female demon we met. Any idea who she was?"

"Not female." Victor raised a hand. "Demons and angels don't have gender the way you do. Even the way I do. They chose to appear as a woman for whatever reason. Perhaps to be underestimated. Perhaps pure aesthetics. I don't know."

"Stop mansplaining angel gender to a Jew," Judy snapped.

Victor blinked. Then nodded. "As for who she was? I don't know. I was using her as a distraction and didn't really look, if you know what I mean. Beelzebub has rivals plural. It was one of them."

"She was behind Dani Martin's death."

"She was a Duke, by Tag's guess?"

Judy nodded.

"Which means she *might* have sent Maurice, but it's more likely somebody higher. Of course..."

"Of course there could be more than one ranking demon involved. I suppose..."

"They don't get on, none of them. But they're perfectly capable of playing it on TV, if you get my drift."

"I suppose that a race of beings defined by excessive questioning..." She emphasized excessive.

"They would say angels don't question at all."

"She tried that line on me. Again; Jewish."

Victor laughed. "Yeah. It's my experience that if you ask two of you people a theological question, you'll get at *least* three answers. More if one's a rabbi."

"Try when they're *both* rabbis," Judy quipped. "But it's our way."

"So you know it wasn't just about questioning."

"It was about trying to take over the world," Judy said, finally.

"It still is."

SHE'D FALLEN silent with that and, in fact, stepped outside to think. There could be worse things than her understanding the stakes.

Why she might have to do what he needed her to do when this didn't work. Maybe he should just...

...she'd taken her gun with her, of course. And it was hard to kill a lilin. Even a bullet in the head might not actually do it. Tag would know what to do if it came to that.

Would know how to deal with Maurice too, if he showed up. If there was even the tiniest chance of this working...

He hadn't entirely told the truth when he said that he didn't know who the Duke was. He had a suspicion it was Asphorel, who had every reason to dislike Beelzebub, and who had ambition for higher rank.

He didn't know who she was working for right now. He had no way to know and no reason to know. As long as it was only her, it didn't really matter he supposed.

He could leave right now. He could walk away. Abandon these people, start the search for Hodges again. He still wasn't feeling the urge and the agony, but he knew what he was supposed to do.

It would be so easy.

It was the easy, wide path. Which might be why he didn't follow it.

The Sibyl had said he could do this. Would do it. Had said he had a choice, to continue to be as he was or set his foot on a different path.

But that he would receive no reward for it. No reward other than the knowledge that he would save lives. He assumed she was telling the truth.

The Sibyl *was* allowed to lie, technically. She rarely did, but it was part of her function, sometimes, to hide a vital piece of knowledge so that somebody would follow their destiny. Or would pass the tests the Heavens set.

If this was a test, he had the simple question of why him.

Or had it been that he was the first to get this far?

The door opened, and Tag came in. "Where's Judy?"

"Back yard. I'm afraid I gave her a few things to think about."

"She hasn't worked it out yet, has she?"

Victor laughed. "No. And when she does I'll want to fly on the wall. I'd imagine she'll be having some really choice words with her God."

"I imagine she will."

TAG POKED his head out and called for Judy. She came out. The car was still outside.

The weather was back to that rain that had lasted for days. A gray gloom settled over Manhattan, the towers looming over the river. They turned away from that, seeking I78 to get them past the craziness that was Jersey City.

Judy was driving.

Victor didn't attempt to help her with navigation, not after last time. Onto the highway, and it was quiet. Too quiet. There was a feeling of faint static that descended over them. He didn't like it. It wasn't familiar, he wasn't sure what it was. He only knew that he didn't like it at all. They drove past New Jersey's historic downtown, with the taller buildings of the actual downtown beyond. Forming a layer with Manhattan and the partially constructed form of the new One World Trade Center. Then they were past that. A peculiar dome showed up on the left hand side.

Victor might be local. He'd never really been here. He'd never had a reason to. He had no idea what it was.

It looked like a planetarium, like a small reality that contained an image of the larger. Containing multitudes, as they said. Right now he felt very small. And very far away from everything he knew. An illusion of how flat and open things suddenly were. Judy drove with her hands tight on the wheel. There was no conversation.

Nothing to break the silence or tension. Nothing to cut through that static in the air. The rain lanced down, suddenly stronger, against the windshield of the car.

If this continued, he idly wondered if the Liberty Island ferry would even be running. They slowed enough to pay electronic toll. Barely. Took the exit and hit another toll plaza.

Screw New Jersey, Victor thought, but it was a surface thought. Everything below the surface was roiling with something which, if he had to admit it, was probably fear.

Judy kept driving. "Sorry. We're on the wrong side of the park." Around a large warehouse. She finally pulled up behind the railroad terminal.

They went to the pier. The rain had eased off. The ferry was running, but it was empty. Maybe that was a good thing.

Nobody was sitting on the deck, certainly, and the only person below was a professorial looking individual who was probably thinking about some research project.

Surprising he was going to Liberty, not Ellis.

The world was shifting. Victor felt it *tilt* for a moment. "Guys."

"I know."

Something didn't want them to get to Liberty Island. He could feel it all of a sudden.

And for the first time he felt the slightest bit of hope. Perhaps this could, even would, work after all...

47

THE BOAT SWAYED. Judy frowned. She saw a look of tension come over Victor's face. "What's wrong?"

"What's wrong is that somebody doesn't want us getting to Liberty Island," he said.

Tag was grumbling under his breath. Judy couldn't hear but one word in three and she didn't like any of them.

She glanced at the professor-looking guy. Was he an innocent person they needed to worry about protecting or was he the culprit?

She sniffed.

He didn't smell of magic, which meant they either had to worry about protecting him or he wouldn't be targeted at all.

She doubted whoever was doing this would care who got in the way.

The boat slowed. The PA system activated. "We're having engine difficulties."

Tag held out the plastic bag containing the holy water and herbs to her. "You *can* both swim, right?"

Judy swallowed. "Yes, but..."

She looked at the distance. She thought she could do it, but the idea of swimming in the filthy water didn't appeal. It was alright for Tag, he could put fur on.

Then the water turned red. "I don't think somebody wants us to swim for it," Victor said.

"We could try doing it here."

Victor shook his head. "If somebody is trying to stop us from getting to the island, we need to get to the island."

Tag shook his head. "It's not actually blood. That's there to put us off."

Judy hadn't thought of it as blood until Tag said it. She glared at him.

Then glanced at the professor type. He winked at them.

"I think we need to do it," she said. The boat was stationary, not far from Ellis Island. If *that* was where they were going it would be a short trip.

It wasn't.

They went out on deck. The driving rain. The blood red sea. None of it felt natural. She reached for her magen David.

The rain eased.

Deep breath.

"Please everyone just be patient. A tug is coming to take us back to Liberty Park."

Of course. Back to Liberty Park, where they didn't want to go. She had no doubt that any boat they tried to take would mysteriously break down.

She looked at the other two, stuffed the spell components into an inside pocket, then she jumped into the bloodstained water. She hit it with a splash that knocked the wind out of her for a moment.

Swim.

Her clothes weighed her down, but they couldn't do this without the components.

Then Victor was on one side of her, spotting her.

With him there she suddenly felt as if she could do this after all.

THE WATER WAS COLD. It sapped everything from her. It also smelled and felt like blood. She knew that wasn't real.

Or was it? It *smelled* like blood, and also like brimstone, like fire. Not the nice kind of fire smell, not a crackling fireplace or a bonfire.

Bonne fire. Good fire. This wasn't that. This wasn't remotely that. She couldn't even imagine this being that.

She cursed it out mentally. But all she could do was keep swimming. If she faltered, one of them would be there.

Perhaps they were thinking the same thing.

Then she wasn't floating in the water at all. Or rather she was, she could still feel herself swimming.

But she was now floating *above* it. A quiet voice, "You risk your life for one who can't be saved. Why?"

The response that came out was "Because I'm crazy." She knew that was the true response at far too many levels.

She was crazy.

"That's not a reason."

"Because I don't want him to go down for something he didn't do."

"As opposed to all the things he did?"

She felt as if she was being held out of time. She had no idea who she was arguing with. "I suppose I've already believed in second chances. How many has he had?"

"The ones he's given to himself."

"None," she said, finally. She was floating higher.

She was drowning, she realized. She'd failed after all. They hadn't been able to save her.

"None," the voice agreed. "At the same time, isn't your life worth more than his?"

"I swore an oath. To protect and serve. To do my best to support justice."

"Besides, isn't his excuse that he was just following orders?"

"The second he wasn't under duress he stopped." And that, she realized, was the deciding factor.

He had stopped.

"He's still going to get pulled back there when the time comes."

"I know. But *he* thinks it's worth it for what he can do until then. Which is all any of us can do."

She was choking. She could feel it now. She was dying. She tried with one more effort. "Let me go."

"Let you drown?"

"I won't drown. You won't let me drown. Neither will they."

Victor. Tag. They wouldn't let her drown. They wouldn't let her die. "If they do, I'll gladly admit I'm wrong."

There was ringing laughter, and then she was flat on her stomach on some surface, coughing up water which tasted like blood.

Tag's voice. "You with us, Judy?"

"I...yes. For now."

Because it was always and only for now.

"WE THOUGHT for a moment we'd lost you," Victor said as Tag helped her up.

"I think for a moment you did," Judy coughed again. The blood taste was fading, leaving salt and something else. "Got anything to keep me from getting sick?"

"If this goes well, I'll brew you up something," Tag promised.

If it didn't, she suspected she wouldn't be worrying about it. They were on the road that ran around the island. "You were only worried," she accused, "Because I had the spell components."

Tag laughed.

Then she glared at him. "You're *dry*."

"Shapeshifter trick."

"That's completely not fair. Where do we need to go?"

"Up to the statue base." Tag murmured a few words, winced. "I hate witchcraft, but that should keep anyone from particularly noticing us, especially the drowned rats.

Victor looked like he wanted to hit him.

Judy shook her head and started walking around the edge of the island. The water was in New Jersey. The land was in New York. Crazy state politics that. All the way around the statue, up to the base, then up onto the base. Up again.

"I think this should do," Tag said.

She could feel a kind of field coming off of the statue. "Until we get attacked again. Or do you think..."

"Technically, this is holy ground," Victor said. "Of a sort. If it was *true* holy ground, I'd have a headache just being here. But it has a measure of the sacred to it."

"Which means that we have some protection." She glanced up at the statue. It loomed and towered high above them. "But likely not enough."

"Likely not. It's slowing them down, though," Victor added.

Despite his words about *not* having a headache, Victor looked particularly uncomfortable with the situation. Judy couldn't think of anything to say.

Actually, he looked scared. He was as worried this would go wrong as they were. He didn't believe it would work.

She did.

But she also had a feeling it could go bad in worse ways than merely not working. They stood on one corner of the second level of the base, like being on a tiered wedding cake.

She handed the bag of spell components to Tag. Then she waited, not sure what to do next.

The sky darkened.

The sky began to turn red.

48

VICTOR WAS HIDING what he had felt when he pulled Judy out of the water. She was the physically weakest of them. If anyone who was going to falter, it was her.

And he was sure she had been dead when he pulled her out. Which made the way she went up the stairs remarkable. Even if she *did* have divine favor.

Which she probably hadn't worked out yet.

The sky was starting to turn red. The next attack was coming. He spoke a few words to her when they got to the top, then stood looking at it.

He couldn't protect her.

Protect? What was *that* thought? Where did it come from? He couldn't anyway. She was the one who had sworn the oath to protect. Protecting her would be wrong, an imbalance in the world.

But right now he wasn't sure he could even stand next to her, and the air smelled sour and wrong. The blood red water hadn't been real. It had been an attempt to intimidate them.

This was equally unreal, but what *was* real was the boat approaching the dock. Maurice was on it. He could feel him.

And their conflict was about to go to its logical conclusion, except that he couldn't fight, couldn't do anything but hope...hope they could somehow hold them off.

Which they couldn't.

"And we've got company," he pronounced.

"Let me guess," Judy said without turning. "Maurice and a boat full of thugs."

He feigned shock, "How did you know?"

"Because it's what I would do. If they can't attack us magically because the statue is protected, they'll just come and shoot us."

Tag laughed a bit. "We need to find a way to buy time."

"We don't have one," Victor said grimly. "Whatever you guys are planning on doing..." A pause. "...even if it works perfectly I won't be in any state to take on Maurice afterwards. I have to deal with him now. You *do* have your gun if you need it?"

Judy pulled it out of her jacket. "I do, but I can't guarantee it will fire safely. It's not drained."

Victor cursed. "Mine's going to be in the same state."

And Maurice would have no such problems. They needed help. "Tag, I don't suppose you have any allies to call on?"

"Not unless your phone works, and that's going to be worse off than the guns."

Judy was doing something with her gun, no doubt trying to drain it faster. He glanced at her then pulled his own out to repeat the process.

It should fire. Once. He was going to need it to fire more than once. "Focus on Maurice. Even a head shot isn't certain, but it will slow him down and then..."

"And then the others might hesitate. But you're going to have to fight him."

It wasn't a question. "I am. And I don't want you in the line of fire this time."

She looked at him, her gray eyes serious. "This time, I promise. How about *you* focus on Maurice and I'll try to scare off the others."

She sounded like she believed she could do it. It made it easier for him to believe in her.

"Okay, then. Tag..."

"...I'm working on the ritual. But I'll wait until you've dealt with him."

Which was more confidence than Victor felt. "If I go down, kill him and burn the body. Make sure, okay?"

Judy hesitated, then nodded. "Okay."

THE BOAT CAME up to the dock. There was a police boat chasing it. Perhaps they would have allies after all.

Maurice was Victor's problem. He didn't bother with the steps. He vaulted down each level, each tier, landing in a roll. It was a hard fall even for somebody like him, especially the first one onto concrete, jarring through him.

Nothing broke, or at least not badly enough for him to care. There was pain. He ignored it.

They were on the end of the dock. The water was blood red again. A warning that he might not want to jump into it.

It was more getting his gun waterlogged again he was worried about. He ran in a low crouch, zig zagging, but the dock was exposed. Very exposed. There was nothing to duck behind. A bullet zinged past. The second one hit him, grazed his arm. He returned fire.

The gun fired once, hit Maurice in the shoulder, jammed. He threw it to one side and hit the deck, letting more bullets fly over him. Somewhere behind him was Judy. He couldn't worry about her right now.

Well, he could, but he couldn't protect her or assist her. She had some kind of plan and he had to trust it.

More gunfire, from the police launch. One of the thugs fell backwards into the water, landing with the kind of dead splash that indicated he probably wasn't worrying about drowning.

Good.

The thugs were now paying more attention to the cops. He charged. Ran down the dock as if he wasn't afraid of what might happen to him. He didn't particularly want to die, but if he did it would at least make everyone's lives easier. His arm hurt. His right leg also hurt, his ankle. From the jumps.

Maurice was out of ammo. Rather than reload, he charged towards Victor. He was bleeding, but he wasn't slowed by it any more than Victor would have been.

His face showed a broad grin, a look of sheer joy. He wanted this fight.

Victor felt his own twist into a similar rictus. "Shall we dance?"

"Indeed. Then I'll have your cop whore."

Victor laughed. "Oh, you have it all wrong. *So* wrong, Maurice." The words were designed to keep each other off balance. They were part of the fight. Then Maurice was throwing a punch at him. He twisted to the side, made a grab for the wrist. Avoided the blow, but didn't manage to get it to go for the throw.

Two of the thugs were charging to join them. "He's mine," Maurice snarled. "Go find the woman. Don't kill her. I have plans for her."

That would give Judy the advantage, but then he didn't have time to think about her as Maurice closed again. The two men became a flurry of fists and feet. The water was below them.

It threatened and beckoned. "Stand down!" came a loud voice from the launch.

Neither man paid any attention.

———

THE COPS DIDN'T FIRE. The two lilin circled one another.

"You know, this isn't even about our bosses any more, is it," Maurice said as he struck to Victor's shoulder.

Victor didn't answer. There was only one language that could pass between them now, only one way for them to communicate. A language older than man. That strike to the shoulder was a feint, as were the words. He took it, sliced towards Maurice's stomach. His gun might be useless, but the knife he had under his coat wasn't.

It sliced a line in the man's belly.

The cops were still there. They'd see two men trying to kill each other. They wouldn't understand what was going on. They wouldn't understand why, and all that was going to happen was that he was going to be arrested for this.

And that was enough of a thought to give Maurice an opening. He grabbed on, and tried to throw Victor into the water.

Victor wrapped his arms around him, and they both went off the edge of the dock, landing in the water. He got his lungs filled with air before they went under.

Keep him under. Keep him under until the cops left. He thought he could hear yelling distorted by the water.

He was sure some of it was Judy's voice. Maurice was going for his eyes, the kind of damage that would take even them forever to heal.

He twisted away, the man leaving a long scratch along his cheek.

There was nothing to be said. They came up for air under the dock, tussling, but out of view of the police.

He had lost the knife somewhere. This had to go past physical, as reluctant as he was. Purple fire grew around him.

Magenta grew around Maurice, as if they'd each been waiting for the other to resort to it. Flames that flowed around them but did not burn. They were resistant to each other's power. Resistant, but not immune. The water wasn't blood red any more, it was carmen, it was colored by their hatred for each other.

"Screw you, Victor," Maurice said, finally.

"You can walk away."

"No, I can't. I was ordered to send *you* back to Hell. Renegade."

He took it as a compliment. It wasn't meant as one, but it became one in his mind. He was a renegade.

He could *be* a renegade. "If I can break free, you can."

"Why would I want to? I can kill as many people as I want this way."

Victor broke his nose.

He heard the police launch roaring away.

49

CHAOS. The police had chased the goons here, and they were now picking each other off. Judy managed one shot from her gun, which would need a thorough cleaning at best, replacement at worst.

"Stand down! He's with me!" she yelled as Victor and Maurice, wrestling with one another, black blood dripping...fell off the dock into the water.

They went under, vanishing beneath the surface.

The cops on the launch didn't seem inclined to listen, but they were now arresting the surviving goons. Judy took a deep breath.

Victor and Maurice did not reappear. She frowned. They had to come back. They just *had* to. Or at least Victor did. She would be just as happy to see Maurice sink to the bottom of the harbor never to return.

Except he'd poison the fish.

These were not charitable thoughts, no, but she was pretty sure he didn't deserve them.

"What's going on?"

"One of the guys who went off the dock is a suspect in a case." She didn't specify which one. "The other is an idiot friend."

"I don't think they're coming back up. I'm sorry."

Judy took a deep breath. As time went past, it seemed less and less likely. They *could* be under the dock, but she didn't hear anything. "Don't be. Like I said. Idiot. And if the suspect doesn't come back up, well, less paperwork, right?"

"Right."

Time dragged further. It was too quiet. She idly wondered how long lilin could hold their breath. Longer than humans? Was it possible they were staying down there on *purpose*?

Finally. "We'll take these guys where they belong, and get divers."

Judy nodded. She knew her face was appropriately worried. "Thank you. Book them for whatever you can."

He gave her a salute and climbed back into the launch. They took the two dead thugs too, but not the blood that soaked the dock, that was definitely in part black. No trick of the light that.

They were probably both hurt. They were probably both dead.

She turned that over in her mind. After all of this, for it to just end? Well, except she was sure Maurice hadn't killed Martin.

She was sure he had hired whoever killed Martin. If he was dead, she would never find out who that was.

A face emerged from the side of the dock like an angel ascending from hell. She whirled.

It was Maurice.

She kicked him in the face, sending him flying back off the dock. "You're under arrest," she said. "You have the right to remain silent, but I'd love it if you sang like a canary."

He spluttered, treading water.

"Who killed Dani Martin and why?"

"You might as well know. It's over anyway. I had her killed, because she was in the way."

"I thought it was something like that." She covered him with her gun, even if she was afraid to fire it again.

He'd killed Victor. She knew that of a certainty. It was the only way he was the only one coming back up.

It hurt.

It hurt a lot.

She let him climb out. Kept her gun on him.

"You can't keep me under arrest on your own. I can't harvest your soul, but I'm going to kill you. Right after I go where Victor was." He looked at her, lascivious.

Judy laughed. "Oh, you have *that* part of things all wrong. Victor Prince is not, I would note, my type. Neither are you."

"I don't particularly care. You're mine."

His type or his property. Both.

"Ah, so you plan rape as well as murder." She smiled. "Come and get me."

She couldn't take him. She knew she couldn't. But Tag was somewhere, she wasn't sure what he was doing. She trusted him.

She trusted him even if he realized what had happened, which would no doubt hit him hard.

She stepped back towards the edge of the dock. "So, why did your boss have her killed."

"Because she's a Guardian and because their time is coming to an end." He said that last part quietly. "Pretty soon, the only people to protect Earth from us will be half-trained fools like you."

She doubted he spoke the truth. Victor had said that Guardians came back. Maybe they were hoping to get a window. A period of time when all the Guardians were kids and the bad guys had free rein.

"I'm probably only a quarter trained if that, but I'm not a fool."

"You think you can take on a lilin. On your own. One who just killed another of his own kind with one hand tied behind his back. You made him soft. You made him *care* and that weakens us."

"No. I don't think that at all."

He stepped towards her.

"I think I'm not remotely, at all, on my own."

And a shadow rose out of the water behind her. She'd expected Tag.

She hadn't expected this. She dropped and rolled out of the way as Victor launched himself at Maurice, pinned him to the dock.

Knocked him against it.

"He's out," Victor pronounced. "Sorry to worry you."

She wanted to throw her arms around him. Victor wasn't a man who encouraged that. "You played possum."

"I did. I was hoping that if he thought I was dead he'd confess."

"Partly. I still don't know who pulled the trigger." She tugged out zip ties from her pocket. Frowned. Tugged out a *second* pair and secured Maurice. "That launch will be back with divers. They can pick up this package."

She couldn't work off of just a confession. She wasn't that kind of a cop. She would let somebody else take care of it. But she knew. She knew all of it, and she could not go back. There was no way back to who she was before.

"I do believe we have some magic to do." Saying it set everything to one side for now. But it didn't make the faint smell of blood go away. Nor did it solve her issues.

"Unfortunately, I think we have more problems." Victor's tone was flat.

Because of course they did.

"I THOUGHT you said this place was protected." Judy could both see and smell the demon.

"I said it was sacred. But it's also open to ordinary people. Even if they bring infernal artifacts with them," Victor grumbled.

"Crap. The two who got past me."

"Indeed."

Tag was up there somewhere. She couldn't see him, but she knew he was holding his own and not dead.

She should have known Victor wasn't dead. She had known. But she'd ignored her instincts in favor of what actually made sense.

"Let's go rescue a wolf," she said. Then she picked up a gun that was lying around on the dock. "The uniforms got careless."

"Is it dry?"

"Mostly." She kept it in her hand as she moved back towards the tier, then frowned. Maybe Victor could get up there. She couldn't. Even with a boost.

She heard a lupine howl.

Tag. Calling for help. Probably calling for spirit help, but also calling for *their* help. Holding his own, perhaps, but in need of assistance nonetheless.

"Excuse me."

And Victor grabbed her. She yelped slightly as he threw her over his shoulder in a fireman's carry, barely managing to keep hold of the gun and not inadvertently pull the trigger. "More warning!"

He was setting off at a run. Rather than expecting her to keep up this time, he was just carrying her. She had no dignity left! It took everything she had not to struggle. She understood exactly why he was doing this. There was the smell of the demon Duke, the smell of Tag, the smell of Victor. The faint static and ozone smell of the statue itself.

She had it all sorted out. But she wasn't sure what she was going to do with a gun against a demon.

She wasn't sure at all how they were going to rescue Tag.

"Brace!"

And Victor was tossing her up onto the second tier. She managed to land and roll to her feet.

"We meet again," she said.

He was behind her. She trusted in that.

He'd sent her first for a reason, even if she didn't know what that was.

But it meant something.

He trusted her. And for somebody like that, somebody who had been to hell and back and wasn't supposed to trust?

That meant a lot more than she wanted to admit.

50

JUDY WAS FACING the demon alone. Victor truly hoped Tag's judgment was right. He wasn't as good as identifying a True Believer as the shaman was. Lilin were generally not granted a huge amount of discernment unless their target was involved.

It took him a little bit to get himself up to the tier.

The Duke manifested in an elegant female form, red hair flowing over her shoulders. He wasn't sure if it was the same form Judy had described, but either way this one preferred the guise of a woman.

It might say something about her personality. Or not.

"Ah, the lilin finally joins the party."

Judy was closed in on herself, her body language defensive. Tag, in wolf form, was behind the demon.

Victor suspected that was part of how she was containing the shaman. His wolf form was powerful and dangerous in a fight, but could not speak. And unlike the true, extinct werewolves, if he stayed in that form too long he would lose himself. Would become a wolf in all the ways that mattered.

"But no, I'm not going to give up my new...pet," the demon purred, turning back to Judy. "Not unless you can give me something of equal value."

"No deal."

The demon was making an attempt on Judy's soul, Victor knew. And she was trying a trick that did, indeed, sometimes work. It was binding. It *would* get Tag free.

Judy knew Tag wouldn't want her to do it. The price was far, far too high.

The air was shading faintly, different colors flowing through it. All any mundanes would see would be three people having a less than pleasant conversation, plus a dog. Nobody would acknowledge that there was a wolf on Liberty Island.

For once, Victor regretted that. He hadn't been alive before the age of reason, back when *most* people had believed in magic and wizards had walked the earth openly. Before the wise women and cunning men had been suppressed.

But it would be nice to have torches and pitchforks come to their aid right now. It would do no damage to the demon, but it would startle her and slow her down.

He mouthed 'good work' at Judy, rubbed his still sore arm, and stepped forward. "If you're going to take anyone, take me."

"Beelzebub would be unamused by *that* particular trick. I'm no fool to fall for it either, lilin."

Victor shrugged. "It was worth a try."

Her eyes narrowed. "Is your leash so loose that you actually *care* about these people?" Her hands flickered to Judy. "Especially the little godservant there."

Judy actually flinched, probably at the idea of being a servant to anyone or anything, God included.

"There's more at stake than our quarrels, Asphodel." He was sure it was her now. The preference for a female form, the mannerisms.

"Indeed?"

He shrugged. "The world's too fun a playground to end it just yet."

"Who said anything about ending it?" Asphodel smiled. "I'm not the one eager to trigger Armageddon."

She might be telling the truth. It was just as likely the one aiming for an end to all things was Beelzebub.

"But somebody is, Asphodel. If you like the playground intact, we should be on the same side."

"Ah." She turned to Judy. "See. He is using you."

Judy actually smiled. "I don't care."

THE DEMON SCOWLED. "Don't care because you, let me guess, *love* him." She flicked long fingers, tipped with red nails, towards Victor. "*That* is an agent of Hell. He might be good in bed if that's your bag, but he will never, can never, be any more than that. He cannot love you. He cannot be your friend. Whatever's left of his mortality is twisted and corrupted and was long before you were born."

But possibly not, Victor thought, before Judy existed. He suspected this wasn't her first rodeo. He said nothing.

Anything he said in defense of himself would make this worse, would make this harder. The knowledge that Asphodel was right did not help.

"Look," Judy said. "I don't care about any of that. I care about this city. I care about the people in it." She indicated Manhattan. "If all of that is destroyed then I've failed."

"So you will deal with a devil, but not with me."

Judy lifted her head.

"You'll let me keep your friend until his mind becomes that of a wolf, at which point I will break his spirit. Oh, I can't take his soul, but he will endure living hell for a very long time."

Tag whined.

"Oh, I have no intention of doing that." Judy's voice was remarkably calm.

Victor knew there was nothing behind Judy's confidence. The demon, possibly, didn't. Bluffing. Not a bad tactic, under the circumstances. When she didn't have anything.

You bluffed in poker.

You bluffed when you had no other alternative, when your only option was to hope that the other person backed down.

It was surprisingly powerful.

Unfortunately, she was trying to bluff a centuries-old fallen angel.

"I have to give you points for courage. But see, there's nothing you can do." Asphodel lifted her hand and Judy gasped.

She was now hovering a couple of inches off the ground. A highly effective way of immobilizing a person. Without harming her.

Asphodel should be blasting her off the island.

Victor laughed. "You can't touch her, can you."

"You can." Asphodel turned towards him.

"Ah, but then you would piss off Beelzebub."

"Maybe not. Why would he want to keep you?"

"Because I'm his and he's an even worse hoarder than most."

"You have a good point."

Tag whined again. Unfortunately, there seemed to be very little he could do.

The look on Judy's face was pure frustration. Apparently she couldn't talk either.

"So, here's how this is going to go down. Beelzebub can't possibly have an interest here." Asphodel smiled. "Kill her and I'll let the wolf go."

HAD it been a mundane asking that question, Victor would have had an answer. But he was pretty sure he couldn't trick Asphodel.

"Ah, so perhaps you *do* care, renegade. Beelzebub will be glad to have you back. In a cell. Or perhaps an oubliette."

Victor couldn't hide the shudder. "More like I was kind of using both of them. You have no idea what Beelzebub is planning."

"You already said you don't want the world to be destroyed. I'm pretty sure that's exactly what Beelzebub is planning."

"Why would he let you know the truth? He knows you're gunning for his rank."

Not that Asphodel had any chance, but she probably flattered herself that she did.

"Ah. So." Asphodel shrugged. "In that case I'll just keep both of them. I can't have their souls, but their bodies..."

"You can't do transformations on Earth and you know it. There *are* rules, Asphodel."

"Who said anything about transformations?"

She dropped Judy, who was looking at her with narrowed eyes. Judgmental, those eyes. Not quite hatred. Then she smiled, pointed at the woman, and Judy was naked. "That's better."

"I have a feeling that won't bother her nearly as much as you're hoping it will."

"Ah, but now I have this." Asphodel was holding...Judy's badge. "I think this is almost as important to her as her faith."

Victor noticed something still sparkling at Judy's throat. "I don't think so. Quite."

"I did say *almost*. I'm betting you feel more naked without this, Detective, than without that coat."

The look in Judy's eyes, though, said a completely different story. And the magen David still glittered, the one thing the demon couldn't take.

It was raining again. Victor wanted to rush to Judy and offer his coat. He knew doing so would make the situation worse. Far worse.

And if Tag had achieved what he had intended, he would be Asphodel's plaything himself right now. The only reason *he* still had clothes on was because Asphodel was afraid of Beelzebub.

"Now, let's see here." Asphodel snapped her fingers, and matching collars appeared around Judy and Tag's necks. "I'll be taking my new pets now. You can't stop me, lilin. And really, you can't even want to."

"You really, *really* intend to take her to Hell with you? Asphodel, I thought you were intelligent."

Leashes appeared. Judy wasn't, for some reason, fighting. Or maybe she had something else in mind.

"Who's going to stop me? You?"

"You already know you can't hurt her. I'm pretty sure this constitutes hurting her."

Asphodel laughed and opened a portal, then started to drag them through it.

Victor took a deep breath and leapt after her.

51

NAKED AND WEARING A COLLAR. With Asphodel taunting her with her badge. The badge that she knew now was tainted with blood, but it still bothered her because of what it *should* have represented.

And now she was in Hell. Or rather, above Hell. They were on a kind of ledge or cliff. Stairs led down. She knew it was all a metaphor of sorts, but it seemed very real. Was she dead?

If she was dead she was pretty sure she would be dry. She felt a warmth at her throat.

This was all because she'd tried to give a demon a second chance. Oddly, she didn't regret it, at least not as much as she had thought she would. She was going to be imprisoned here, but the demon couldn't take her soul.

Or Tag's.

"So, *now* I can make the bitch what I need her to be."

Judy felt herself curl inwards, dropped to hands and knees. No, to paws. Asphodel was turning her into a wolf.

Or a dog. She couldn't tell which. Her vision became less colorful. The smell of brimstone infinitely stronger. There was heat under her paws.

"That's better." To her disgust, Judy felt Asphodel pet her head. She snarled.

"Oh, you'll come to enjoy it. At least once you forget you were ever human. Your God will get your soul back, but he might not want it after I'm done."

Her chest felt warm. Asphodel tugged on her collar. "Come. Let's get you settled in, my pets."

Judy resisted, but the collar had spikes on the inside, that dug into her fur and her throat.

Where was Victor?

Still on Earth.

Was there a way she could communicate with Tag? He was in the same boat she was. And could they really, truly, expect rescue from somebody like Victor Prince? He hadn't tried to save her.

Well, no.

He'd refused to choose between her and Tag. Maybe he should have done it, it would have been a way out of the situation. And right now, she wasn't sure she wouldn't be better off dead.

They were going down the stairs. And then?

Something hit Asphodel in the back of the head. "What?" she demanded, turning around.

Victor was on the ledge above, another rock in his hand. "I see I have your attention."

He *had* followed them. Judy had to think of a way to help him. It was rather hard when she had no hands, no voice, and was wearing a collar with spikes on the inside.

There had to be something she could do. Something other than pray. Trying to do so felt like ashes in her soul.

She tried anyway.

THE SMELL OF BRIMSTONE DIMINISHED. Above them, Victor was just rolling his eyes. "You're breaking the rules, Asphodel."

"Isn't that what we are, *Renegade*? You're breaking all the rules too. Beelzebub will consign you to the depths."

"Nothing compared to what's going to happen to you if you don't let them go. Bringing the living to Hell, harming somebody over who's soul we have no *imaginable* rights."

He meant her.

Not Tag.

Her.

And she'd faced court before. The problem was, she didn't know the rules.

"I haven't harmed her."

"Perhaps by the letter of the law, but certainly not by its spirit. Do you *really* want Heaven to come down on you?"

"Heaven can't come here."

Victor was smiling.

Heaven can't come here.

Her chest felt warm. Had she been human she might have produced one of the bitter laughs for which she was coming to know Victor. It was perhaps what she would remember the most about him.

Unless they managed to stay friends.

Victor finally spoke, "Asphodel, you're a fool."

"And your boss is coming."

Judy could smell it. Not brimstone, not sulphur, not any smell she would have associated with Hell. All of the nuances of it. The signature of a demon prince, of one of the rulers of Hell, was tar and city smell oddly mixed with cedar and the hint of burning flesh. Of death and destruction and the aftermath of war.

Of New York destroyed.

Anger flowed through her. No, there was a better term for what she felt in that moment.

Wrath.

The kind of anger that brought destruction but which also cleansed and strengthened.

Victor shrugged. "What happens to me doesn't matter."

"He'll..."

There was another smell. Ozone. Or.

Lightning.

She smelled the building of a storm. *Heaven can't come here.*

There was a second half to that sentence.

Heaven can't come here unless somebody brings it.

Tag couldn't. He was a wild thing, a wolfman, a *good* man and one she cared about deeply, but he couldn't do this.

She could.

And she had no idea what the consequences of doing it would be. Except they would probably be bad. Not just for the demons, but for her.

The energy built. She threw back her head and howled.

Tag joined in, an eerie descant. Wolf and dog howling together, the sound which had once driven humans to gather around their campfire as the wolves howled. Then the wolves had come to the fire and become dogs, but they had never quite forgotten that they were wolves. Wolves who had made a choice.

She was a *wolf* and she was a conduit. The lightning flashed downward through the upper levels of Hell.

Asphodel screamed. And fell from the stairs, dropping their leashes as she did so. She fell down into the darkness as the area lit with lightning, with ozone. It flowed through her.

Asphodel wasn't the problem now.

What came up from below was.

AND SHE WAS on her own two feet again. Still naked except for the magen David at her throat. But alive and human.

Tag was standing up too, although he shook himself like a wolf. Unfairly, *he* still had his clothes.

"Well, that was..."

"A prime sign of a demon being an idiot. Judy, are you okay?" Victor asked.

She noticed he didn't ask about Tag. "Yes, but I think we need to get out of here before Beelzebub shows up."

She started to go back up the stairs, then frowned. "Except that somebody closed the door behind us."

Tag nodded. "You can open it. But it might take you a few."

She took a deep breath. "Watch my back, then. We need out of here before Beelzebub shows up."

"I'll take care of that," Victor said.

"And he'll throw you into the deepest pit."

Victor shrugged. "I was hoping for a few years before that happened. But there's no saving me. The two of you need to get back to Earth and take care of things. I can slow him down enough."

"No," Judy found herself saying. "That is not acceptable."

"There are rules. God has to follow them too, or the entire system falls apart."

"We had a way to save you," she said.

"No, you thought you did. The best you could have done was hide me from Beelzebub for a few years. Which I would have appreciated."

The ozone smell was strong again, it was flowing through her. But Tag was right. She had to get the door open. "Dammit, Victor."

"That's pretty much accurate."

Tag reached for him. Whispered something. They kissed and Judy looked away. She was going to have to leave a friend here, even if it was his choice, and she rebelled against that. The scent of Beelzebub's approach was no weaker than when she had been a dog. It filled her nostrils, mingling with the ozone. She couldn't smell Tag or Victor at all, their signatures drowned out by it.

She could open the door. She *had* to open the door. And then they could grab Victor and pull him through it.

Nothing less was acceptable.

She could see the outline of it, could feel the energy flowing through her. And instinctively, suddenly, she knew the words. In the Hebrew she had barely learned, but they were there for her when she needed them.

Godservant, the demon had called her.

She would have some *very* choice words for God after this.

52

JUDY WAS CHANTING IN HEBREW. She probably didn't even know why.

She didn't want to leave him here. He couldn't let her risk herself getting him out.

Beelzebub didn't bother with the stairs. Under other circumstances he probably would have. He rose out of the depths as a horned shadow of smoke, looking almost more like a djinni in fire form than a devil.

The intimidation tactic wasn't aimed at Victor. It was aimed at Tag and Judy, to put them off their stroke. Perhaps.

Beelzebub would know better than to try and hold them, but at the same time he could pretend he thought they were intruders. Pretend he hadn't seen Asphodel's fall.

She was going to take a long time to climb back up.

"I'm here," Victor said. "Let them go. Asphodel overstepped."

"Indeed," came the great, rumbling voice. "She's going to spend the next few centuries as a succubus if she's *lucky*."

"Nah, she wouldn't consider that a demotion."

"Perhaps the pits, then. But no, I suppose I have to let them go. You, on the other hand..."

Judy turned. The door was cracked open. "He comes with us."

Beelzebub smiled. "Leave, little one. He's mine. Even your God won't argue with that."

Victor nodded. "Judy, just go. I can handle this."

He couldn't, but perhaps she would believe him. But the hardest people to bluff are those who have come to care for you. It's easy to fool and stand up to your enemies. A lot harder to fool your friends.

"I..." Her face was streaked with tears.

"Go. I'm not worth it."

She was still naked. Victor hesitated, then he pulled off his trench-coat and handed it to her. "You'll need this."

She nodded, her face a little pale, then turned back to the door. Even Victor could smell the faint scent of ozone.

At his heart, under everything else, the God of Abraham, Isaac, and Jacob was a storm god. And He was present. Not directly, no, but in her. She was going to have to come to terms with that.

And he couldn't help her.

He couldn't help her anyway. He turned back to Beelzebub. "You can turn off the special effects. I don't think you'll scare her."

The smoke faded. "And you've always been more afraid of this." A slender man, walking up the stairs. Absolutely no demonic features to him. His skin was light brown, his hair black, slicked back.

Desire and fear warred within Victor. He wanted to run. He wanted to be taken by this man. By this being.

This being who had pulled him out of the pit, said he was special. Said he could have a modicum of freedom in return for absolute loyalty.

He owed everything to him, and slowly, he began to kneel.

"That's better," Beelzebub said.

ONE KNEE TOUCHED THE GROUND. He was abject, he was nothing again. He was a damned soul and he existed solely at the pleasure of the Lord of Flies. Said flies buzzed up out of the darkness, around him. They were comforting and terrifying.

"Ah. Not so hard to doubt now, is it. Of course, doubts must be punished."

Fire and barb wire closed around Victor. He screamed. Judy had the door open. She turned, he saw it in the corner of his eye. He did not look towards her face or Tag's. With what small part of him could still resist he willed for them to go. To leave.

To get out of here and not to watch this.

"To whom do you belong, Thomas?"

His original name. He hated it. "To..." He gasped. He was dying now, he could feel it. "To the Lord of Flies."

"Better." The agony eased off a little. "But you understand that I can't let you keep this form."

His heart was beating unsteadily, but it was just the pain. The pain that intensified again. It was setting fire to his veins, overloading his nervous system as Beelzebub forced his body to channel more pain than anyone could bear.

He tried not to scream. But he couldn't.

And a grey streak dived past him towards Beelzebub's form. "Tag no!" His voice was ragged.

Beelzebub stopped the wolf with a hand. "And now, *now* I have every right to tear this one apart."

Victor dropped to the ground. His head sank to it.

"But I won't just yet." Beelzebub tossed Tag aside, he landed with a whimper. "I think a fair punishment on him is to watch the end of this."

The agony had eased, but it wasn't to his benefit. Beelzebub was punishing him by making it take longer. "Maybe I'll spin this out...I can give you a little more strength to endure it."

Victor felt a warmth through him. "Ah yes, there."

He had no idea what Judy was doing.

He hoped running. He was having difficulty breathing now, but his heart felt stronger, beating through him. Betraying him by keeping him alive. Tag was just kind of lying there, broken. Perhaps paralyzed.

He couldn't hear anything other than his own heartbeat, the rushing of the blood between his ears. There was nothing left to him but the pain. Nothing but to endure his punishment. Which he deserved.

But Tag didn't.

Tag didn't deserve any of this. Judy didn't deserve any of this.

The rules said you didn't harm a true believer.

Something rose up within him.

Something new.

THE OZONE SMELL GREW STRONGER. And Judy. The trenchcoat wrapped around her like tattered wings. Something glowing at her throat. Stepping between him and Beelzebub.

"Ah, so now..."

"You can't hurt me. You can't *touch* me. He's coming with me and there's nothing you can do about it."

Beelzebub laughed. "Who do you think you are? One of your God's prophets? No, I can't hurt you, but these two are mine."

"I'm not a prophet." Calm, casual. "There has never been a woman who has claimed that and I'm not going to start now."

She was almost full of light.

"I'm not a *prophet*, you idiot demon."

Victor managed a harsh laugh.

"I used to be a cop." Used to be? "But that's about enforcing law, and absolutely not about justice."

"You can't have his soul. You can't have it now and you can't have it ever."

"Souls are rather out of my jurisdiction," Judy admitted. "But... Lives are *not*. And he's still alive." Whatever she was now, it was more than just a cop.

Semantics, Victor thought. But she made a good argument. Because of course she did.

Because of course she wasn't a prophet.

Tag was picking himself up, shifting back human. "She's got a point there."

"Then I will just kill him."

"I don't think so."

The lightning crackled on the heights again, not around them.

"Really. Is he worth the arguing? To you?" Judy added. "As an example, maybe, but don't you have hundreds of souls you can mold as you did him?"

Victor felt that same odd feeling.

"Does your God want him?"

"No, but He would rather like me to be safe. And I'm not leaving without him."

"You acknowledge that you have no claim on his soul. And you know what he is. You'll end up having to put him in jail. You'll probably end up sending him right back to me."

"That's his choice. Not yours. Not mine."

Do you have to be evil?

No.

It wouldn't matter. He would be back here, but he would save lives in the interim. And without Asphodel, whatever the others were planning in New York would fall apart.

"I'm going with her." He said it raggedly, through agony.

"You're still mine. Never forget it."

And the agony dissipated.

Tag immediately grabbed him, lifted him and bodily *threw* him through the portal back to the real world. He landed hard on the concrete, not able to protest the treatment, wind thoroughly knocked out of him.

He lay there, not sure about anything except that the urge to kill Christian Hodges was completely gone. Then he wasn't sure about anything at all, because he had passed out.

53

THEY WERE IN A HOTEL ROOM. Judy wasn't even clear on whether it was hers or Tag's. Victor was unconscious on the bed.

"Will he be okay?"

"He still has his...abilities, including his healing. Beelzebub couldn't take them away without relinquishing his claim, and if he did that the ripple effect would be huge." Tag looked at Victor. "But Beelzebub fried a good chunk of his nervous system. He'll recover, but he's going to need time and rest."

She nodded. "Whose room are we in?"

"Yours."

"Excuse me, then." She found her clothes, slipped into the bathroom and got dressed. She set Victor's coat down on the bed for him. "That's better. I suppose that outfit's a dead loss."

Tag nodded. "Asphodel destroyed it."

"I don't know what to do now."

"With the case?"

She knew what would happen. There was something inside her now that screamed not for law, but for justice. "I'm done."

Tag turned to her. "You've always been a good cop."

"I've always tried to make sure I catch the right person." A pause. "Dani Martin's killer."

"Is probably already in custody. I'm sure whoever it was was on the boat with Maurice."

Judy nodded. "Maurice was the one really responsible anyway. And *he* is in custody at least until somebody breaks him out." Who else would go down, though? What excuses would be made.

"Hopefully nobody will."

Judy let out a breath. "And hopefully..."

"Are you sure you should quit? We need cops like you."

She shook her head. "There are no cops like you think I am. Like I thought I was. Something in that place burned it all out of me. Made me realize that everything I've done, everything I've tried to do was tainted."

"So, what? Private investigator?"

Judy considered that. "I suppose. Monster hunter?" She made a face. "I *like* being a cop. But..."

Tag nodded. "But you know too much of the truth now."

"I saw faces in the hellfire. They were cops. I don't think God wants me to do it any more, and for once in my life I agree with him." A pause. "So, I'm going to work towards justice some other way. Some way that isn't compromising who I am for a tarnished badge." She fell silent.

Tag looked at the sleeping Victor.

"Do you love him?" Judy asked.

"I don't think he's my soulmate but yes, I love him. For now. I'm not looking for a husband and I doubt he is either."

Judy frowned. "You might be surprised on that latter."

"We'll work it out. I certainly don't plan on leaving him right now."

"Until Beelzebub comes to get him back."

"He agreed to leave him alone until he dies."

"Which means that he's going to be dodging assassins for the rest of his life." Judy sighed. "I'm not stupid."

"Do *you* love him?"

"I like him. I value him. I respect him. I could call him a friend."

"You're only dodging the love word because it implies s e x." Tag spelled out the word.

"You're right. I am." A pause. "But I need to take care of some things. Call me when he wakes up."

"It might be a couple of days."

She smiled. "I know."

Leaving the hotel room, she noted that the weather was clear again.

Her steps took her away from it. At first she thought she was going to a synagogue.

Then she realized she wasn't. Because she didn't need to. She didn't need to be anywhere but where she was.

The smells of the city washed over her.

54

Victor regained consciousness in a bed. "Where am I?"

"Judy's hotel room. She's been sleeping in mine. I didn't want to move you again."

He stretched. Checked. All of his limbs were in place. He could still feel the fire within him. But he also couldn't feel any urges. "Well...I guess..."

"It worked. It wasn't the way we planned on doing it, but it worked. Until Beelzebub finds a way around it."

Victor frowned. Then, quietly, "Judy..."

"...has very definitely been chosen by her God for something. She's quitting the force."

He nodded, soberly. "For the best. She has too much of a sense of justice to last any longer."

"Which sucks. She should be able to..." Tag tailed off. "Maybe she'll be a rabbi."

"Nah. Rabbis are mostly teachers. Can you imagine Judy doing that?" Victor grinned. "No. She's going to do something to fix things. She can't do it from the inside. I don't think she knows it yet, but...."

Tag kind of blinked. "Politics. Nah, that would..."

"She managed this long as a cop without being corrupted. She could do it. Or maybe she'll hunt monsters. I don't know."

"No." Tag looked thoughtful. "No, she's going to find a way to fix things so she can be a good cop again. How, I don't know. And perhaps not in time for this life. The next, though..."

"So, what about *this* life?"

Tag shrugged. "You can do whatever you want, although Judy's probably right that you'll be dodging people trying to kill you."

"You should walk away."

Tag shrugged again. "Not unless you are going to say you don't want me." He glanced at Victor's pants. "Of which I see evidence to the contrary."

Victor actually blushed. "I suppose you probably already have to dodge people trying to kill you."

"I'm going to be honest. I'm not looking for a husband. I'm looking for a steady for a bit, but I make no promises beyond that."

"Neither do I. We can see what happens."

"As for what you should do." Tag shrugged. "You need a job that uses your skills but stays within the law. One you'll enjoy. And one that might be good..." A pause.

"I intend to save as many lives as I can before Hell comes to get me. I can't save myself, but I can make this worth it."

"Oh, come on. You're not going to stop being a hunter any more than Judy's going to stop being a cop."

"Then I'll just have to hunt people who deserve it."

Tag slid something over to him.

His old private investigator's license.

"You're right, I should dust this off. Maybe see if I can get a license as a bounty hunter. Go straight."

Tag shook his head. "I don't want you to go straight."

Victor laughed at the pun.

Then he kissed Tag.

Then he found several other things to do with Tag.

EPILOGUE

JUDY WAS NOT ENTIRELY sure why she was in Hell's Kitchen. Nor was she sure why she was knocking on a certain door. She knew she was there for a reason. She would have words with God about it later.

An older woman opened the door. "Come in, Detective."

She didn't ask how they knew. They smelled of patchouli and herbs, and everything smelled, and she was learning to tune it out.

She stepped inside. "You called me here."

"No. You were sent to me." She sat down. "I think for you, no need for any trappings. I am the Sibyl."

"The Seer."

"They used to call my predecessors the Oracle, but that's a database software now."

Judy couldn't help but laugh. "So, I'm assuming I was sent here to get...a prophecy?"

"I think there are some things you need to hear that will help you."

"Help me save the world."

The Sibyl lifted a hand, then indicated a chair. Then she held out a plate of cookies to Judy.

Judy took one.

"You already played your role in saving the world."

"I saved Victor Prince and he's going to do something...it's a chain. A butterfly effect."

"Precisely."

"I think I did need to hear that." Judy munched on the cookie. "But I can't go back to being a regular cop. I don't think I could..."

"You were *never* a regular cop, Judy." The Sibyl studied her. "You were a good cop. Are a good cop. There's no current place in this land for good cops.

"So, what can I do?"

"Fix it. It's not in your power alone, but it's in your power."

Judy felt a weight lift from her. "It's the work of the rest of my life, isn't it? Pushing. I can't do it from inside, not any more. But I..."

"It's not your job to save the world, Judy Eisenberg. Not any more. It's your job to be one of the people who makes sure it stays worth saving."

"It always has been."

"The only difference is that now you know. You know what you were doing before wasn't enough, was the opposite of enough."

They talked into the night.

The next morning, Judy Eisenberg handed in her badge.

The morning after, she began the rest of her life.

AUTHOR'S NOTE

This book is a prequel of sorts to the Lost Guardians series. I wanted to dive into the past of our fascinating anti-hero, Victor Prince.

What came into this book was a trip to New York (I want to go back at some point, when everything has recovered from the pandemic), the desire to establish a previous romantic relationship between Victor and Tag (readers of the series will know it ended quite amicably), and the character of Judy.

I wrote this book before the protests of the summer of 2020, and made some changes. Victor's arc is redemption from being a demon. Judy's arc is redemption from being a cop, from thinking she can change the system from within. She can't, any more than Victor can somehow reform Hell.

But maybe in her future she will.

As a note, this book is set in about 2011, and I hope that I didn't introduce any inadvertent anachronisms. Of course, everything before 2020 feels like a bit of an anachronism from here, although I have every confidence that the future will see a return to crowded bars, conventions, and travel. In the interest of that, I'm calling on all of my readers to get vaccinated against COVID-19, if your health allows, as soon as the vaccine is made available to you. Please.

We can defeat this particular demon, and we don't even have to fight thugs or do complicated rituals on Liberty Island to do it. We just have to wear masks, be patient, and trust science.

Not hard at all, right?

ACKNOWLEDGMENTS

As usual, acknowledgments go to my wonderful editor, Jennifer Melzer, to my cover artist, Starla Huchton, and my husband and primary proofreader, Greg Pearson. I would also like to acknowledge everyone I know who lives in New York. In fact, I would like to shout out to the city of New York, in all of its wonderful resilience, in all of her ruined places.

All mistakes and problems are, of course, entirely on me.

OTHER BOOKS BY JENNIFER R. POVEY

The Silent Years (Mother, Crone, Maiden)

The Ky Federation novels

Transpecial

Araña

The Lost Guardians Series:

Falling Dusk

Fallen Dark

Rising Dawn

Risen Day

Daughter of Fire

The Lay of Lady Percival

Tales of Yirath:

Firewing

The Friar's Tale

www.ingramcontent.com/pod-product-compliance
Lightning Source LLC
Chambersburg PA
CBHW052034240626
47153CB00006B/2071